TWILIGHT IN DELHI

Novelist, poet, critic, diplomat, scholar, Ahmed Ali was born in Delhi in 1910. He became famous in 1932 with the publication of *Angaray* in Urdu and co-founded the All-India Progressive Writers' Movement. After the Indian subcontinent was divided, Ahmed Ali had to live in Pakistan, and established Pakistani embassies in China and Morocco. His many works include the well known anthology of classical Urdu poetry *The Golden Tradition* and *Al-Qur'ān, A Contemporary Translation*. Ahmed Ali died in Karachi in January, 1994.

DATE DUE

DEMCO, INC. 38-3012

By the Same Author

NOVELS
Ocean of Night
Rats and Diplomats

SHORT STORIES
The Prison-House

POETRY
Purple Gold Mountain
Selected Poems

TRANSLATIONS
Al-Qur'an: a contemporary translation
The Golden Tradition
Ghalib: Selected Poems
The Flaming Earth

CRITICISM
Mr. Eliot's Penny-World of Dreams
Muslim China

Twilight in Delhi

A NOVEL BY *Ahmed Ali*

Delhi was once a paradise,
Such peace had abided here;
But they have ravished its name and pride,
Remain now only ruins and care.

BAHADUR SHAH

A New Directions Book

First published by the Hogarth Press, London, 1940.
First published as New Directions Paperbook 782 in 1994.

Manufactured in the United States of America
New Directions Books are printed on acid-free paper
Published simultaneously in Canada by Penguin Books Canada Limited

Library of Congress Cataloging-in-Publication Data
Ali, Ahmed, 1908–
Twilight in Delhi / Ahmed Ali.
   p.   cm. — (New Directions paperbook ; 782)
ISBN 0–8112–1267–X (pbk.)
1. Delhi (India)—History—Fiction. 2. Muslims—India—Delhi—Fiction. 3. Family—India—Delhi—Fiction. I. Title.
PR9499.3.A465T95 1994   93–45363
823—dc20   CIP

New Directions Books are published for James Laughlin
by New Directions Publishing Corporation,
80 Eighth Avenue, New York 10011

To
Laurence Brander
and
the memory of my parents

Contents

Introduction   xi

Twilight in Delhi   1

Introduction

The *Raison d'Etre* of *Twilight in Delhi*

The damage done by colonial powers to the heritage of conquered peoples is irreversible; yet racial memory is a collective storehouse that time and history cannot eradicate. In Mexico and Peru, the Spaniards conquered the vast Aztec and Inca empires in the early part of the sixteenth century, and became the rulers of millions of human beings, sanctified by Papal bulls to convert heathen peoples to Christianity and impose their languages upon them, which the Portuguese also did in Brazil. In Africa, the British, Dutch and Portuguese captured, enchained, baptized and shipped twenty million able-bodied men, women and children as slaves to the Americas, of which only twelve million reached alive. And on the lands they had captured they imposed their rule and languages . . .

When the Europeans came to the Orient, it was to an Islamic World; and they had been awed by Islam since the conquest of Spain, Sicily and parts of France in the eighth and ninth centuries. Islam had come to symbolize for them "terror, devastation, the demonic hordes of hated barbarians," as Edward W. Said says in his incisive analysis, *Orientalism*. "For Europe," he continues, "Islam was a lasting trauma. Until the end of the seventeenth century the 'Ottoman peril' lurked . . . to represent for the whole of a Christian civilisation a constant danger."[1]

The British arrived in India at the beginning of the seventeenth century when the Mughals were in power, having been preceded by the Portuguese who came to Calicut in 1498 in search of "Christians and Spices," followed by the Dutch, who sent a fleet to the East in 1595. During the reign of the Great Mughals the British expanded their trade and competed with their rivals the Portuguese, Dutch and French. Their territories were confined to a few miles within the island of Bombay and Madras city, a few factories and warehouses in the Bay of Bengal, with a fortified post set up at Aramgaon about 1625. For fifty years after the death of Aurangazeb in 1707 the English merchants kept away from politics and fighting. Though commercially astute, the Company's servants were not trained for politics or war. But after the Battle of Plassey in 1757 and the capture of Delhi by the Afghan Chieftain Ahmad Shah Abdali, when Mughal power began to decline, the East India Company's forces were built up by the wily robber baron Clive, who changed the mercantile character of the Company to that of war lords. After the successful Battle of Baksar in 1764 and the maneuvering of the revenue collection (*Diwani*) of Bengal from Shah Alam in 1765, the British could look to mastery of India. They succeeded in establishing virtual control by 1818.

Though elated by their achievement, the British were afraid of the hidden fire of religion that had been revived by the movement of Shah Waliullah (1703–62). The great scholar and theologian of Delhi, who had gone to the Hedjaz in 1730 and studied the conditions of Europe, Africa, and Iran, as well as Turkey and its European empire, had seen the shadows of decadence lengthening over the Muslim world. Returning in 1732, he issued warnings against the corrupt social system, addressing admonishing letters to the princes and lords demanding the abolition of the entire decrepit feudal order, warning against the danger from foreign powers which he described as "stars glowing in the darkness like the eyes of serpents or the stings of scorpions." And even though he wrote secretly for help to Ahmad Shah Abdali, the Afghan King, in 1761, he failed to call the "Muslims to rally round the throne" (in the words of Percival Spear in his *History of India*) "and took refuge in the concept of the community of the faithful looking only to God."[2] Yet the impact of his movement was so great and lasting that it continued to be felt till the end of the nineteenth century. It was vengefully suppressed as the "Wahabi"[3] conspiracy by the British Indian Government (which replaced the East India Company after the fiasco of 1857) with mock trials of Muslim scholars, many of whom were hanged or condemned to penal servitude in the Andaman Islands, where most died of hardships greater than anything suffered by American prisoners at Alcatraz in San Francisco Bay . . .

The danger was real enough to awaken the British after their successes in the eighteenth century to the urgency of what was to be done to consolidate their position, and led to open debates and discussions at the dinner tables of publicmen over how best to revamp the policies of governing and of reshaping India into a new

Western mold. Conservative Tories like Warren Hastings and W. W. Wilson stood for non-interference in the prevailing religio-social institutions of the country. Warren Hastings (Governor 1772–85) tried to locate himself within the Orient, and laid emphasis on Indian institutions of learning. But the Tories were challenged by the Evangelicals of William Wilberforce, who, with William Pitt and Charles Grant (Chairman of the Company's Board of Directors) supporting them, were hungry for souls, like the Spaniards and Portuguese in the sixteenth century, and wanted to save the Indian people from idolatry and Islam by preaching the Gospel. They were joined by the Radicals in denouncing Indian customs. Thus, while the Evangelicals preached Christianity openly in schools and market places, the Radicals denounced Indian culture, beliefs and religious practices as barbaric and superstitious. Suppported by reformers and helped by sympathizers like Ram Mohan Roy, they became responsi ble for evolving a policy that changed the face and mental attitudes of India to what we—the splintered pieces of a whole—have inherited, warped and distorted into a *new* image of Prajapati (with the sacrifice of himself to himself at the behest of the gods who, it so happened, were his own offspring).

With the coming of William Bentinck, a Benthamite, as Governor-General (1825–35), the framework of "anglicizing" was completed with the planting of Western ideas through education, in order to fulfull, with typical English imperialist arrogance (overlooking the state of ignorance and immorality at home) "the great moral duty to India," and to introduce and promote "knowledge of the sciences," to which Bentinck added in 1829 the British language, "the key to all improvements." Thus Persian, the centuries-old court language, was abolished as well as Arabic and Sanskrit, with the object of producing (in the words of Thomas Babington (Lord) Macaulay's Minute of 1835) "a class of persons, Indian in blood and color, but English in taste and character, in morals and intellect." Hence schools and colleges were set up to convert Indians to brown Englishmen through knowledge imparted in the English language, a tradition which has been followed by the surrogates to this day.

This change was, however, confined to the sophisticated urban population; village life continued undisturbed by the so called "civilizing" influence of *Westernization* and remained as unenviable as it had been under the time-old tyrannical caste system and Brahmanic domination, untouched by the "benevolent" British rule. That is why, it seems, the Hindu English novelists of the thirties and later, in search of the real India, turned to the countryside for "copy," as here alone lived the India of "Brahma and Prajapati; of Varuna, Mithra; of Rama . . . and Yagnavalkys" (in the words of Raja Rao), symbols of the India the West preserved but did not ostensibly understand, in glaring contrast to their unseating of the Mughals and erasing of everything Islamic . . .

                              *   *   *

In the meantime, the ghosts of the past, roused by our readings of works by the radical writers of Europe and Russia, stirred romantic feelings of freedom and patriotism that led us to look around us and find the social order in shambles. In spite of Bentinck's Westernization and Macaulay's painting our faces brown with a pigmentless brush of anglicization, ignorance had increased a hundred fold and people had forgotten their own mother tongues. Ashamed and demoralized by the distorted pictures of India presented by British historians, Orientalists, and trained propagandists from missionaries and civil servants to Anglo-Indian journalists like Rudyard Kipling, we suffocated in an atmosphere of inferiority. The plan of brainwashing the Indians, especially the Muslims from whom the British had wrested power, and implanting a sense into their minds of being a backward, uncivilized, and conquered people through manipulated propaganda like Vincent Smith's *History of India* (which contained a good deal of falsification of Muslim history and was taught in all schools as a compulsory text) was well-planned and successful.

And yet, rising from within, a tide of revolt led some of us to contemplate the state of inanity and indifference into which the social order had sunk. It was the beginning of the third decade of this century, almost a hundred years since Macaulay wrote his infamous Minute of 1835. A few of us, filled with dreams of freedom and independence, made bold to publish in 1932 a collection of our short stories in Urdu, *Angaray (Burning Coals)*, to show a mirror to society. Our enthusiasm was immediately dampened by a cold shower of denunciations, from the pulpit down to the social and political platforms. Though it made us famous overnight, the government banned the book as subversive, and our names were listed in the Intelligence Bureau as communists and dangerous characters. The mirror had warped our own image into its reverse. The social order we had set out to reform, pronounced us West-stricken devils! In the process of transformation from Indian to "brown Englishman," I found that I had lost not only my freedon but also my culture and individuality, and I have been engaged ever since in search of my self, my identity. Where between the heart and mind had it been waylaid? Slowly, through the years, light began to filter through the pictures of Delhi to which I turned for my past. The story of my immediate ancestors held the key to a treasure trove of mysteries. My grandmother was five and my grandfather eleven when the *ghadar* of 1857, the blind persecution and massacre of the citizens of Delhi, took place. The triumphant British held an orgy of blood and terror, all mention of which has been dropped by their historians,[4] but is mourned by an eyewitness, Bahadur Shah (the last of the Mughals who was imprisoned and, ironically, accused at a farcical trial of "treason" by the usurpers of his own throne, and then banished to Burma with all his surviving male descendants) in one of his pathetic poems:

> Ravished were the people of Hind,
> So unenviable their fate.
> Whoever the ruler of the day saw fair
> And free was put to sword.

As though this had not been enough to quench the bloody thirst of the conquistadores, the whole Muslim population of Delhi was banished for five years, their homes dug up by the Prize Agency for buried treasures, the women molested and searched for ornaments and gold by red-faced Tommies. Even the cloth bags in which they carried areca nut and betel leaves for chewing were opened and searched for money, and being found empty of valuables were shamelessly urinated upon by the brutes of Tom Atkins. Suffering hardships of every kind, wandering from jungle to jungle, village to village, in search of food and shelter, they trudged back from exile to find that they had neither roof nor walls nor doors to protect them from wind and weather, and that they had to restart life as paupers and a vanquished people, like the Aztecs and Incas of Mexico and Peru three hundred years before them . . .

With my short story, "Our Lane" (*Hamari Gali*), the mantle fell apart. It was the year 1935, the centenary of Bentinck's making English the medium of instruction and of Macaulay's Minute. The vista changed completely. My search had found a direction, India her neglected cause. This cause deserved a world-wide audience. If presented in Urdu, it would die down within a narrow belt rimmed by Northwest India. There were many instances to show that British injustices in India were dismissed as local matters. But if a case were brought to London, the home government became involved, which depended on public good faith and was answerable to King and Parliament. Ram Mohan Roy had presented the case of restrictions placed on the rights of Akbar Shah II in London, which had restored the King's rights and changed the entire perspective . . .

My decision to write *Twilight in Delhi* in English, then, turned out to be right, with critics saying: "It may well be that we shall not understand India until it is explained to us by Indian novelists of the first ability, as it was that we understand nothing of Russia before we read Tolstoy, Turgenev and the others. Ahmed Ali may well be vanguard of such a literary movement."[5] This judgment was re-echoed by *The Oxford History of India* in 1958 when it said in reference to Mulk Raj Anand, R. K. Narayan and myself: ". . . it can be said that they have taken over from E. M. Forster and Edward Thompson the task of interpreting modern India to itself and the world."[6]

*   *   *

The novel had been written after the eventful years following the publication of *Angaray,* the collection of short stories which had led to the founding of the All-India Progressive Writers' Movement and Association. Finished in 1939, I took it to England and showed it to E. M. Forster who liked it and eventually associated it with *A Passage of India,* in the Preface to its Everyman's Library edition. It was accepted for publication by the Hogarth Press.

The Second World War having intensified, I received a letter from the Publishers one morning enclosing the galley proofs of the novel but regretting that the printers found some portions of the book "subversive" and were unable to print it. John Lehmann, then a Director of the Hogarth Press, expressed his disappointment at the printers' decision, and suggested that I should delete the chapter and the passages the printers found objectionable. I could not agree to this, as they were the historical portions dealing with the War of Independence of 1857 (labelled by the British as the "Mutiny") and the reactions of Mir Nihal to the John Company and British rule, which were basic to the theme of the book and Mir Nihal's character. Nevertheless I agreed that, if Mr. Forster thought so, I would revise them. When the matter was referred to him he reacted inevitably and said that the portions were quintessential to the book and he did not see how they could be deleted without emasculating the whole.

Whereas this satisfied Lehmann, the situation with the printers remained unchanged; and the prospects of publication became as bleak as the wartime blackout. One day, having gone with Forster to the London Library, we met Desmond McCarthy, and Forster mentioned the problem to him. He came up with a solution and suggested to Virginia Woolf, who was the moving spirit of the Press, that the book be submitted to Harold Nicholson, the official censor. Nicholson passed the book; the printers collapsed; and the novel came out but not until I had left England in the autumn of 1940. When the book reached India it was hailed as a major literary event and soon acquired the position of a legend, generally influencing the writing of fiction there. But when most of its stock was destroyed in the Blitz, the book was forgotten in more momentous events.

Two decades later in 1964, some chapters of the book were prescribed by the Willimentick College in the U.S., and specially published for this purpose with the help of James Laughlin, who had earlier published my short story *Before Death* in *New Directions 15*. The Oxford University Press then brought out an edition from Bombay, London and New York in 1966, followed by an Indian paperback a few years later. During the seventies, it was assigned in various courses such as History, Comparative Literature, Asian Studies and "Masterpieces of World Literature" at a number of American universities including Columbia and Oakland in Michigan, and included in such exclusive anthologies as *Modern Islamic Literature*.

During the quarter century of its existence out of print, it was read in my wife's exemplary translation in Urdu published in 1963, which in the opinion of some critics restored the natural language to the book. Those who read it in the translation said it could not have been written in English, while those who had read it in the original English said it was untranslatable. This curious controversy was put to an end by an American critic, David D. Anderson, when he said that the novel "transcends language as any substantial work of art ultimately must do . . ."[7]

*   *   *

In this world of shadows nothing ever remains the same. *Twilight in Delhi,* I suppose, served in its own way some small purpose. But what are a few insignificant pages in the undying ocean of words? Life's workshop is busy night and day. I remained an exile in search of what I had lost. India won her freedom. The British found an escape and left in a hurry, degrading the East to the Third World, leaving behind a series of intangible ethnic, social, politico-economic and geographical problems, a crisis of identity into local and refugee, and a burden of hatred that will keep the countries of South, Southeast and Far East Asia involved for generations to come.

I was in China on foreign service, sent by the British Government of India as British Council Visiting Professor to the National Central University of China in Nanking, when the subcontinent was divided into two, Bharat (now India) and Pakistan. A sea of people moved up North, a sea of them moved down with the turning of the tide. I was prohibited by the overnight-turned-Hindu Indian authorities in 1968 to come back to India, and for no other reason than because I was a Muslim. As their Ambassador in China, K.P.S. Menon (member of the British-India Civil Service) told me, "It's a question of Hindu and Muslim." And when I protested he added, "All that I can do is write to New Delhi, *but I can tell you* nothing will come of it!—" demonstrating a living repetition of history ninety years after the banishment of my grandparents and the Muslim citizens from the vanquished city by the British. Yet while their exile was temporary, mine was permanent, and the loss not only of home and whatever I possessed, but also my birthright, when I had no hatred of any caste or creed in my heart. Yet even as Time takes away, it also reconciles the mind to the alternations of night and day, wearing out grief into regret, the throb of pain into a sigh of the heaving breast . . .

*   *   *

In 1966 when the Oxford University Press brought out its edition of *Twilight in Delhi,* its author was on the other side of the border, and the book was not allowed by Customs to cross the frontier of Pakistan. Later, when it was suggested that a televised version of the novel be presented from Karachi (as once the Radio version had been broadcast from Delhi), the manager of the local station refused on the grounds that its scene was laid in the forbidden city across the border and so could not be telecast in Pakistan. There was no John Lehmann to suggest a change of title from Delhi to Lahore, nor an E. M. Forster to uphold its right to be what it was, nor a Virginia Woolf to intercede, nor even a Harold Nicholson to exorcise the ghost. It seemed that the fate of the great city, once the heart of Hindustan and symbol of its glory, was dogging the shadow of its memorial, like Time the ruthless destroyer, into the frontiers that did not accept its historicity or its representational personality, or even its human identity now lost forever in the forced amnesia of plucked-out memory. . . . And so today, the Oxford University Press of Delhi could change its character completely by saying in the blurb of the "Golden Jubilee" edition of the novel that " it describes a culture and . . . way of life in the *predominantly Muslim areas of the city,"* while *The Oxford History of India* itself says that "Delhi never figured largely in Hindu History. It was ordinarily the Head-quarters of the Sultans of Hindostan from 1206 to 1526 but did not become the established Mogul capital until Shah Jahan moved his court from Agra in 1648. It continued to be the usual residence of his successors until 1858 when their dynasty was extinguished . . ."[8]

Yet beyond the ravages of unpredictable fate, my purpose in writing the novel was to depict a phase of our national life and the decay of a whole culture, a particular mode of thought and living, values now dead and gone before our eyes. Seldom is one allowed to see a pageant of History whirl past, and partake in it too. Since its publication, the Delhi of the novel has changed beyond nostalgia and recognition. For its culture was born and nourished within city walls that lie demolished today; and the distinction between its well-preserved, jealously guarded language and the surrounding world has disappeared in the rattle of many tongues, even as the homogeneity of its culture has been engulfed in the tide of unrestricted promiscuity.

The British had only built a new capital outside the city walls.

The present rulers have removed the last vestige on which the old culture could have taken its stand and are moving it farther away towards Indraprastha, affirming the prophecy of the book: Seven Delhis have fallen, and the eighth has gone the way of its predecessors, yet to be demolished and built again. Life, like the Phoenix, must collect the spices for its nest and set fire to it, and arise resurrected out of the flames.

Ahmed Ali
Karachi
December 1993

ENDNOTES

1. Edward W. Said, *Orientalism* (Pantheon Books: New York, 1978) p. 54.

2. Percival Spear, *A History of India 2* (Pelican Books: London, 1974) p. 72.

3. *Wahabi:* follower of the puritanical movement started in Arabia by Muhammad Ibn 'Abdul Wahab (1703–92) which became the driving force behind the military expansion of the Saudi family and remains the official ideology of the Saudi Arabian kingdom. The *wahabis* had no reverence for saints and their tombs, and tried to demolish the dome over the holy Prophet's tomb, which was saved, however, and restored by the Turks. It was considered a term of abuse in India and used for renegades amd disloyal persons. Duncan Forbes says in his *Dictionary of Hindustani and English* published in 1866: "in India the term is equivalent to 'infidel' or 'unbeliever,' just as we good Protestants are called 'heretics.'" The British used it in the sense of *baghi,* that is, a mutineer or traitor and rebel.

4. Its nature could be sensed from the exultation with which Sir Alfred Lyall wrote to his father: "I am quite well now, and will start for Delhi tomorrow morning at 4 a.m. in order to enjoy the pleasure of seeing the imperial city of Mussulmans in ruin . . ." quoted by Mortimer Durand in his *The Life of Rt. Hon'ble Sir Alfred Lyall,* 1918, p. 70; and from the Diary of William Howard Russell, the India correspondent of the Times during 1858–59: "It has been warmly suggested that we should destroy the Jumma Masjid. . . . The fact is that the Mohammedan element in India is that which causes us most trouble. . . . Our antagonism to the followers of Mohammed is far stronger than that we bear to the worshippers of Shiva and Vishnu. They are unquestionably more dangerous to rule. . . . If we could eradicate the traditions and destroy the temples of Mahomed by one vigorous effort it would indeed be well for the Christian faith and for British rule." See *My Diary in India, Vol. II,* 4th edition (Routledge, Warne & Routledge: London, 1860) pp. 77–78. This cry is being heard again, and has been intensified since the demolition of the Babari Mosque in Ayodhya by M. M. Joshi and L. K. Advani of the *Bharat Janta* Party and their followers in December 1992.

5. Maurice Collis, *Time and Tide* (November 30, 1940).

6. *The Oxford History of India,* 3rd edition, edited by Percival Spear (Oxford, 1967) p. 838.

7. David D. Anderson, *Mahfil; A Quarterly of South Asian Literature,* vol. VII, p. 86.

8. *The Oxford History of India,* p. 211.

PART I

The night is dark, the waves rise mountains high,
And such a storm is raging!
What do the pedestrians know of my plight moving
Upon the shore that's safe and dry?

HAFIZ

1

NIGHT envelops the city, covering it like a blanket. In the dim star-light roofs and houses and by-lanes lie asleep, wrapped in a restless slumber, breathing heavily as the heat becomes oppressive or shoots through the body like pain. In the courtyards, on the roofs, in the by-lanes, on the roads, men sleep on bare beds, half naked, tired after the sore day's labour. A few still walk on the otherwise deserted roads, hand in hand, talking; and some have jasmine garlands in their hands. The smell from the flowers escapes, scents a few yards of air around them and dies smothered by the heat. Dogs go about sniffing the gutters in search of offal; and cats slink out of narrow by-lanes, from under the planks jutting out of shops, and lick the earthen cups out of which men had drunk milk and thrown away.

Heat exudes from the walls and the earth; and the gutters give out a damp stink which comes in greater gusts where they meet a sewer to eject their dirty water into an underground canal. But men sleep with their beds over the gutters, and the cats and dogs quarrel over heaps of refuse which lie along the alleys and cross-roads.

Here and there in every mohallah the mosques raise their white heads towards the sky, their domes spread out like the white breasts of a woman bared, as it were, to catch the starlight on their surfaces, and the minarets point to heaven, indicating, as it were, that God is all-high and one. . . .

But the city of Delhi, built hundreds of years ago, fought for, died for, coveted and desired, built, destroyed and rebuilt, for five and six and seven times, mourned and sung, raped and conquered, yet whole and alive, lies indifferent in the arms of sleep. It was the city of kings and monarchs, of poets and story tellers, courtiers and nobles. But no king lives there today, and the poets are feeling the lack of patronage; and the old inhabitants, though still alive, have lost their pride and grandeur under a foreign yoke. Yet the city stands still intact, as do many more forts and tombs and monuments, remnants and reminders of old Delhis, holding on to life with a tenacity and purpose which is beyond comprehension and belief.

It was built after the great battle of Mahabharat by Raja Yudhishtra
in 1453 BC, and has been the cause of many a great and historic battle.
Destruction is in its foundations and blood is in its soil. It has seen the
fall of many a glorious kingdom, and listened to the groans of birth. It is
the symbol of Life and Death, and revenge is its nature.

Treacherous games have been played under its skies, and its earth
has tasted the blood of kings. But still it is the jewel of the eye of the
world, still it is the centre of attraction. Yet gone is its glory and
departed are those from whom it got the breath of life. Where are the
Kauravs and the Pandavas? Where are the Khiljis and the Saiyyeds?
Where are Babur and Humayun and Jahangir? Where is Shah Jahan
who built the city where it stands today? And where is Bahadur Shah,
the tragic poet and the last of that noble line? Gone they are, gone
and dead beneath the all-embracing earth. Only some monuments
remain to tell its sad story and to remind us of the glory and splendour—a Qutab Minar or a Humayun's Tomb, the Old Fort or the
Jama Mosque, and a few sad verses to mourn their loss and sing the
tale of mutability:

> I'm the light of no one's eye,
> The rest of no one's heart am I.
> That which can be of use to none
> —Just a handful of dust am I.

And, as if to echo the poet king's thoughts, a silence and apathy of
death descended upon the city, and dust began to blow in its streets,
and ruin came upon its culture and its purity. Until the last century it
had held its head high, and tried to preserve its chastity and form.
Though the poet who sang its last dirges while travelling in a bullock-
cart to Lucknow, city of the rival culture, managed to keep silent and,
to preserve the chastity of his tongue, did not indulge in conversation
with his companion yet when he reached that other town and sat in the
crowd to be asked to recite his verses no one extended to him the
invitation. For no one knew him, until, seeing his plight, one man asked
him where he hailed from, and thus he replied:

> Why do you ask my native place,
> O dwellers of the East,
> Making mock of me for the poor plight I am in?
> Delhi, which was once the jewel of the world,
> Where dwelt only the loved ones of fate,

Which has now been ruined by the hand of Time,
I'm a resident of that storm-tossed place. . . .

But gone are the poets too, and gone is its culture. Only the coils of
the rope, when the rope itself has been burnt, remain, to remind us of
past splendour. Yet ruin has descended upon its monuments and
buildings, upon its boulevards and by-lanes. Under the tired and dim
stars the city looks deathly and dark. The kerosene lamps do light the
streets and lanes; but they are not enough, as are not enough the
markets and the gardens, to revive the light that floated on the waters of
the Jamuna or dwelt in the heart of the city. Like a beaten dog it has
curled its tail between its legs, and lies lifeless in the night as an
acknowledgement of defeat.

Still a few shops of the milk-sellers are open, and someone comes and
buys a couple of pice worth of milk, drinks it, and throws the earthen
cup away to be licked by cats who steal out of dark corners. And still a
beggar or two goes by singing in a doleful voice his miserable song,
tap-tapping the slab-paved streets with his bamboo stick, or whining in
front of doors:

'Give in the name of God, mother, and may thy children live long.'

Or a belated flower-vendor sells jasmines in a singsong voice putting
one hand on his ear, holding the basket to his side with the other,
shouting in resonant tones: 'Buy the flowers of jasmine'.

But the city lies indifferent or asleep, breathing heavily under a hot
and dusty sky. Hardly anyone stops the flower vendor to buy jasmines
or opens a door to satisfy the beggar. The nymphs have all gone to
sleep, and the lovers have departed.

Only narrow by-lanes and alleys, insidious as a game of chess, inter-
sect the streets and the city like the deep gutters which line them on
either side, and grow narrower as you plunge into them, giving a feeling
of suffocation and death, until they terminate at some house front or
meet another net of by-lanes as insidious as before.

Such a net of alleys goes deep into the bowels of the city shooting
from Lal Kuan, and going into Kucha Pandit turns to the right and
terminates at Mohallah Niyaryan, which has a net of by-lanes of its own.
One branch of it comes straight on, tortuous and winding, growing
narrower like the road of life, and terminates at the house of Mir Nihal.
As you look at it only a wall faces you, and in the wall a door. Nothing
else. As you enter the house through the vestibule you come into an
inner courtyard. Right in front is a low kotha and under it two small

rooms. On the left is an arched veranda opening on to a raised platform
made of bricks, and behind it a long room. On either side of the
veranda and the platform are small rooms, and by the side of the
entrance is the lavatory, a narrow bathroom, then the kitchen black
with smoke. In the centre of the courtyard an old date palm tree raises
its head up towards the sky, and its long leaves clustering together
conceal a part of the sky from view, and its trunk, curved and sagged in
the middle, looks ugly and dark. At the foot of the date palm a henna
tree is growing, and sparrows have built their nests in its branches. Two
earthen dishes hang from it, one full of water the other of grain for the
sparrows and wild pigeons who have built their nests in the cornices of
the veranda and in the thick red and white curtains hanging above the
arches.

By the wall of the kotha are flat wooden couches with a red cloth
covering them; and on the platform and in the courtyard are beds
covered with white bed sheets which glow in the dim light of a kerosene
lantern.

An old lady in her fifties is lying on one of the beds in the courtyard
with her head-cloth lying near her. On another bed are Mehro Zamani,
her youngest daughter, a girl of fourteen, healthy and plump, and
Masroor, a young boy of about thirteen, her nephew, a cousin's son.

'It must be eleven o'clock, and your father has not come back yet,'
Begam Nihal says to her daughter. 'You'd better go to sleep. It is very
late.'

'No, mother,' her daughter says to her, 'the story you were telling us
was so good. I am not sleepy. Tell us another.'

The old lady fanned herself and said:

'You have heard enough for today.'

'But, aunt, do tell us the story of the king who had turned into a
snake,' said Masroor turning on his stomach and looking at his aunt
expectantly.

'We have heard that,' said Mehro Zamani as she fanned herself.
'Amma, tell us what happened in the Mutiny. You were once telling us
how the Farangis had turned all the Mussalmans out of the city. Why
did they do that?'

'It's a long story. I will tell you some other day,' the old lady replied.
'Your father will be coming soon. And the heat is so oppressive. . . .'

The young folk feel disappointed. It is late and they are sleepy.

Mehro lies on her bed and looks up at the stars, and vague thoughts
come into her mind, thoughts of kings and princes and soldiers. She

thinks of a man far away whose proposal has come for her hand. What can he be like? She wonders. She has never seen him. They are extremely rich people, she has heard; and Meraj—that is his name—is very fond of shooting. And she associates him with the Prince in the story with whom the Princess was in love. But the thought of leaving the home, her father and mother, brothers and relations, comes into her mind. She heaves a sigh, and feeling dejected and downcast closes her eyes.

Masroor has already gone to sleep.

Begam Nihal sits up, draws her dome-shaped paan-box, puts lime and katha on a betel leaf, then adds finely cut areca nut, some cardamom, a little tobacco, rolls it up and puts it in her mouth. Then she lies down again and begins to fan herself, occasionally fanning her daughter too. . . .

*   *   *

'Hai, hai, what has happened to my fan? Bi Anjum, are you awake? Have you seen my fan?' comes a voice from the kotha.

'What do I know of your fan?' the other voice replies. 'It must be on your bed.'

'It is not here.'

'Then it must have fallen down. . . .'

Then a silence descends upon the house. A gust of hot wind blows, and the leaves of the date palm rustle. The lantern flickers, but the flame steadies again.

*   *   *

Shams's newly-married wife, the grand-daughter-in-law of the house, who sleeps on the platform with her husband, wakes up, and taking the bowl fills it with water from the earthen pot and goes to the latrine. As she goes back and lies down, the front door creaks and a man clears his throat in the vestibule. Begam Nihal sits up on the bed and covers her head with her head-cloth, and calls to the maidservant: 'Dilchain, O Dilchain, get up. The master has come.'

Dilchain gets up with a start and Mir Nihal comes in. He is tall and well built, and is wearing a white muslin coat reaching down to the knees, and an embroidered round cap is put at a rakish angle on his bobbed head. His white and well-combed beard is parted in the middle, and gives his noble face a majestic look.

'You went out today without a meal,' Begam Nihal says to him in a slightly annoyed tone, 'and have kept me waiting. It must be past midnight.'

'It is only eleven,' he replies in an apologetic way. 'I heard the clock strike at the corner of the by-lane.'

Dilchain brings the food from the kitchen. Begam Nihal spreads the food-cloth on the wooden couch. Mir Nihal takes off his coat, washes his hands and sits on his haunches, not cross-legged, to take his food. Begam Nihal begins to fan him.

'Asghar is now twenty-two,' she tells her husband. 'It's time you thought of his marriage lest the boy starts keeping bad company.'

Mir Nihal clears his throat and says:

'Yes, I was going to speak to you about him myself. Has he gone to sleep?'

'No. He went out after dinner and has not come back yet.'

'Where has he gone?' Mir Nihal demanded.

'What do I know? He must have gone to see some cousin.'

'No. He does not go to see his cousins often,' Mir Nihal said with annoyance. 'He must have gone again to Mirza Shahbaz Beg's as usual. I have told you I don't like his friendship with Bundoo, the Mirza's son.'

'He is a boy, after all, and must mix with people of his own age,' Begam Nihal explained. 'Bundoo and Asghar have studied together in childhood. Besides, Ashfaq lives there, and he is your nephew.'

'I had never approved of Ashfaq's marriage to Mirza Shahbaz's daughter,' Mir Nihal said angrily. 'And I do not approve of Asghar's friendship with Bundoo. Why don't you stop him?'

'He is your son too. You could tell him yourself. That is why I say you should think of his marriage. And there is another thing that is weighing on my mind. . . .'

Begam Nihal turned and looked at her daughter who had fallen asleep. As she turned the light from the lantern fell on her face and lighted up her brown forehead which was fairly broad in the middle but on the sides her hair had made it narrow, and showed three light wrinkles which had formed there.

'Yes. I was saying,' she continued, 'that a letter came again from Bhopal about Mehro's marriage. They are in a hurry about it.'

Mir Nihal frowned, and in the dim light of the lantern his fair-complexioned face and his wide forehead showed signs of anxiety.

'Mehro is too young to be given away to strangers,' he said. 'I do not know what sort of people they are. I do not seem to like them.'

'You always jump to conclusions,' Begam Nihal said in a reprimanding tone. 'You do not know them; but I have heard praises of those people. And then Mir Wahajuddin has property worth a lakh. . . .'

'But I can't think of marrying Mehro before Asghar. Have you thought of any girl for him?'

'Why, there are so many girls,' says Begam Nihal looking relieved. 'But I like brother Naseeruddin's daughter.'

Mir Nihal muttered 'Hm,' looked thoughtful for a while, and said: 'Well, have you spoken to Asghar? What does he say?'

From the pigeon house in the corner comes a sudden fluttering of wings.

'What is that?' Mir Nihal asks.

'It must be a cat.'

The pigeons flutter again. Mir Nihal gets up and, picking up the lantern, rushes to the pigeon house. He raises the lantern high and throws light inside through the bamboo structure wall of the pigeon house. He sees nothing wrong and comes away. But in a moment the pigeons flutter more frightened than before.

Mir Nihal goes back, opens the door of the pigeon house and putting the lantern inside looks all around. Something like a black rope creeps behind a wooden pigeon box.

'It's a snake. Bring my stick, Dilchain,' Mir Nihal shouts to the maidservant who rushes into one of the low rooms under the kotha. As she goes in the noise of a pot falling comes from the room and a woman's frightened 'Ooi!' The snake creeps from behind one pigeon box to another.

'Hurry, Dilchain. Hurry up,' Mir Nihal shouts excited.

Before Dilchain arrives with the stick the snake has moved to the bamboo structure side of the wall. Kicking against a bowl which is lying in her way Dilchain hurries with the stick. Mir Nihal moves a box from its position to get the snake into open ground in order to hit it with the stick. But it wriggles out into the courtyard. Mir Nihal hurriedly comes out of the pigeon house and rushes after it. Before he can strike the snake creeps into a gutter. Throwing away the stick Mir Nihal puts his hand into the gutter. From the wooden couch Begam Nihal shouts:

'What are you doing? Look out!'

But Mir Nihal has managed to catch hold of the snake's tail, and pulling it out with all his force he jerks his hand backwards with a quick movement. The snake is seen flying in the air and the next moment Mir Nihal strikes it on the ground and leaves it. It lies there trying to move, but it is only the front half of the snake which is curling and twisting.

The back half wriggles but cannot move forward. Its spine is broken.
Taking the stick he crushes the hood, and wriggling and moving pain-
fully for a while it becomes motionless and dies.

From the kotha Begam Jamal, Mir Nihal's widowed sister-in-law,
shouts:

'Hai, hai, what was it?'

'Just a snake. I have killed it,' Mir Nihal replies in a laughing voice,
and the flesh on his cheeks quivers with pleasure, and there is a merry
twinkle in his eyes.

'Thanks be to God. He saved your life. . . .'

Shams also gets up disturbed by the noise, and comes to see the
snake. Dilchain, who is still inspecting the reptile and poking it with the
stick, relates to him the whole story, emphasizing how the master
brought it out of the gutter with his hand and broke its back.

Mir Nihal smiles and goes to the pigeon house. He finds that one of
the young ones of his rare Shirazi pigeons had died. The snake had tried
to swallow it but had failed. This pigeon house contained Mir Nihal's
breeding pigeons. His flying pigeons were housed on the kotha of the
adjoining house which belonged to the widow of his late brother-in-law,
and was lying vacant.

He feels sorry for the young one of the pigeon which had been reared
after a great many of the same pair had died. But he throws it on the
heap of refuse, and washing his hands comes back to finish his meal.

Having finished it he picks up his coat and goes out to the men's part
of the house. As he reaches the vestibule Asghar enters quietly walking
on tiptoe. He is a tall and handsome young man with his hair well oiled
and his red Turkish cap cocked at a smart angle on his head. The upper
buttons of his sherwani are open and show the collar of the English
shirt that he is wearing under it. He looks an aesthete, and has a
somewhat effeminate grace about him. And round his wrist is wrapped
a jasmine garland. As he enters his pumps creak. Mir Nihal stops and
turns to Asghar and says in an angry tone:

'You are again wearing those dirty English boots! I don't like them. I
will have no aping of the Farangis in my house. Throw them away! . . .
And where have you been so late in the night? I have told you I don't
like your friendship with Bundoo. Do you hear? I shouldn't find you
going there again.'

But he is not in a very bad mood and goes out. Asghar takes the
lantern and goes into a room, leaving the house in the dark, lit only by
the dim and hazy starlight. From the platform comes a woman's voice

saying in an angry whisper: 'Please, what are you doing? You never see the time nor the opportunity. . . .'

But Asghar comes out of the room, and all becomes quiet again. The date palm leaves quiver in the wind, and a shooting star leaps and is seen falling towards the earth, but is soon lost to sight behind the date palm leaves; and night holds sway over the sleeping earth.

2

ASGHAR sleeps on the roof all by himself. He goes up, lost in thought, and lies on the bed, first turning from side to side on account of the heat, then as a cool breeze begins to blow, for the night is on the wane, he fixes his gaze at the sky.

The stars shine in clusters, so many of them, ever so many, little bunches of light, twinkling away with a white radiance, holding court, as it were. There are big stars and small stars, stars shining with a lonely lustre, and stars glowing in bunches like pearls strung together in a necklace or like the forehead ornament of a beautiful brow. There are bunches of them shaped like a semicircular purse, and stars shaped like a nose-ring studded on a delicate nostril. And there are stars and stars, and inside the stars are cool, green worlds, and every star is a lovely maid.

As Asghar lies on his bed he feels as if he is rising slowly on the viewless wings of the air. He is lifted up and up towards the sky, floating in the stratosphere, free like a bird which floats without effort or difficulty. He goes up without let or hindrance, just as he is lying on his bed, with his back towards the earth and his face towards the sky. But suddenly an unknown fear shoots through his brain. He sees the stars grow big and come down towards him from their places, huge green rocks of incandescent stone. They come down until they grow so big that he cannot see the sky. Fear overcomes him and he is hurled back and falls through empty space, and a sinking sensation comes upon him. He falls and cannot feel anything solid under his back, and he is mightily afraid.

Then he falls no more, and moves up again instead. He becomes light and travels with ease up towards the sky. He flies upwards and the stars do not seem big, nor do they come down. At last he is up there, and one by one the stars seem to move and begin to dance, and out of every star a beautiful maiden is born, and the starry maidens dance around him. Their glowing bodies are shapely and naked. Their breasts heave with a gentle motion as they dance, round and round and round, and their long dark hair waves in the breeze. They all come towards him, and with beautiful twinkling eyes tempt him towards them. He resists, but unconsciously, against his will, he too begins to dance and moves his legs and arms in the graceful gestures of the dance, until he finds that he is dancing all alone with his erstwhile sweetheart, Mushtari Bai, the graceful dancing girl. He is oblivious of the other stars, oblivious of himself and of Mushtari Bai who comes near him dancing around, but he turns away, and is interested in his own body, in love with his own flesh and the movements of his own arms. . . .

But as slowly as it had come upon him the vision vanishes, and when he awakes he finds himself on his bed gazing at the stars. But where is the Milky Way? he says to himself. It used to be here just over his head. Where has it gone? . . . Thinking of the Milky Way he falls asleep.

But he awakes again. Or was it a continuation of the vision or the dream? He looks up at the sky. There was the Milky Way stretched out from one end of the sky to the other, a bright line of incandescence, broadening out or narrowing to a straight line, going on and on until it faded in the far distance near the horizon.

He thought how the Prophet Mohammad had walked on the Milky Way for that eternal moment in Paradise, consecrating the very path on which he walked, making it holy and pure and white with his feet that trod to God. And he too was walking on the Milky Way, on and on, until he became conscious of another presence, a lithe and handsome figure walking ahead of him on the other white track. He recognizes the figure to be Bilqeece, his friend Bundoo's sister, walking with a heavenly grace, her hair spread out and her gaze fixed in front of her. His heart begins to beat and he follows her until he overtakes her, and arm in arm they go. But soon the road comes to an end, and in front there is a void, deep and dark and dim. As he looks down its abysmal depth his head begins to reel, and beads of perspiration come upon his brow. He turns to say something to the girl, but she is not there. Upon the brink of that void he finds himself alone, and an unknown fear grips his heart.

As he turns a big star, greener and brighter than any he had seen, floats before his vision. He moves towards it and the star smiles. Arms and legs and breasts form themselves out of the star. They become a beautiful woman and she begins to dance. He also starts dancing. And as they dance they come near, and as they come near he sees in the star the face of Bilqeece; and dancing they fall into each other's arms. Their mouths search each other and meet in a kiss. But the star vanishes and the sky melts, and he is one with his sweetheart, knowing a heavenly bliss which is not on this earth. . . .

Asghar opens his eyes for a while and sees the Milky Way stretched out above him, and by the side of the Milky Way a green, big star, twinkling bright; and he falls asleep with the picture of the star dancing before his eyes. . . .

3

THE world came to consciousness with the resonant voice of Nisar Ahmad calling the morning azaan. Far and wide his golden voice rang calling the faithful to prayer, calling them to leave their beds and arise from sleep, in a rippling voice full of the glory of a summer dawn. As yet it was dark and the stars twinkled in the cool and restful sky. Only on the eastern horizon there was a sense of birth, but as yet far away, hidden from the prying eyes of men. But the azaan carried forth a message of joy and hope, penetrating into the by-lanes and the courtyards, echoing in the silent atmosphere.

Men heard his voice in their sleep, as if far away in a happy dream. Some woke up for a while then turned on their sides and curling once more about themselves fell into a fresh slumber. Or they got up from their beds and, rubbing their eyes, groped for their bowls, and went to attend to the calls of nature.

In response to the azaan, as it were, the sparrows began to twitter one by one, in twos and threes, in dozens and scores, until at last their cries mingled and swelled into a loud and unending chorus. The dogs were awakened from sleep and began a useless search for refuse and offal, going about sniffing the very earth in search of food.

A cool green light crept over the sky. The stars paled, twinkled awhile, then hid their shy faces behind the veil of dawn which opened out gradually and the waxing light of day began to illumine the dark corners of the earth. A forward sun peeped over the world and its light coloured the waters of the Jamuna, dyed them rose and mauve and pink. Its rays were caught by the tall minarets of the Jama Masjid, glinted across the surface of its marble domes, and flooded the city with a warm and overbearing light. The sky was covered with the wings of pigeons which flew in flocks. These flocks met other flocks, expanded into a huge, dark patch, flew awhile, then folded their wings, nose-dived, and descended upon a roof. The air was filled with the shouts of the pigeon-fliers who were rending the atmosphere with their cries of 'Aao, Koo, Haa!'

This went on in the air and on the house-tops. Down below on the earth the parched gram vendors cried their loud cries and, dressed in dark and dirty rags, went about the streets and the by-lanes, with their bags slung across their backs, selling gram from door to door. And the beggars began to whine, begging in ones and twos or in a chorus. They stood before the doors and sang a verse or just shouted for bread or pice or, tinkling their bowls together, they waved their heads in a frenzy, beating time with their feet, singing for all they were worth:

> Dhum! Qalandar, God will give,
> Dhum! Qalandar, God alone;
> Milk and sugar, God will give,
> Dhum! Qalandar, God alone. . . .

They were ever so many, young ones and old ones, fair ones and dark ones, beggars with white flowing beards and beggars with shaved chins. They wore long and pointed caps, round caps and oval caps, or turbans on their heads. And there were beggars in tattered rags and beggars in long robes reaching down to the knees. There were beggars in patched clothes and beggars in white ones. But they had deep and resonant voices and all looked hale and hearty. The house doors creaked, the gunny bag curtains hanging in front of them moved aside, the tender hand of some pale beauty came out and gave a pice or emptied the contents of a plate into their bowls and dishes, and satisfied they went away praying for the souls of those within. . . .

Men went about their work with hurried steps; and from the lanes the peculiar noise of silver-leaf makers beating silver and gold shot forth like so many bottles being opened one after the other. To cap it all the tinsmiths began to hammer away at corrugated iron sheets with all their might. And the city hummed with activity and noise, beginning its life of struggle and care.

*   *   *

Begam Nihal had already got up, and, having finished her prayers, sat on a small wooden couch reading the Koran in rhythmic tones, moving gently to and fro. Mehro had also got up and sat on the platform performing her ablutions; and Masroor was getting ready to go to school. Shams was still asleep; but his wife was in the latrine. From the kotha could be heard the voice of Begam Jamal saying angrily to her widowed sister-in-law who lived with her:

'You have made my life a misery, bi Anjum. I have neither rest nor peace. . . .'

As the parched gram vendor came near the house Begam Nihal turned round and without opening her lips began to attract Dilchain's attention by muttering something like the dumb. One who was not accustomed to her habit could not have made head or tail of what she said. But Dilchain understood her. She was cleansing the pots sitting in the kitchen, fumbling with her hands in the ashes, then crunching the inside of the pot with the help of hemp string made into a knot. As Begam Nihal mumbled again Dilchain dipped her hands in a bowl of water and grumbled:

'There is no peace for me, O God.'

She got up and came near her mistress, who took out a pice from under her prayer-cloth and gave it to Dilchain, and asked her to buy gram.

Masroor came out of the room, books under his arm, wearing a dirty sherwani, dirt and oil on the lower part of his Turkish cap, and quietly went out by the door. Mehro, having finished her ablutions, was busy at prayer. Shams's wife came out of the latrine and vanished into the bathroom.

The sparrows chattered on the henna tree and on the date palm perched a crow and croaked in a hoarse and heart-rending way his monotonous cries. . . .

* * *

Mir Nihal went to the kotha where his flying pigeons were kept. He released the birds, and as they all came out he rushed at them with a flag tied to a bamboo stick in one hand, the other stretched out, and shouted at the birds: 'Haa, koo!' and off they went. They were ever so many, black ones and white ones, red ones and blue ones, dappled and grey, beautiful wings stretched out in flight.

The pigeons circled over the roof, then seeing their master's flag pointing towards the east where Khwaja Ashraf Ali's flock of rare, dappled pigeons was circling over the roof, they flew in a straight line shooting like an arrow. As they neared the Khwaja's flock they took a dip and suddenly rose upwards from below the other flock, mixed with the pigeons and took a wide detour. They would have come home, but Mir Nihal put two fingers in his mouth and blew a loud whistle, and the pigeons flew away in one straight line.

Khwaja Ashraf Ali began to rend the air with his cries of 'Aao, aao', but to no purpose. Mir Nihal's flock along with Khwaja Saheb's flew far away, mixing and intermixing with other flocks, forming a huge mass which grew smaller and smaller in the distance. The other pigeon-fliers were also shouting, calling their pigeons home. Many pigeons separated from the flock and, joining their wings together, shot towards the roofs. Only just a few of Khwaja Saheb's pigeons came home in ones and twos; the others were still flying with the rest, far away. Mir Nihal stopped whistling and sat looking in the direction where his flock had flown. Khwaja Ashraf Ali stood there peeping over the parapet, still shouting to his pigeons to come back home.

After a long time a dark patch appeared over the house tops in the distance, growing bigger and bigger as it neared. With its approach the noises increased and became more hysterical. As it drew near Mir Nihal's house Khwaja Ashraf Ali bellowed and howled, calling his pigeons home. He could be seen standing there shouting and waving his hands. He was throwing handfuls of grain in the air instead of water to attract the attention of the birds. But as the flock drew near home from the west it had to pass over Mir Nihal's roof; and he put his hand in an earthen pot which was full of water and grain and threw some water in the air. His pigeons descended on the roof; but many other pigeons, recognizing that it was not their home, separated. A small flock went towards Khwaja Saheb's house, and many others flew away in other directions.

As Mir Nihal's pigeons sat on the roof picking grain he saw that some new pigeons were also there, and a few of them were dappled. Mir Nihal smiled to himself, a smile of satisfaction and victory. He threw a little grain inside the loft and the pigeons rushed in, the new ones included. He shut the door, and catching the new ones he put them in another loft and released his flock.

Khwaja Ashraf Ali stood there and his close-cropped head could be seen peeping over his wall towards Mir Nihal's house. Now and then as some pigeon of his which had gone astray came into sight he shouted. But Mir Nihal sat there happy beyond measure, giving his pigeons grain

mixed with clarified butter. Other pigeon-fliers were shouting, and the
sky was full of wings, ever so many. . . .

As the heat became intense and a hot wind began to blow, the voices
died down one by one, and the pigeons were not seen in such great
numbers. The sky became bronzed and grey, dirty with the dust and
sand which floated in the air. The kites shrilly cried, and the grating
noise of tram cars far away sounded more dreary. A heart-rending
monotony and a blinding glare crept over the earth. People went inside
the rooms and closed the doors. Drowsiness came upon every living
thing. The dogs hid in cool corners, and the sparrows found shelter in
the shade of trees or inside their nests in the walls. Only now and then
the wild pigeons flew in and out of the veranda, cooed awhile, and
added to the feeling of monotony.

Even when the sun stood lower down in the sky, the heat remained
intense, and the glare hurt the eyes. The wind moaned through the
houses and the by-lanes and rustled heavily through the desolate trees,
and the sound of tinsmiths beating iron sheets and the cries of vendors
and ice-cream sellers sounded more disquieting and dull. But when
the sun went still lower down people came out and went about their
work. . . .

4

AT five o'clock in the evening Asghar went out. It was still very warm,
and the hot wind blew in gusts. As he came into the street the shopkeepers were sprinkling water in front of their shops, and the vendors
were shouting their varied cries, bellowing at passers-by or commend-
ing their wares in singsong voices—melons and water-melons, cucum-
bers and mulberries, plums and quinces, ices and sherbets—putting
their hands on their ears, raising their voices in loud melodies.

Asghar went past them, avoiding little pools of water, or banana
skins. At the corner of a by-lane some urchins had flocked round a mad
woman. She was naked. Her close-cropped head looked like a walnut
on her plump and pulpy body, and her breasts hung loosely and
dangled as she walked. As they pelted her with stones she shouted 'Ain,

ain,' helplessly, and saliva ran down her mouth. A grown-up boy went
up to her and asked her in a mocking tone: 'With whom didst thou
spend last night?'

The woman began to prance and caper and turned to Asghar for
help. But he made a wry face and quickened his step to avoid her.
From the barber's dark and dingy shop came a loud guffaw which
proceeded from the barber himself, a wiry man with a black curly
beard and long hair reaching down to his waist, well oiled and combed.
As Asghar's eyes met his the barber looked at him with his collyrium-
blacked eyes longingly, and Asghar turned his face away. Just then
was heard the gruff voice of Mirza, the milk-seller, shouting at the
urchins:

'You illegally begotten ones, run away. Why are you teasing the
helpless woman? Go home!'

Asghar went hurriedly past and was lost in the crowd which flowed
outside the mohallah.

His eyes fell on an oldish man in the crowd. He was dressed only in a
shirt and paijama, and on his head rested a round cap stiff with starch,
and flowers were embroidered on it in brown thread. His long beard
fell over his chest in a fine array. There was something sad and unknown in his eyes and they seemed to be looking for someone, a friend
who had been separated, or a loved one far away. Asghar was reminded
of his life at Bhopal and of those happy days when he had love to
receive and nothing to give at all. He had just to cast a glance and there
were many who would have given their lives to do his bidding. At the
least sign from him they would have done anything. There he was the
bestower of favours; there he was the loved one and not the lover. To
be loved is sweet, he thought, whereas to love is full of sorrow and grief
and pain. He had never known that the path of love was fraught with so
much hardship and frustration.

As he saw this man in the crowd he suddenly realized that he must
have caused so much pain to so many. He had never known what it
meant, so he did not do it knowingly. Even if he had known, would it
have changed his attitude? He did not know. He was filled with the
pride of youth, and the wine of life was coursing in his veins. He did not
ask those people to lavish love and care on him. If they burnt themselves like moths he was surely not to blame.

Still, he could not help thinking of one of them especially, Huzoor
Ali, who resembled the man in the crowd. Time and again he had seen
the same sad look in his eyes. Huzoor Ali was so devoted to him, but he

had always ignored him. If Asghar had happened to look at him kindly even once there had appeared such joy on his face.

But though Asghar had behaved more kindly with others he was always, somehow, indifferent to Huzoor Ali. He wanted him to do things for him, perhaps, but he did not wish to please him even with a kind word.

He realized all this today when he was himself in love and there seemed no way of compelling his sweetheart to take notice of him. Yet an insidious wave of optimism swept over him and he repeated to himself the line of Hafiz:

Love is created first in the heart of the beloved.

But it was so short-lived. Huzoor Ali had not succeeded in making Asghar love him. And he thought of an evening when Huzoor Ali had insisted on his coming to dinner at his place. He had refused and refused until the old man was broken-hearted and, heaving a sigh, he had cursed him gently by repeating the lines:

Would to God that you
Might also fall in love and suffer
As I am suffering now.

The curse had come true, Asghar thought; and there seemed no way out of it.

Engrossed in thought he reached the house of his friend Bundoo. As he saw the familiar massive gate leading into it, with a huge door curving into an arch at the top, and the two raised stone seats on either side of it where he had sat and chatted with his friend so often, his heart began to flutter. The thought that within those four walls lived his sweetheart made the blood course more quickly in his veins. There, inside that house is Bilqeece, thought he, scenting the very air with her presence, and here am I standing outside like a beggar with no one to give him alms.

He hesitated whether he should call on his friend or not. He was feeling shy; but he made up his mind and with a beating heart clanked the chain on the door. No response. He knocked again, and from inside came a gentle voice saying: 'Chanbeli, will you see who is at the door?'

The voice was sweet, and Asghar's heart beat more loudly as he thought it may be Bilqeece's. As he stood there a child went past him riding a stick, running joyously; and a man came singing from a by-lane in a rich and golden voice:

They'll steal the kohl clean from your eyes.
O friend, such thieves live here:
They've stolen all your goods and now
It is my turn, I fear.

As he took a turn in the by-lane the singer's voice died down and
mixed with the other noises of the city and the eternal cries of the
pigeon-fliers. Just then Chanbeli peeped out to see who had come, and
as she saw Asghar she smiled. He asked for Bundoo, but he was not at
home, nor was cousin Ashfaq, who was married to Bundoo's elder
sister, and lived with his parents-in-law.

Disappointed, Asghar made to go. But Chanbeli said: 'But your
sister-in-law is there. Shall I tell her you have come?'

Asghar felt self-conscious, and was undecided for a while. Then his
passion overpowered him and he decided to go in.

In the centre of the courtyard was a fountain around which jasmines
and tube roses were growing. Water had just been sprinkled, and it was
cooler inside the house than in the by-lane. His sister-in-law was sitting
on a bed covered with a clean white sheet, and by her side was the
paan-case and near the pillow were kept some jasmine flowers which
she was threading into a garland. She was slim with a golden complexion and black eyes with eyelashes that naturally looked blacked
with collyrium. Her gold ear-rings full of fresh jasmine flowers con-
trasted so well with her black hair and looked becoming on her olive
brown face. The palms of her hands and her fingers dyed red with
henna looked beautiful.

As Asghar sat down he felt awkward. He thought that he was an
intruder, superfluous like an unbidden guest.

His sister-in-law asked Chanbeli to bring sherbet; and from a room
in the courtyard came a woman's voice asking Asghar:

'Is everyone well at home? . . .'

His sister-in-law asked him:

'When are we going to hear the good news of your marriage?'

Asghar felt very self-conscious. There was a peculiar sadness in his
heart, and he felt restless. Somewhere inside the veranda Chanbeli
upturned a pot; two sparrows hopped and chattered on the wall, and a
pigeon misbehaved in its flight and the dropping fell near Asghar's
foot. He felt he should not have really come. But overcoming his
shyness he began to praise the border of his sister-in-law's head-cloth.
'It is so pretty,' he said. 'Did you make it yourself?'

She smiled, feeling flattered.

'Do you like it?' she said. 'It was made by Bilqeece.'

That name was a knell to Asghar's ears. He began to praise the needlework more, exaggerating its qualities. Inside him there was a stir, and he looked with furtive glances at the door of the room, hoping he might catch a glimpse of Bilqeece. But Chanbeli brought the sherbet in a silver cup, ice cool and delicious. Asghar drank it and as it went down his throat the stir within him increased. He felt restless and sad, and taking his leave went away.

*   *   *

As he came into the by-lane a strong gust of hot wind blew dust into his eyes. A small cyclone formed itself, and particles of dust, stray bits of paper and feathers rose in the air circling and wheeling, rising up above the house-tops in a spiral, and as the force of the cyclone died down they descended limply, fluttering and tumbling back towards the earth. Somewhere nearby two women were quarrelling inside a dilapidated house:

'O God, give me death. I am tired of this life. . . .'

In a grey mood Asghar went to his friend Bari who lived nearby. Slowly, one by one, he went up the stairs as if his feet were sore. The staircase, full of cobwebs, dust and pigeons' feathers, seemed long and unending. When he reached the roof he found his friend flying a kite, and the floor was littered with torn kites and the string lay in knots and coils all over the place.

Bari was a young man with a sallow complexion and light-brown hair which looked, somehow, so artificial. Young moustaches were growing on his lip, and beautiful flowers were embroidered on his white muslin shirt whose buttons were of gold, heart-shaped and joined to each other with a fine chain; and he wore a charm tied round his biceps. As he saw his friend come in Bari said to him without taking his brown eyes off the kite up in the sky:

'I say, where have you been all these days? You have come after a long time.'

'Don't ask me,' Asghar replied sadly, and then quoted the lines from a poet:

> 'Life has become a burden, the time is ripe for death;
> The space of existence has shrunk into a narrow cell.'

'But what has happened to you?' Bari enquired.

'Nothing has happened, and yet everything,' Asghar replied as if from far away in a breaking voice. 'Life is a storm.'

'Don't talk rot,' Bari said, and shifting his position suddenly began to pull the string.

The sky was full of kites, black kites and white kites, purple kites and blue. They were green and lemon coloured, red and peacock blue and yellow, jade and vermilion, plain or of various patterns and in different colours, black against yellow, red against white, mauve alternating with green, pink with purple, striped or triangular, with moons on them or stars and wings and circles in different colours, forming such lovely and fantastic designs. There were small kites and big kites, flying low and kites that looked studded in the sky. They danced and they capered, they dipped down or rose erect with the elegance of cobras. They whirled and wheeled and circled, chased each other or stood static in mid-air. There was a riot of kites on the sky.

Bari was flying a zebra-striped kite and it had formed a painch with another. His opponent's kite was circling round itself far away as he slowly released the string with gentle twists of the finger. Bari bit his lip and began to pull hard at his string. Then he suddenly let it go and the kite flew fast with the force of the wind. But his string had got worn out under the strain, and as the other fellow stuck to the same tactics of 'release' Bari lost his kite, and it flew far away, cut from the string. A number of kites began to hover and circle round it in an attempt to get it entangled in their strings and pull it home.

A shout went up from his opponent's side, a loud chorus of voices: 'Shame on the zebra, boys, sha-a-a-me.'

And a boy drolled out a tune from a nearby roof:

> With one twist I've cut thy kite,
> O my darling boy. . . .

Bari began to pull and draw his string home, but someone caught it far away. He stretched it and released it, thinking that it had got entangled in something. Then, realizing that someone had caught it, he cursed under his breath and pulled the string hard. It snapped from the middle and Bari got the remainder safely home.

Trying to get away from the mess of string around him, Bari said, more to himself than to his friend:

'I say, that was a rotten painch. Would you care to fly one?'

Saying this he hurriedly went to a heap of kites lying in a corner. All of them seemed to be torn. He looked for gum, but there was none. A shout went up again from his opponent's side:

'Shame on Bari, boys, sha-a-a-me.'

Bari cursed aloud, and blowing at his nose loudly he began to repair the kite with the mucus.

Asghar said 'No' to his friend's query and sat down on the parapet, immersed in thought. The sun was setting and the western horizon was dyed a dirty red for the atmosphere was not clear and the dust and the smoke of engines far away had made the air dirty and black. Flocks of pigeons rose from house-tops and were lost in the toneless colours of the darkening sky. Far and wide wherever the eye could see, houses stretched for miles, their roofs and walls dim with dust and years. Here and there some new house was being built, and its scaffoldings looked hazy and dim. On one side the long low hills stretched, rugged and dark in the hazy distance, one dreary line of monotonous rocks. On the other side the ugly Clock Tower jutted its head towards the sky, and by its side the dull red building of the Town Hall looked drab. Wild pigeons circled and towered above the two buildings and, beating their wings for a while, settled down on the roof of the Hall and in the crevices of the Tower. The Jama Masjid looked diminutive and shrunk, and its red-stone plinth and the marble domes all looked grim in the austere light.

Suddenly in the midst of this dreary scene was flung a stone. A moazzin from a nearby mosque raised his voice, calling the faithful to the evening prayer. Other moazzins called from the other mosques. As their voices were nearing an end there rose on the wind the voice of Nisar Ahmad, for Asghar's mohallah was not far away from where he sat. His resonant voice came bringing peace and rest, and a sense of the transience of life, that all that we do is meaningless and vain. Asghar sat listening to the azaan until it died away, leaving a sense of silence and a buzzing sound in the ears.

As it was getting late Asghar performed the ablutions and began to offer his prayers. Bari also joined him. As they finished Asghar's eyes fell on a lonely star shining in the sky. The heat was still intense and the floor on which they had spread the prayer-cloth was warm. But as they rose a gust of wind blew and brought with it freshness and life.

Putting down a bed which stood against the wall Asghar lay down on it and began to gaze at the sky. A green light had crept upon it and it looked restful. Bari was putting his kites away, and as he came back

Asghar heaved a sigh and said to him, obviously wanting to attract his attention:

'Is there anything else besides grief in this world? Is there no happiness, no joy for us human beings?'

'What has happened to you?' said his friend. 'You have been like this ever since you came.'

'Nothing has happened,' said Asghar. 'What can happen to me?'

'After all,' said Bari, 'there must be a reason for your mood.'

'Nothing,' Asghar replied, heaving a sigh, and his beautiful eyes looked deep and sad with pain, and his fresh skin looked wrinkled and old. 'It's all a question of fate,' he said. 'There are sorrows and miseries which grip you in their claws, and there seems no escape from them. We struggle, but we cannot get out of the net which fate has cast about us.'

Bari slapped him on the chest and said:

'Why, what on earth is the matter? Tell me.'

'But can you understand? Can anyone understand?' Asghar replied, and then quoted from the Persian Hafiz:

'The night is dark, the waves rise mountains high,
   And such a storm is raging!
   What do the pedestrians know of my plight moving
   Upon the shore that's safe and dry?'

'Well, are you in love?' said Bari, hitting the nail right on the head. 'Who is it this time? Are you no more interested in Mushtari Bai? Which reminds me, she was inquiring about you last night.'

'She can go to hell,' Asghar replied with annoyance. Then he cooled down, and said: 'Listen, Bari. It's a matter of life and death for me.'

'Who is she?' his friend asked sympathetically. 'I am at your service if I can help you.'

'She is beautiful, Bari, very beautiful,' Asghar said. 'She is graceful as a cypress. Her hair is blacker than the night of separation, and her face is brighter than the hours of love. Her eyes are like narcissi, big and beautiful. There is nectar in their whites and poison in their blacks. Her eyebrows are like two arched bows ready to wound the hearts of men with the arrows of their lashes. Her lips are redder than the blood of lovers, and her teeth look like pearls studded in a row. . . . I tell you she is beautiful.'

'Is she a living being or a poem?'

'You have started joking, and for me it's a matter of death,' Asghar said, and quoted from a poet again:

'Betake your way, O breeze of the Spring,
Frolic not with me:
You are in a playful mood,
But I in none of ecstasy.'

'Then tell me who she is,' Bari said, showing a trace of annoyance.
'It shouldn't be difficult for you to win her.'

'That is the difficulty,' Asghar persisted in avoiding the issue. 'Fate seems to be against me. Had she been any other woman it may not have been so difficult. But now...'

'Who *is* she?' Bari asked impatiently.

'She is Bilqeece, Bundoo's sister,' Asghar replied in a whisper.

'Then why are you worrying? What difficulty can you have in marrying her?' Bari said hopefully.

'No. There you are wrong. What have I that they should care for me?'

'They would accept you with open arms,' said Bari. 'It's not easy to get a young man of such a good family and charm. Besides, they all like you.'

Asghar heaved a sigh and looked at the stars. He was reminded how so very often Bundoo's mother had entertained him. Whenever he had gone inside she had talked to him from behind the purdah. She had even said once that she scarcely felt it necessary to observe purdah with him. He remembered how she had expressed the wish that he should teach Bilqeece, about a year ago. But Ashfaq had opposed it.

He thought of the day when he had seen Bilqeece a few weeks ago. It was evening and he had gone to see his sister-in-law. The staircase was just in front of him. Perhaps Bilqeece did not know that he was sitting there, for she came down into the courtyard. It was not until she stood face to face with him and their eyes met that she became aware of his presence. Seeing him she rushed inside. He had sat there wonderstruck, overpowered with her beauty.

Sometimes a fleeting glance goes more deeply home than a meeting. For Asghar this glance meant all the world. He thought it was nothing and that he would forget it. But her thought was with him day and night, following him wherever he went like his shadow or the memory of happy days and beautiful dreams. In the daytime he carried the secret joy of her loveliness hidden in his heart; and at night when he lay down to sleep the stars brought to him a message of love and happiness. She came to him dancing in his dreams, and in waking hours he could not forget her face.

As days went by this chance meeting became a malady and he could get neither rest nor peace. He thought of marrying her, but the thought of his father and mother stood in his way. They would never allow the marriage, he said to himself. For not only was her father a Mughal, but because somewhere in her line someone had married a prostitute or maidservant. The different race and caste (his people came of Arab stock and prided themselves on being Saiyyeds, direct descendants of the Prophet Mohammad) and this low blood in her veins were bound to stand in the way of his father giving his consent to the marriage. His mother could, perhaps, be brought round; but he could not speak to his father, firstly because it was not done, secondly because with his pride of family and blood, and his inherent conservatism, the old man would never listen and only get angry.

Asghar was between the devil and the deep sea. On one side of him stood the wall of the Family, on the other his deep and incurable passion. He spoke to his friend about his difficulties and doubts and fears. Bari saw his point and agreed. But he was not to be defeated so easily. He suggested that if Asghar gave him some money he would get him some charms which would help in subduing his father. Asghar did not much believe in charms, but Bari said: 'It's all the word of God and has efficacy. You cannot deny that.'

'That is true,' said Asghar. 'But I have no money to give you.'

'It wouldn't be much. Only about twenty rupees or so for the prayers to the dead and a feast to the poor. I tell you, I shall get you a charm which will act like magic. Take my word . . .'

The moazzins began to call the night azaan, and realizing that it was late Asghar got up to go. The by-lanes were narrow and dark, lit only by kerosene lamps here and there at the turns. Heat exuded from the walls and the cats stole out of doors. The hum of the city still came from far away. A flower-seller went past him and scented the air for a while. Then again the stink of gutters filled the nostrils as before. As he passed a house he saw a young woman remove the gunny bag curtain hanging in front of the door to give alms to a beggar. As he received it, the beggar began to bless her:

'May God keep thee and thy children alive, daughter. May He give thee plenty. . . .'

As he took a turn in the lane Asghar came to the main road and mixed with the crowd, still lost in thought, thinking of his sorrow, and of finding a way out. Already a scheme was forming in his head, and he thought of winning some people over to his side. He could not give up the fight, but the task was by no means easy.

5

BEGAM WAHEED, Asghar's eldest sister, had been married to Saiyyed Waheedul Haq in Bhopal. But she had become a widow at the age of nineteen, soon after the birth of her second child. She was religious by nature; and, not to arouse unnecessary suspicions, she had decided to live with her husband's people. For though Islam permitted her to marry again, the social code, derived mostly from prevailing Hindu practice, did not favour a second marriage.

There is no doubt that she missed her own people and wanted to go home. But she had other responsibilities now, and being very fond of her children, like all mothers, she sacrificed her own pleasures to the interests of her children, a boy and a daughter. She felt very lonely in an alien land and often wept silently. But Asghar had been the soothing element in her life. He had stayed with her ever since she had been married, and, in fact, Begam Waheed had brought him up like a son.

So now when he was in distress he wrote to his sister to come to Delhi, for his going to her would not have helped him at all. He was in great distress, he had written, without mentioning its cause. The letter was gloomy, and pictures of death flashed through it like lightning in a night dark with storm. His sister could not really make out what it was all about. But she was filled with anxiety for Asghar, and her motherly instinct was aroused.

So one morning the old postman brought a letter from her announcing her arrival. Mir Nihal was just going out when he got the letter. An unconscious smile appeared on his face and his lips trembled with happiness as he read the news. She was his eldest daughter and Mir Nihal was very fond of her.

He had already gone into the by-lane, but he came back. His servant, Ghafoor, was sitting on a bed in front of a small room by the side of the gate of the men's part of the house. He was somewhere in his thirties with a black beard, oval in shape, with the hair on the cheekbones shaved off. He put a good deal of oil in his hair which was bobbed and it trickled down to his forehead. There was kohl in his eyes and a charm hung round his neck by a string. He had just started smoking his hookah, and on its smoking-stick sat a parrot, part of its wings and back all yellow because of the attar which Ghafoor rubbed on its feathers. Seeing Mir Nihal come back he got up and asked him if he had forgotten something. But Mir Nihal smiled and said that his eldest daughter was coming home. Then he went inside the house and gave the letter to Begam Nihal; and happy and smiling he went to his work walking lightly with quick steps.

Begam Nihal was also happy. It was an event if one of the children came home. Their two eldest sons were in Government service and lived far away from them. But being nearer home than Begam Waheed they often came to Delhi, at least two or three times in the year, or their families came. Their daughter lived in Bhopal, far away, and she could not come so often. In fact, she came only once in a year or so. That is why both of them were happy to get the news of the arrival of their daughter. Mehro was bursting with happiness, and Asghar, of course, could not expect anything better. He waited for his sister's arrival with impatience, counting the days; and as each day passed he heaved a sigh of relief.

Things went on as before in the house. Mir Nihal flew his pigeons in the mornings, then went out to work. He had a share in a shop of lace dealers. He had some property, no doubt, a bit of land in a village nearby and some houses in Delhi; but his growing family—he had had nine children, but two daughters and two sons had died—had necessitated some kind of business to increase his income. He was an aristocrat in his habits, a typical feudal gentleman, as his hobbies testified. Besides pigeon-flying he was fond of collecting old china and he had devoted some time to alchemy and medicine.

But most of his time was now spent at the shop, from ten till four. His pigeons he could not really give up. Every morning and afternoon he would be heard flying them, crying himself hoarse or beating the roof with his shoes to drive the pigeons away from home. In the evenings many a pigeon-flier would come, asking his pigeons back if he happened to be an amateur, or just to talk things over.

At night after dinner he usually went out. At home he had given out that he went to see his friend Nawab Puttan, but he went to his mistress, Babban Jaan, a young dancing girl. Since she had become Mir Nihal's mistress and was in his employ, she had given up living in the Chaori Bazar. Mir Nihal had rented a house for her in Dareeba. She lived there and entertained him with her conversation and songs and her lithe figure and young body. He came back home at twelve or one in the night and went to bed.

By this time his servant Ghafoor would be away. He too was a gay bird. He was not only strong and virile, but possessed great charm. With his Tartaric ferocious eyes, his hairy chest, the oil trickling down over his brow, and his fine white long coats smelling of strong attar, he was a favourite with the prostitutes. Many of them had engaged him to entertain them at night when their paying customers had departed. For the prostitutes were of two kinds, the cultured ones and whores. The cultured ones were patronized by the rich and well-to-do. Young men were sent to them to learn manners and the art of polite conversation; and the older people came to enjoy their dancing, music, and their company in general. They had, thus, two kinds of lovers, one who came for their own entertainment, and the other who entertained them. Ghafoor belonged to the second category, and was a favourite with the dancing girls.

He never ate at home, but took flour and had fine bread made at the baker's and supplied the ghee himself. He took exercise in the morning to keep fit, and ate well. But he was a good and conscientious servant. That is why Mir Nihal did not mind his nocturnal absences.

                                   *   *   *

In the zenana things went on with the monotonous sameness of Indian life. No one went out anywhere. Only now and then some cousin or aunt or some other relation came to see them. But that was once a month or so or during the festivals. Mostly life stayed like water in a pond with nothing to break the monotony of its static life. Walls stood surrounding them on all sides, shutting the women in from the prying eyes of men, guarding their beauty and virtue with the millions of their bricks. The world lived and died, things happened, events took place, but all this did not disturb the equanimity of the zenana, which had its world too where the pale and fragile beauties of the hothouse lived secluded from all outside harm, the storms that blow in the world of men. The day dawned, the evening came, and life passed them by.

The time passed mostly between eating, talking, cooking, sewing, or doing nothing. Every day Begam Jamal and Anjum Zamani, her sister-in-law, came down and, peeling potatoes or some other vegetable for dinner, or just sitting idle, cutting areca nut into small bits which they collected in circular purses, they let their tongues loose, and talked and talked, of marriage and death, of this and that, but mostly of people and the family. Now and then tempers rose, first one voice raised its pitch, then another, and for no cause, over nothing, a quarrel ensued, between Begam Nihal and her sister-in-law, or Begam Jamal and her sister-in-law, or Dilchain, who always sat near the ladies. Sometimes Begam Jamal would shout at Shams's wife or at Mehro or

Masroor. She would stand there, handsome still, with her broad forehead, prominent nose, fair complexion, and waving her hands in the air she would curse and shout and bellow. She could shout, and if anyone interfered then tears began to flow, breasts were beaten, and heaven and earth made one.

Now and then Mehro and Masroor came to blows, but Mehro had the upper hand. Their quarrels mostly started with Masroor's teasing Mehro by mentioning the name of her fiancé. When Masroor would be annoyed with her he had just to mention 'Meraj' to throw her in a bad temper. She, of course, liked it in her heart of hearts; but the name brought her hidden wish to the surface with a rude suddenness that not only disturbed her emotional balance, but also exposed her inhibitions which grow in the repressed lives of Indian women like cobwebs and mushrooms. To conceal her consciousness of sex she flew into a temper, without, of course, realizing its unconscious and hidden cause. Meraj's name fell upon her ears with a splash like a stone in the midst of the stagnant water of a pond which sets up a whirlpool of waves rushing one after another. From nowhere a storm wells up for a while and disturbs the placidity of the pond's static life, but soon it subsides and the water becomes calm again. In the same way was Mehro's equally static quiet disturbed, wrenching her wish out of the darkness of the mind into the broad daylight of consciousness. She would then threaten Masroor, saying that it was her house; but it all became quiet again like the pond.

Masroor would shed a few tears and, filled with self-pity, would think of his dead parents and of his aunt, Begam Nihal's sister-in-law, who had brought him up and had left him in Delhi for the sake of education as she lived with her daughter and son-in-law, Mir Nihal's second son. But patience is another name for helplessness and he would become quiet and resigned.

His life passed mostly between school and home, or he was sent on errands or to the bazar to change this cloth and buy that lace. Mehro's trousseau was being prepared little by little, although there was no sign of the marriage yet. Often it happened that he came back tired from the school, ate whatever was kept for him, thin round bread, cereal and, if it was left over, a little soup with meat in it, and was sent to buy something in the scorching heat of a May noon. . . .

Shams, of course, got up late, went to the office—he was employed in a Government office—came back at five, went to the mohallah mosque to offer his prayers, or now and then to the bazar. Sometimes a cousin or an uncle dropped in—they came often, in fact—and Shams would talk shop or of saints and Sufis and religion. Often on Thursdays, the Muslim sabbath day, he would go to pray at the tomb of some saint, especially to Nizamuddin where, on these days, qawwals would gather and sing mystical and religious songs with an amorous flavour. But mostly he was absorbed with his wife. . . .

Every morning and evening the water-carrier shouted: 'I have brought the water.'

And he came in without waiting to be asked, covering his face with a red veil, doubled up under the weight of the water-skin, his hands looking frost-bitten, and went up to the earthen pots and emptied his watery load.

The four walls stood high, shutting them all in from the world, protecting them from noise and life. The sparrows hopped on the henna tree, drank water from the earthen dish hanging from it or ate grain, and chattered, chattered unendingly. On the date palm paper kites got entangled, crows cawed, or real kites sat and shrilly cried. The wind blew the leaves to and fro, dust floated in the air, and at night the cats quarrelled over bones under the wooden couches or miaowed and caterwauled on the roofs. In the by-lanes, in the streets, the gutters stank, beggars whined, vendors shouted, and life went on. . . .

6

ONE day Begam Waheed arrived. They had all been expecting her, and when the kahars shouted: 'Receive the guest,' they all rushed to the door. Begam Waheed had hardly got out of the doli when she was caught hold of and one by one they all pressed her to their breasts. Her pretty daughter went through the same ceremony, and her son also had his cheeks stroked by loving fingers. Then a chatter, chatter, filled the house. They even forgot to pay the kahars off who shouted from outside until someone thought of them and Dilchain was sent to pay them off very much against her will. For she too did not wish to leave the guest even for a while.

Asghar had gone to the station to receive her. In the afternoon Mir Nihal came home beaming with happiness. He brought a water-melon, big and bulky, on the head of a coolie. When it was cut it turned out to be red, and everyone enjoyed it and collected the seeds to be dried and eaten.

Masroor was also happy, and when Shams came home from the office he too felt gay and instead of closing himself up in the room with his wife he sat with everybody talking. Even Ghafoor was affected, and he put a little more attar on his clothes and his beard, and besmeared the parrot with it. Even the sparrows seemed gay, and the leaves of the date palm fluttered and beat their heads with joy....

*   *   *

With her small eyes Begam Waheed looked at Asghar anxiously.

'You have grown so thin and pale,' she said to him, and then to her mother: 'What has happened to Asghar? He looks only bones.'

Asghar looked away from his sister, smitten with self-pity; and Begam Nihal remarked:

'It's nothing but this terrible heat.'

Begam Jamal started complaining against God, fanning herself frantically:

'The heat is simply awful this year. There is neither peace at night nor rest in the day. My whole body is full of sores.'

And she bent down and, pulling her shirt up at the back, began to show the heat sores. Then she turned to her sister-in-law:

'For God's sake, will you please fan my back, Anjum.'

As she began doing so Begam Jamal blessed her:

'May God keep you alive....'

*   *   *

It was not until after dinner that Asghar found an opportunity of talking to his sister. It was past ten o'clock and from all around came the strains of qawwali and of hectic clapping as the singers' party clapped together beating time. Then all sang in a chorus mystical love poems which could be taken as addressed to God or Mohammad or to some earthly sweetheart, to the accompaniment of a harmonium. The leader of the chorus would sing a line at the top of his voice, then the others would begin to sing, repeating the same line over and over again as some religious person worked himself up into a frenzy and beat his head and shouted loudly: 'Haq Allah, Haq' (God is true). With these shouts the singers would raise their voices and clap more loudly. But the song would end at last, and there would begin the sound of the harmonium, the drum, and clapping as the singers prepared the audience with their orchestra for the next song, playing the tune for a while before they began to sing.

'You know, Sister,' Asghar said to Begam Waheed, 'there are some people who are lucky; but there are many unfortunate creatures in this world who have never known any joy or happiness. There is only sorrow written in their kismet.'

Begam Waheed heaved a sigh and said:

'Who can interfere in the ways of God?'

'Ever since I have set foot in the world,' Asghar continued, 'I have known neither love nor happiness. Right in our childhood, you remember, mother had lost her reason. I shall never forget those terrible days. She used to sit there staring in front of her, reciting verses. Then in a fit she would tear her clothes and wander about the house, blacking the walls with verses. . . .'

'Those were terrible days,' said Begam Waheed. 'Forgive us our sins, O God. . . .' And her eyes moistened with tears.

'I forget why we were sent to live in that deserted house near the graveyard,' said Asghar.

'You were too small to remember it. Mother's illness started when Dilchain had a son who died later. . . .'

'Oh, yes I have heard that father and Dilchain . . .' Asghar put in, but Begam Waheed quickly hushed him into silence and continued:

'It was then that mother and father had a quarrel. I remember one day father wanted to make up with mother. He used to smoke a hookah then. He sat in the veranda, and asked mother to light the hookah for him, but she retorted: 'I know only how to burn: I don't know how to light the fire.'

After that she became worse and wanted to run away into the streets. Father consulted so many hakims, but nothing did her good. One day came Kambal Shah, the faqir, and he suggested that she should be left alone and he gave some charms and amulets. That is why father decided to send her away with Uncle Bashir who had houses at Roshan Chiragh Delhi. She was loath to go and was persuaded with the greatest difficulty. She caught hold of you and wouldn't go without you or me. . . .'

'Yes, I remember now. It was evening when we were sent away in a bullock-cart, you and I sitting frightened in a corner, and Uncle Bashir (may God rest his soul) walked by our side. We were left in that lonely house. There were graves all around, and it was all deserted. The house smelt of dung and refuse, and bats flitted in and out of the long uninhabited rooms. Leaving us there Uncle Bashir went away to his house. Mother got on to the neem tree, you remember, and dangling her legs recited verses loudly. There was not a soul about, and we were frightened to death. . . .'

Asghar stopped for a while, and seemed to be lost in thought. The qawwals were singing loudly, repeating the same line over and over again:

'Cares and miseries, grief and sorrow.'

And a man in frenzy was rending the air with his cries of 'Haq Allah, Haq.' Begam Waheed would have liked to change the topic, but the hidden trait in feudal character which made people dwell on the macabre had hypnotized her, and she listened on to Asghar. The qawwals changed the line, repeating the second of the couplet:

'What is there I have not known in love.'

But the shouts of 'Haq' became more piercing and poignant, coming in a quick succession, and the qawwals began to repeat the first line again.

'Every day Uncle Bashir would bring us food,' Asghar continued. 'We would ask him when he would take us home, and he would only comfort us and go away. Mother would order us to collect neem twigs, and we would wander among the graves. She did not eat anything but dry bread soaked in water, and we could hardly eat the food for fear. The hot wind blew in the daytime raising dust, hissing through the trees and howled in the empty rooms. At night the owls cried, the dogs wept, and the donkeys brayed, and we were so frightened. One day, you remember, when mother was worse and having torn her clothes she climbed the neem and wanted you also to get there, you were terrified. It was night and you sent me to Uncle Bashir's house to see if someone was awake so that we could go there. I would never have gone, but fear drove me to go. I managed to reach his house, but they had all gone to sleep. When I was coming back I saw some people bringing a dead body on their shoulders and the shroud glowed in the dim light of a lantern. I thought it was death itself. I closed my eyes and ran. . . .'

Heaving a deep sigh Begam Waheed said: 'Yes, I remember. You came and cried and would not tell me anything. . . . But God was good and mother got better, and one day father came and took us home. How happy we were then.'

A gentle breeze stirred up, and another party of qawwals began to sing. Their voices rose on the wind and fell, carried away by the breeze. They were singing a poem addressed to Mohammad, and as they were a little distance away on the windward side only the refrain could be heard clearly. Their voices and the sound of clapping came together:

Ya Mohammad, Mohammad, Mohammad. . . .

'Then you were married,' Asghar continued, 'and I was sent to live with you. Those were happy days.'

Begam Waheed heaved a sigh, and the glow of memory brightened up her face.

'Do you remember how after the birth of your daughter,' said Asghar, 'I was playing with a nail-cutter and it fell on her breast and she howled and blood came out? . . .'

Begam Waheed laughed a dry laugh and said:

'Yes, I remember. And how afterwards you were ashamed and didn't like to come near her again.' And she began to gaze into vacancy.

'Then one day,' Asghar related, 'came the terrible news of brother-in-law's death (may God rest his soul). I had just come back from school when that most unfortunate telegram arrived. When I read it the earth seemed to slip from under my feet. I looked at the telegram and I thought of the two little children. Who was going to father them? They were left orphans. . . .'

Begam Waheed began to shed tears. Asghar also heaved a sigh, and continued: 'Then your in-laws blamed you for his death. . . . You and I are the two most unfortunate creatures on this earth.'

He stopped for a while, and Begam Waheed wiped her tears with the corner of her head-cloth.

'But you have been very brave,' Asghar said with admiration, 'and have fought all through your life courageously. God will reward you for your sufferings and sorrows. Father and mother wanted you to come back home after brother-in-law's death; but you were wise in staying there. Now they all admire you. But I am very unfortunate. Who will help me in my need? No one would ever see my point.'

'You should not worry,' said Begam Waheed. 'So long as I am alive I shall always do all I can for you. But tell me what is the matter? Your letter was also full of anxiety. . . .'

'You know,' Asghar said in a voice full of bitterness and self-pity, 'that father has never been sympathetic towards me. He is always shouting at me and getting angry. I must not wear pumps or English

shirts; I must not grow my hair in the English fashion. If I had stayed in
Delhi he wouldn't have even allowed me to learn English. Worse than
this I am not allowed to have any friends. I must not even meet Bundoo.
Knowing all this how can I expect him to have any consideration for my
happiness. You have perhaps some influence with him. But who will
speak on my behalf? . . . I am the most unfortunate creature in the
world. . . .'

He spoke with great pathos. Tears of self-pity rushed to his eyes; and
he looked away from his sister. Nearby on the roof of Sheikh Fazal
Elahi, karkhandar, a party of qawwals were singing. They sat in a row
and behind their backs were fat bolster cushions. In front of them sat
the leader of the chorus on a carpet. In the light of lamps and lanterns
the white clothes of the listeners looked eerie; and their shadows came
and played on the wall of Mir Nihal's house. A young man was beating
his hands on the floor in a frenzy. He would rise on his knees and throw
himself on the ground with all his force, shouting frantically 'hai, hai' all
the time. Asghar recognized him. He was Hameed, Sheikh Fazal
Elahi's nephew, who had been his friend in childhood. . . .

'Tell me what it is,' Begam Waheed said to Asghar. 'I will speak to
father and persuade him.'

'It concerns my marriage,' Asghar said in a whisper.

'I am so glad to hear the news,' Begam Waheed said with joy. 'May
God show us that auspicious day soon when I will see you a
bridegroom. Has there been some talk about it?'

'Not in particular,' said Asghar. 'But mother wants me to marry
Uncle Naseeruddin's daughter, and I don't want to marry her.'

'Is that all?' Begam Waheed asked.

'No. I want to marry another girl.'

'Who is that fortunate one?'

'There is the difficulty. She is Bundoo's sister, brother Ashfaq's
sister-in-law.'

Begam Waheed's face fell a little at this, and she said: 'But you can
get much better girls.'

'I won't marry any other girl,' Asghar said peremptorily. 'I will marry
her or no one else. You know that none of my wishes have been
fulfilled. I wanted to go to Aligarh to study further; but father put his
foot down. He wouldn't hear the name of Aligarh. It is after all a Muslim
institution, but he says that it is all the evil-doing of the Farangis who
want to make Christians and atheists of all of us. But that is finished
now. I have given in to him. But in this matter I won't listen. . . .'

The qawwals began to sing a Persian song:

> She aimed a poisonous arrow
> Straight from her eyes at me.
> She looks at one and hits another,
> How cruel and clever is she!

And Hameed began to shout more loudly.

'You know I have always put my trust in you,' Asghar said after a pause. 'I have always got love from you alone. You cannot forget your childhood when we used to play together, how I always did your bidding. You cannot forget how I have always been with you in your troubles and sorrows. In the name of all this and all that beautiful past I ask you to help me in my need. If I am not able to marry Bilqeece I will commit suicide. . . .'

'Don't say such evil things,' Begam Waheed said with fear. 'May God preserve you from harm. . . .'

Asghar had already touched the tender chords in his sister's heart; and the mention of suicide was the last arrow in his quiver which he used to such advantage. It decided his sister's attitude. She would do anything for him and she promised to persuade Begam Nihal to consent to the match. . . .

As Begam Waheed left Asghar heaved a sigh of relief, and a faint smile flickered on his face. The qawwals were repeating the lines continuously and Hameed was beating his hands and head on the floor more loudly than before. After a while they changed the lines, but Hameed became more frantic and they began to sing again:

> She aimed a poisonous arrow
> Straight from her eyes at me.

And it seemed that Hameed was soothed a little.

Asghar got up from the bed on which he had been sitting and stood by the parapet and looked at the scene on the other roof. The lines the qawwals were singing fitted in with his own mood and created a sadness in his heart. As he looked at the sinister shadow which the beating body of Hameed cast on the wall his thoughts moved away from himself to Hameed and his life flashed through his mind.

*   *   *

Hameed and Asghar had played together and studied in the same maktab in childhood. He was a simple boy, well behaved and gentle. He was not only the first to memorize the portion of the Koran which he was asked to remember by heart in one day, but he also washed the Molvi Saheb's dishes, swept the house and ran errands for him. When he was about eighteen years of age and there was talk of his marriage he suddenly went mad. He was a handsome boy and people began to say that some fairy or jinn had fallen in love with him. Others said that it was some evil spirit which had possessed him. They called all sorts of Molvis to treat him for these supernatural ailments and took him from one tomb of a saint to another, but to no purpose.

Now someone had suggested that qawwalis could cure him. But instead of soothing his overwrought brain they tortured him the more. The wild music and the songs touched him to the core. His emotions were aroused, the blood knocked heavily at his heart, and vague and unconscious memories stirred within him. At such moments his soul contracted into a point with pain, and he was filled with an ecstatic agony, and he beat his hands and head on the floor without being conscious of pain. The more mystically passionate the poem was the greater was his rapture and greater the agony. They all thought that the fairy or the jinn was being charmed, but they knew not what pain it caused Hameed.

Asghar was filled with religious awe. The music was going deep into his soul also. As he watched his old friend in frenzy, from nowhere, as it were, came before his mind the picture of Budho, Durgi Chamari's daughter. He had seen Hameed very often standing in the by-lane talking to her. She was a pretty girl, and there was something enchanting in her unusual grace. As she sat there in front of the small and dingy room in which she lived where even the light of day hardly penetrated, she did not look a low-caste woman but a fairy. She wore blue and green loose and wide paijamas, and the colours suited her. She was very fond of goats, and as one passed by her room the smell of the gutters and the damp was mixed with the pungent odour of uncastrated goats which dirtied the air for yards around and followed him right to the turn of the lane.

As one passed by her she looked at him unconcernedly, and smiled an uncanny smile, following him with her eyes a long way off. She would be cleansing the pots and utensils or just sitting on the bed over the gutter in the lane and at its foot would be sitting a fat and greasy goat. Often as Asghar passed that way she would begin to caress the goat, then she would throw a glance at him and look straight into his eyes. And there would be a hint of invitation there. Yet with all her charm there was something unwholesome and repulsive in her eyes and about her ways. Her mother was also pretty, as only Chamaris round about Delhi are. And it seemed that her daughter was not so fresh as she looked at first sight. There was an air of the night about her, something of a newly built house in a lonely place which has never been inhabited and is allowed to fall into ruins. Her face, though pretty, communicated a sense of the barrenness of the soul; and about her ways there was something of the women who have gone astray.

Asghar remembered how one day as he had passed by her he had heard two boys, one small, the other grown up, laying a wager with her. The bigger boy was saying: 'All right, let him box you anywhere he likes,' and he pointed at his companion, 'and I will give you two pice.'

'All right,' the girl had said.

The boy bared his arm and showed his fist. As he did so she put her hand on her breasts and said: 'Make one condition. He won't hit me here,' she said, pointing to her breast.

But the boy said: 'No. This was not settled. He can hit you wherever he likes. You can't go back on your word. . . .'

Asghar did not know what happened for he had come to the turn of the lane and from the other side he saw an uncle coming. So he moved on, sorry not to have seen the end of the wager.

As he thought of this he was filled with pity for Hameed. He was too gentle for her, too good and simple. No wonder he had gone mad. This sense of pity was deepened as Asghar thought of his own life, wondering if the same fate were in store for him. Hameed had at least had the pleasure of talking to his sweetheart. What about him who could not even see his? . . .

He stood there thinking of all these things, and the shadow rose and fell with the movements of Hameed. The stars looked down with knowing eyes. A gentle breeze blew, and the qawwals were still singing, and though the song was different now yet the feeling of pain was the same:

> If her heart has now become soft it matters not;
> If the strong one has become weak it matters not.
> Granted your red lips are the source of life,
> But if they serve not the lover they matter not.

Their voices rose and fell and rang through the silent night. Only now and then a dog barked somewhere, or an engine shrieked far away touched by the beauty of the voluptuous song. . . . A pigeon disturbed out of its nest by some greedy cat flew heavily in the night and struck against the wall, fluttering its wings for support. The Clock Tower struck ding-dong twice; and Asghar found his bed. . . . .

7

IN the morning Begam Waheed sat talking to her mother. She was tacking gold lace on a head-cloth and the cloth lay on her lap as with deft fingers she sewed quickly. Begam Nihal was peeling a pumpkin and was cutting it into bits, taking out the seeds.

'You know, mother, Asghar will be twenty-three in the month of Eed. You should now get him married,' Begam Waheed said leaving her sewing for a while and looking at her mother.

'Yes, I am also anxious about it,' said Begam Nihal. 'I was telling your father about it some time ago.'

'What did he say?'

'He was going to say something when that dirty snake came out, and he got busy with killing it. . . . I like brother Naseeruddin's daughter.'

'She is quite a nice girl,' Begam Waheed replied. 'But she won't be the right wife for Asghar.'

'Why not?' Begam Nihal said sharply. 'She is a nice girl and will be a very good housewife. She sews so well, and she is a very good cook. She will make Asghar very happy.'

She finished her work and kept the peelings in one side of the basket and the peeled white bits in the other, and called Dilchain to take it away. Then turning round to her daughter she said:

'I think we should not delay in this matter. I must take your father's consent and send the proposal.'

'But, amma, I don't think she is the type of girl who would keep Asghar happy.'

'What defect has she got? She is not one-eyed. Is she?'

'She is too plain-looking for Asghar.'

'Then will he bring a fairy from the Caucasus?' Begam Nihal said sarcastically, and then added in a tone of annoyance: 'I have never heard of such things before. You know how I selected their wives for your elder brothers, and they have never complained. On the contrary they were pleased. . . .'

Begam Waheed looked at her mother anxiously. Three wrinkles had formed on Begam Nihal's brow.

'But, amma, somehow the pair does not fit. Asghar is tall and handsome, and Surayya is short and plump and she has such a screeching voice and a bad temper.'

'What has happened to you, daughter?' Begam Nihal said with anger, and then quoted from a poet: '"Not so much should one go beyond his limit." It never pays to think so highly of oneself. It's a matter of a small mouth and tall talk. As for her being short, your eldest brother's wife is short, and she has borne him eight children—may God keep them alive. . . .'

'No, amma, it's not a question of that, but of Asghar's happiness. I know Asghar very well and I am sure he will not be happy with Surayya.'

'It has been the custom from the time of our elders,' Begam Nihal said, annoyed with her daughter for being persistent, 'that the girls the parents have selected for the boys have been accepted by them.'

'There is no question of Asghar's not accepting the girl,' Begam Waheed said in a persuasive tone. 'But you should see to his happiness. If he is not happy, then? . . .'

From the vestibule came a man's voice: 'May I come in?'

'Who is it?' Begam Nihal asked her daughter.

'It sounds like brother Saeed.'

Saeed Hasan came in. He was a man nearing forty, of medium height. He had a beard and a four-cornered cap was on his head. He was Begam Nihal's son-in-law, but his wife had died in child-birth two years ago. He was jovial, with an abundant stock of stories and a sense of humour. He came and sat talking of the family and other domestic matters. The talk came to marriage and Begam Waheed asked what sort of wife should a man like most.

'A man should give preference to moderation,' said Saeed Hasan. 'A wife should be of moderate stature, neither short nor very tall nor too fat. She should not be short because then she would give birth to many children. She should not be very tall as she would bend down soon after the birth of one child. She would not be too fat for then she will never have a child at all. That is why a man must give preference to one who combines all qualities harmoniously and proportionately. . . .'

They began to laugh, even Begam Nihal, who remarked: 'You are incorrigible, Mian Saeed.'

'Am I wrong in what I say, aunt?' said Saeed Hasan, and continued: 'And a man must marry a girl who would love him and serve him faithfully, one whom he could worship himself. For a man must worship his wife. And a man must marry. Once a man went to the Prophet and said that he was in great distress. Get married, the Prophet advised him. He went away and got married. But his worries did not cease. So he came again for advice. Marry again, was the Prophet's reply. The man got married a second time. When the Prophet met him next he enquired how his affairs stood. The man had no worries now....'

Saeed Hasan went on to relate some other story, obviously unconnected with the topic under discussion but having some hidden allegorical meaning. That was his way; and he seemed to be in love with his own voice. Perhaps what he said about worshipping a wife was true. He had himself been a good husband, and was heart-broken when his wife had died. But he did not wish to waste his youth and was anxious to have a son so that his name could live. His first wife had not given birth to a living child.

Having been very much in love with his wife he now wanted to marry her younger sister Mehro. His proposal had come for her hand. But, although no definite reply had been given, Begam Nihal did not very much want to give another daughter to Saeed Hasan. Not because she did not like him, but she was more attracted by Meraj. The young man himself had nothing much to commend him, perhaps; but his father was a wealthy person. He was in the service of the Bhopal State and had amassed a good deal of money. Besides, they also came of good stock, and were related to Begam Waheed's husband. That is why Begam Waheed was acting as the match-maker, and Saeed Hasan had hardly a chance.

Mother and daughter had already had a talk about Mehro's marriage. Meraj's people wanted the marriage to take place soon, and they had sent another reminder through Begam Waheed. Begam Nihal had spoken to her husband, but Mir Nihal had not given any definite answer. He did not wish to banish another daughter to far-away Bhopal, and Mehro was the youngest. She had got to be married, and Mir Nihal could not close his eyes to facts. But she could not be married away before Asghar....

*   *   *

When Saeed Hasan left, they came back to their conversation. Begam Waheed quietly suggested to her mother: 'What do you think of Bilqeece, brother Ashfaq's sister-in-law? I think she will be a nice wife for Asghar.'

'No,' Begam Nihal said with an air of indifference as if she did not consider the thing at all serious. 'We and they can't mix well.'

'But, amma, she is a nice girl and those people have money.'

'Money is not everything. It's blood that matters. Their blood and ours can never mix well. The good-blooded never fail, but the low-blooded are faithless.'

'But brother Ashfaq is married there, and they are very happy.'

'I am not going to marry my son to Mirzaji's daughter,' Begam Nihal replied, raising her voice a little in anger. 'They are Mughals, and we are Saiyyeds.'

'Brother Karim had also married a Mughal.'

'Yes, but she came of the family of Nawab of Loharu. In Mirzaji's wife there is the blood of a maidservant. I am not going to bring her daughter as my daughter-in-law. No. I like Surayya, and she is my cousin's daughter. I will get her for Asghar.'

'But if Asghar himself wants to marry Bilqeece?'

'How can he!' Begam Nihal said with anger. 'He will marry the girl I like and not a girl of his choice.'

'But Asghar wants to marry Bilqeece,' Begam Waheed said in a low voice, as if afraid.

'Hai, hai,' Begam Nihal shouted, shocked out of her equanimity; and as she said this she beat her breast with her left hand. 'Has the boy gone mad? If your father only comes to hear of this he will eat him up alive.'

'Asghar has set his heart on marrying Bilqeece. He says that if he is not able to marry her he will commit suicide.'

'That Begam Shahbaz has cast some spell on my boy. I was fearing it all the time,' Begam Nihal said with anger. 'He used to go to her house every day, and she has done something to him. Or she has given him some charm through Begam Jamal. . . .'

At this moment Begam Jamal came down from the kotha. As she heard her name being mentioned she asked: 'What are you saying about me, Sister-in-law?'

'Who was talking about you?' Begam Nihal said in a loud and self-conscious voice.

'I just heard you call my name,' Begam Jamal replied in an angry voice. 'What crime have I committed after all?'

'You always misconstrue things,' Begam Nihal said in a conciliatory tone, 'and imagine people to be calling you bad names.'

'There was something surely, that is why you were mentioning me. Why don't you tell me?'

'What has happened to you?' said Begam Nihal in a tone of disgust. 'You should not behave like this to me. . . .'

Two crows sat on the edge of the wall and cawed, eyeing a bone. Mir Nihal cleared his throat in the vestibule. As his voice penetrated the house Begam Waheed sat prim and adjusted her head-cloth, and Begam Nihal also covered her head. Begam Jamal mumbled something to herself and went towards the kitchen. . . .

8

THE heat was oppressive with a temperature of one hundred and thirteen in the shade. The sky was bronzed and covered with dust. It was late afternoon, and the kites, who had gathered from nowhere, circled high up above the earth, circling and moving a little forward, wheel within wheel and circle above circle in a big swarm. They came slowly and gradually from the west and the sky became reddish-yellow with sand. The loo had been blowing; and as the kites came near the wind increased in velocity.

Suddenly the western horizon became coppery, and it seemed that some hidden power was shooting tons of burning sand from below the earth towards the sky. The sunlight fell on this sand and gave the horizon the colour of shooting flames. The kites up above circled and cried and moved forward.

There was a lull for a while, a sense of tension as before a birth. Then the storm burst suddenly. Like a swarm of locusts the sand came forward making a gyrating noise. The wind struck against houses and roofs and trees; blew with a vengeance through openings, banging the doors and windows, wrenching the roofs, beating against the walls. It howled through the courtyards, in the by-lanes, in the streets, and a loud clatter of corrugated iron sheets filled the air.

The sparrows hid in the henna tree, holding on to the twigs; and a crow perched on the date palm holding a leaf with its talons for all it was worth, bending low. The sand had come to the centre of the sky and, like locusts when they espy a patch of green, it swooped down upon the earth and filled the rooms, and blinded the eyes. The wind swished and lashed the henna tree, and bent the date palm low down over the roof. The sun hid his face, and light began to fail. It became darker and darker as the sand spread over the sky. And the atmosphere became oppressive and suffocating.

Begam Nihal shouted to Mehro and the children to come inside the room. Dilchain hurriedly gathered the rags and clothes which lay scattered in the courtyard. Begam Jamal and her sister-in-law came down from the kotha, and everyone found shelter inside the big room behind the veranda. The wind howled and moaned, sand floated in the air, and it grew dark as the night.

'For God's sake, put a broom under the leg of a bed,' shouted Begam Jamal. And Begam Nihal cried: 'Where is Majeed? Has anyone seen the boy?'

A lantern was lighted and the eyes found some rest.

'I am here, grandmother,' Begam Waheed's eight-year-old son said as he bent down to put the broom under the leg of Begam Nihal's old wedding bed. But he could not lift it, and Dilchain came to his aid.

Begam Waheed's daughter Ruqayya's head was uncovered; and Anjum Zamani said to her:

'Cover your head, daughter, or some evil spirit may harm you.'

Mehro said to Majeed:

'You come to me, child, lest some evil eye strike you.'

'Why do we put the broom there, aunt?' asked Majeed.

'Because, our elders say, if you put a broom under the leg of a bed the wind-storm abates. . . .'

'It's the marriage party of some great jinn that's going,' said Ruqayya.

Masroor tried to go outside to watch the fun. But Begam Jamal shouted:

'Hast thou lost thy reason, boy! Dare to go out and I will break thy legs!' And she began to complain, beating her breast with one hand: 'These boys fear neither the wind nor rain. . . .'

The sand got inside clothes and stuck to bodies wet with perspiration and pierced the skin. The hair became tousled and rough with sand which came between the teeth and produced a strange sensation in the mouth. But soon the wind fell. Only the sand floated in the atmosphere, and the darkness held sway over the prostrated earth. The family settled down in the room, waiting for the storm to blow over and the sun to light the world again.

'I have become worried on account of Asghar,' said Begam Nihal to
her daughter in a whisper.

'Yes, amma,' Begam Waheed said. 'I am also very worried lest he
really does something evil. You know, he is so self-willed. And the fact
is that he has been unfortunate. Never has any one of his wishes been
fulfilled. . . .'

* * *

From the other corner of the room came the voice of Begam Jamal complaining:

'Allah is also restless. Every day new worries crop up.'

'Hai, hai, sister, what has happened to you?' came the shocked voice
of Anjum Zamani. 'You will never learn to keep your tongue inside
your mouth. . . .'

* * *

'What happens when a dust-storm comes?' came a child's voice from
the semi-darkness.

'You know, our elders say, when a dust-storm blows it means the
jinns are going to celebrate a marriage.'

'But we don't see the jinns, do we? Who are they?'

'No. The jinns are invisible. They are also creatures of God like us.
There is only one difference: God made us with clay and the jinns were
created out of fire.'

'Then they must be very hot.'

'They are not hot. You can't feel them.'

'Are they evil?'

'No. All of them are not evil. There are some evil spirits among them.
But most of them are Mussalmans like us, and some are holy. . . .'

* * *

'But your father will get angry and will never give his consent,' Begam
Nihal was saying to her daughter in a whisper. 'He doesn't even like his
friendship with Bundoo. How can he agree to Asghar's marriage with
Mirzaji's daughter?'

'We might lose the boy. You must persuade father.'

'It's easy to say a thing, but it's difficult to do it. You know your
father's temper. He will begin to shout.'

A little light came in through the doors and fought with the light
of the lantern for supremacy. Begam Waheed said to her mother:

'But Asghar's life is more important. He might really commit suicide.'
Begam Nihal heaved a sigh and said:
'I will try.'
The light grew strong, and things became visible in the room. Dilchain, who sat nearby listening to the whispers between mother and daughter, rose, and mumbled to herself:
'Let me go and see to the cooking.'
Then she opened the doors. The dark corners were lighted up and the lantern burnt dimly, its flame looking pale and yellow. The clouds of dust passed away, but the atmosphere was not yet clear.
The lantern was blown out, however; the broom was taken away from under the leg of the bed, and they all got busy with different things. And soon was heard the voice of the water carrier:
'I am bringing water.'
And he walked in and emptied his water-skin into the pots. . . .

9

IT was the middle of June and the heat was intense. Begam Nihal was mustering courage to speak about Asghar's marriage to her husband. The fear of the boy's committing suicide was preying on her mind.

Asghar was her youngest son, and since Mehro had been born about eight years after him she had lavished a good deal of care on Asghar. The other sons had grown up, found employment, and had settled down. Asghar was not so lucky. He had found a job in Bhopal a few years ago. But he had been called home soon after on account of the death of his sister, Begam Saeed Hasan. And things had so happened one after another that he had not been able to go back to his job. She was, therefore, more concerned on his account. She wanted to make up for Asghar's misfortunes, exaggerated, surely, as only a mother's heart can exaggerate the ills of a son, by arranging this marriage for him to his satisfaction.

But it was not entirely in her hands. Mir Nihal could not be ignored. Begam Nihal thought of the pros and cons, thought of what she could do if her husband refused to give his consent. She had to speak of it at first to him and then see how things turned out. She did not want to make a mountain of a mole hill for no cause.

Two days after the dust-storm she sent for Mir Nihal. He came in, noble, towering, with his white beard parted in the middle, his bobbed hair curled at the nape.

'Why did you send for me?' he asked his wife as he sat down by her.

'You never seem to take any interest in the house,' said Begam Nihal.

'Then what shall I do? Shall I start cooking?'

'Your ways are always so funny: either on this pole of the earth or on the opposite.'

The skin on Mir Nihal's cheeks began to quiver with a smile and he said good-humouredly:

'Then what do you want me to do?'

Begam Nihal also caught the contagion from her husband's good mood.

'I want you to give up flying pigeons.'

Mir Nihal began to laugh in a gentle voice and said:

'All right, tell me what is the matter?'

'Nothing is the matter. I wanted to talk to you about Asghar's marriage. Have you thought about it?'

'But you are also there to do it. After all, you selected their wives for your elder sons. You can select one for Asghar too.'

Begam Nihal mustered courage and spoke out:

'What about Mirza Shahbaz Beg's younger daughter?'

'Now leave this joking aside. Naseeruddin's daughter is all right. Better send the proposal.'

A seriousness had crept into Begam Nihal's face and made her look worried.

'I am serious and not joking,' she said.

'What!' Mir Nihal said with angry surprise.

'Asghar does not wish to marry brother Naseeruddin's daughter. He wants to marry Mirza Shahbaz Beg's second daughter Bilqeece.'

'How can he! It is impossible,' Mir Nihal said with an air of finality. 'He must be mad to think of it.'

Begam Nihal's face became dark with anxiety. Mir Nihal looked red with anger, as if he had been insulted.

'But what's the harm?' Begam Nihal put in, as if decided to fight the battle. 'She is a nice girl.'

'What is the harm, indeed!' Mir Nihal burst out as his temper rose to a high pitch. 'Have you gone mad along with him? How can my son marry Mirza Shahbaz Beg's daughter? You don't want to bring a low-born into the family? There are such things as the family honour and name. I won't have the marriage. . . .'

The dung-fuel seller had been shouting in the by-lane: 'Dung for fuel. Buy fuel.' And one of the donkeys suddenly blared forth an ugly bray, and another caught the contagion from his companion.

'But, after all—' Begam Nihal tried to put in in a tone which suggested persistence merely for its own sake and showed an acknowledgement of defeat. She had hardly said the words when Mir Nihal thundered:

'I can't hear of this. I have told you I don't give my consent to the match. I had asked you to stop him from mixing with those loafers and low-borns. But you did not listen. Now you want my name and honour to be damned!'

'But the boy threatens to commit suicide.'

'It would be a good riddance,' Mir Nihal thundered again. 'Is he my own offspring? My children cannot do anything against my wishes. If he marries Mirza Shahbaz's daughter I will disown him. I shall have nothing to do with him. Tell him that. Do you hear? Tell him I should have nothing to do with him, and that he could not look upon me as his father. . . .'

Raging, Mir Nihal went out. The by-lane was blocked with the donkeys belonging to the dung-fuel seller. Livid with rage he shouted:

'Why hast thou blocked the way? Get out!'

The dung-fuel seller, wearing a short loin cloth, a half-sleeved jacket of homespun and a dirty turban, began to beat the donkeys to drive them away. In the hurry a donkey rubbed against the wall and its load upturned. A strong gust of wind blew and fine particles of fuel dust filled Mir Nihal's eyes and nostrils. He began to sneeze loudly and shouted at the chamar, who began to apologize slavishly.

With difficulty Mir Nihal reached the *mardana*, the men's part of the house. His mood was thoroughly spoilt. The sky was overcast with dust and sand. The kites circled and cried; there was dreariness in the atmosphere; and a dust-storm was brewing. Mir Nihal walked up and down, raging like a lion. The pigeon-fliers shouted their eternal Koo Haas; and Ghafoor's parrot screeched: 'Say, parrot, talk.'

Finding there was no peace at home Mir Nihal put on his coat and went out. As he set foot in the by-lane the parrot imitated a man's laugh and gave out a peal of laughter and then added: 'Allah be thanked,' and began to twist its neck and turn its eyes up and down, screeching all the time. Ghafoor filled his hubble-bubble and began to smoke in a self-satisfied way. . . .

10

EARLIER in the day Dilchain had reported what she had heard Begam Nihal say to her daughter during the dust-storm to Begam Jamal in a confidential way. Begam Jamal had spoken of it to her sister-in-law. In the evening, long after Begam Nihal had a talk with her husband regarding Asghar's marriage, Begam Jamal came and said sarcastically to her:

'Congratulations, sister-in-law. I hear Asghar's marriage has been arranged.'

'Who has told you that? Nothing has been arranged.'

'What is the use of concealing things. I won't run away with your daughter-in-law.'

'But who has told you these lies?' Begam Nihal said in a self-conscious way, wanting to conceal the truth.

'I am not your enemy that you must hide your secret from me. As far as I am concerned, may you live a hundred years to enjoy the flowering of your children.'

'I should like to know the name of the person who has told you all this,' said Begam Nihal in an angry voice. 'God is my witness that Asghar's marriage has not been settled.'

'Oh, leave these things aside. I know even the name of your future daughter-in-law. Bilqeece is a very nice girl, and her presence will add grace to your house. . . . But I am surprised that Brother-in-law gave his consent.'

Begam Nihal would have liked to keep the matter secret, not because she really wanted to conceal it, but because she did not think it wise to make a thing public which had not taken a definite shape, and there seemed no hope of its coming about. But now that the cat was, somehow, out of the bag, she decided to talk it over. And she told Begam Jamal:

'There was only a suggestion about Bilqeece; but your Brother-in-law won't listen to such a thing. When I told him about this some time ago he shouted at me and got very angry, and said he would disown Asghar if he marries her.'

Begam Jamal showed such an interest in it not only because it was a family matter, but because Ashfaq, who was married to Bilqeece's elder sister, was her cousin. Mir Nihal had said sarcastic things to her about Ashfaq at the time of his marriage and had never approved of the match.

If Asghar was married to Bilqeece a little of what had been flung into her face would be washed off. That is why she began to discuss the matter seriously with Begam Nihal and, knowing the situation, she suggested:

'The best thing to do is to settle the thing quietly. Brother-in-law will come round in the end. If you wait for his consent nothing will ever come off. . . .'

Begam Nihal seemed to agree with her sister-in-law. For though women hold a subordinate position in Indian life yet in certain matters they can take the law in their hands, and marriage is one of them. She knew her son very well, and was afraid lest the boy really did something desperate. Thinking that one day her husband would surely give his consent to the match if she persisted, she thought of Begam Jamal's suggestion seriously. She spoke to her daughter about it, and she too was of the same opinion. So it was all settled behind Mir Nihal's back, and they thought of speaking to Begam Shahbaz about the match.

11

ASGHAR was restless. He cursed his fate and cursed himself. He went from home to Bundoo with his heart all a-flutter; and from Bundoo to Bari in a dark and pessimistic mood. His sister saw him a picture of grief and shed silent tears. His mother noticed that his appetite had deserted him, and she felt a great pity surge in her breast.

On the eventful day when his fate was being decided he had gone to Bari in a despairing mood.

'How are things progressing?' asked Bari.

'Can there be any hope for the unfortunate like me?'

'Don't despair. Things will come out all right in the end. Only don't forget what the poet has said:

"You are just beginning to climb love's hill;
Wait and see what hardships there are still." '

And he persuaded Asghar to go to Mushtari Bai, thinking that it might take his thoughts away from his troubles.

The night was warm and the moon shed a pale lustre over the weary world from behind a film of sand. The shadows lay across the roads, and the dark by-lanes looked mysterious in the moonlight. Beggars went about, tap-tapping the pavements, whining in front of doors. The flower-sellers shouted, and here and there the saqis, hookah-bearers, emerged from some corner and offered puffs at their hubble-bubbles to needy passers-by. Some people detained them, put the tubes in their mouths and pulled, puffing out the smoke. Having satisfied their want they paid a copper pice to the saqi who began to bless them, or else they went away without paying anything and the saqi did not complain.

They went through the Chaori Bazar, the quarter of ironware and brassware merchants, second-hand dealers in lace, and prostitutes. On either side of the narrow and noisy street sat the girls in balconies, ornamented and well dressed, and small lamps or lanterns shed light on their tempting faces. From all around came the sounds of song, whining of sarangis, muffled drums and the tinkling of bells, as the dancing girls entertained their customers.

The music made Asghar feel more sad, for it reminded him of his love. He wanted to turn back, but Bari forced him to go. As they turned into the dark alley lighted only by the moon where Mushtari Bai lived, for she was one of the cultured dancing girls and did not live in the quarter of the common whores, they heard two cats quarrelling on the roof. They purred angrily for a while then miaowed and caterwauled. And from nowhere, as it seemed, a man appeared singing a verse from Dard in a resonant voice:

> The wounds of love had made me
> A lighted tree aglow in the night:
> But even then—ah, pity me
> You did not come to see the sight. . . .

As he climbed up the staircase, lighted dimly by an earthen lamp, Asghar thought how he was happy once with Mushtari Bai. Her love was better, for it had its reward and did not cost him pain. But now he seemed married to grief. The world was a vast and dreary cave, he felt, and life was a misery.

As they reached the landing and stepped into the courtyard Mushtari Bai, who was lying on a bed, got up to receive them. As Asghar saw her he suddenly felt lonely and his heart seemed to burst. Mushtari Bai salaamed them and took them inside the room.

She was a beautiful woman, young and tall; and in her dark eyes there was something piercing and poisonous. But her face was gentle, and she looked a respectable woman. She was dressed simply but with taste, in a white tight-fitting paijama, a muslin shirt with flowers embroidered on it in white thread, and a pink head-cloth well starched and plaited. There was a fine nose ornament studded on her nostril, and in her ears were gold ear-rings filled with fresh jasmine flowers, and on her arms she wore gold bangles of a beautiful design. The palms of her hands and the soles of her feet were dyed red with henna.

As they sat down Mushtari Bai turned to Asghar and said in a sweet voice:

'You have become the moon of Eed. The eyes long for a sight of your face, but in vain.'

'I was so caught in the worries of life that I did not have time even to die.'

'I do not complain. The world is a selfish place,' said Mushtari Bai with a sad sincerity. 'Who thinks of such unfortunate persons like me?'

'Why must you have cause to complain?' said Bari. 'God has given you beauty and you have love. What else can a woman desire?'

'But when old age knocks at the door,' Mushtari Bai said with sadness, 'beauty of the body dies. Only virtue is beauty which I do not possess.'

'The beauty of the body is like a flower,' Asghar philosophized, 'which attracts the bulbul to itself and breaks his heart, like a candle which tempts the moths and burns their wings.'

'The real beauty of the flower lies in its smell,' Mushtari Bai replied. 'But I am such an evil-smelling flower that I repulse everyone. I am that candle which burns its own self, shedding tears of blood, and blackens the walls of the niche with its smoke. . . . No one cares for me. I am like a caravan-serai where people come, rest their tired bodies for a while and depart.'

'There you are wrong,' said Asghar. 'You are an oasis in the desert for which the eyes look and the heart yearns, a light put in the night to guide the weary travellers on their way. . . .'

'No, no,' Mushtari Bai said with a sigh. 'My life is a desert in which no oases exist. It is just a mirage, a will-o'-the-wisp. You think there is water to quench your thirst, that there is light to guide you on the way, but, in fact, there is nothing. . . . And even if I am what you say, I haven't succeeded in attracting you. . . .'

Bari, who was looking bored with this talk, said: 'Oh, leave this philosophy of life aside. Give us a song, my dear.'

Asghar was feeling guilty, for he knew that Mushtari Bai cared for him, and he also agreed. She began to sing and there was pain in her

voice and sadness in Asghar's eyes. She sang a poem of Bahadur Shah
written in his banishment:

> When as you came in silks and dazzled
> Me with the beauty of your Spring,
> You brought a new flower into bloom,
> The wound of love within my being.
>
> You lived with me, breath of my breath,
> And did not part from me a while;
> But now the wheel of Time has turned
> And you have left without a smile.
>
> You pressed your lips once on my lips,
> Your heart upon my beating heart,
> But all my trust and pride in you
> Lies crushed and shattered now, alas.
>
> And now I have no wish to fall
> In love with the faithless fair again,
> For they who sold love's remedy
> Have shut their shop for good and gone.

Mushtari Bai sang with great feeling, and Asghar was filled with the
unknown sadness that is love. As the song finished he looked out. The
moon shone in the sky and its green rays came through the sand, and its
light split into the different colours of the rainbow and formed a halo
round the moon. Asghar said: 'Beautiful, beautiful,' in appreciation of
the song and heaved a sigh. And he thought how his love had formed a
halo round his sweetheart.

Mushtari Bai also looked out and thought that it was her passion
which had dulled the sky. Then she began to make paans, and, rolling
them up beautifully into conical shapes, put them in a silver platter
and offered them to Asghar and Bari. Bari sat cross-legged like a
contemplating Buddha, and now and then he massaged the sole of his
foot with his hand. His round stiff cap embroidered with silver and
gold was kept tilted on his head showing half of his well-oiled and
well-combed hair. As he stretched his hand to take the paan the palm of
his hand showed a circle where it had been dyed red with henna, and
part of his little finger was also dyed red. On his face there was the hard
look of a rake, and his light brown eyes looked white. Bending a little
forward he said to Mushtari Bai: 'You are looking beautiful tonight;
and you sang most wonderfully well.'

Mushtari Bai seemed to blush, but she heaved a sigh and quoted from a poet with pathos:

'We are but travellers on the road;
It matters not if we die or live;
Our life is like a candle flame:
You had put us out and we had died;
You have lighted us and we are alight.'

Asghar sat quiet, nursing the pain in his heart. As he heard Mushtari Bai quote the lines he felt more guilty and annoyed. He felt that he was the cause of her despondent mood and he resented it. He was in love, but not with her; and she had no right to love him. As he sat with her, heard her familiar voice, he felt conscience-stricken, for he had loved her once and now he could not give her anything. Her presence was a reminder of the past, and Asghar was in no mood for it. So he said to Bari:

'Let us go.'

'Are you angry with me?' asked Mushtari Bai.

'Not at all. Why should you think so?' Asghar replied as he stood up to go.

'Our hero is in love,' Bari said sarcastically.

'Don't jest, Bari,' said Asghar suddenly flaring up. 'What's the use of such things?'

Mushtari Bai turned a little pale, but steadied herself and with the perfect training of her art she concealed her emotion, and remarked lightly with the air of turning a serious thought into a jest, although there was still a ring of disillusionment in her voice:

'Never fall in love. It's better to commit suicide than fall in love. . . .'

* * *

Saying good-bye Asghar went out alone, for Bari had wished to stay on. The night had advanced and few people were about. The city lay restless in the heat under the yellow moon, casting shadows across the roads and on the walls. Sounds of singing still came from some of the top-storey houses on either side of Chaori Bazar. Now and then someone got down from a dark staircase stealthily and walked away. The dogs were still about and the cats quarrelled on the roofs and cater-wauled. The street, covered with broken earthen cups, dry leaves out of which men had eaten something and thrown away, and all sorts of rubbish and refuse, looked dirty and drab.

When Asghar came to Hauz Qazi an old man coming from Ajmeri

Gate began to walk in front of him, slightly to his right. Engrossed in thought Asghar walked on swinging the stick in his hand with a gentle motion. When they reached Lal Darwaza the old man suddenly turned to the left to go into a by-lane. As he crossed Asghar, his stick unwittingly touched the old man's behind. At once he turned round and remarked:

'I say, moon-bridegroom, even with an old man? . . .'

A eunuch who still sat on the balcony just above in the hope of some stray customer, clapped loudly in a vulgar way and gave a loud guffaw. Asghar felt abashed. The remark was so spontaneous and witty that he could not give any reply, and, hanging his head in shame, he walked on.

As he turned into Kucha Pandit he saw the kababi closing his shop. Mirza the milk-seller's shop was still open and some people had collected there and sat on a dirty wooden bench talking. From the dark and dingy shop of the barber, lighted only by a dim earthen lamp, came the sound of a lewd Punjabi song:

O Lachhi thy soft and rounded thighs,
Lachhi thy soft. . . .

Asghar turned into Jangli Kuan and the sound died behind him in the night. . . .

12

EVERYONE had gone to sleep at home except his sister, Begam Waheed, who was waiting for him. As Asghar entered the house on tiptoe and emerged from the vestibule into the courtyard his eyes fell on the dark and ugly trunk of the date palm and rising along it upwards reached the sky. The moon shone with a pale light and Asghar could see the end star of the Great Bear as the rest of the constellation was hidden behind the clustering leaves of the palm tree. Some trick of memory brought to his mind the story of the Constellation, called in Persian the Daughters of the Corpse. The bed on which the corpse lies is warped; and as the daughters press it from one side the other end is raised upwards. Asghar thought of his own life, how trying to straighten it up at one end he unbalances it at the other. . . . Not a breath of wind stirred, and the date palm stood expectant, as it were, against the sky. . . .

As he went upstairs his sister followed him.

'You are still awake?' Asghar asked her from behind the veil of his mood.

'I was waiting for you.'

'Why, has something happened?' Asghar asked in a voice filled both with fear and expectancy.

'Amma had a talk with father. . . .'

Asghar's heart contracted into a point with expectancy and he asked: 'What did he say?'

'He got very angry and was not even prepared to listen to the proposal. . . .'

Asghar heaved a deep sigh and looked up at the moon. The halo had vanished and the moon looked frightened, trying to hide her wan face behind the sand. Asghar caught his head between his hands and looked down. Tears appeared in his eyes and he said with pain:

'Death is much better than this life. I . . .'

But his sister intervened.

'You must not become despondent for nothing,' she said. 'Amma says that she is willing. In fact she has made up her mind, and has agreed to speak to Begam Shahbaz. Father will come round in the end. . . .'

A cock, awakened from its sleep, crowed in a house nearby. Asghar raised his head and a smile lit up his face. 'You are my very dear sister,' he said with happiness, and embraced her warmly. Begam Waheed's arms also went round Asghar and they embraced. Tears rushed to their eyes and both of them began to weep, overcome with emotion.

Drying her tears Begam Waheed said:

'May God keep you happy and make the marriage a success.'

And Asghar said: 'Amen.'

'It would be better,' Begam Waheed suggested, 'that you come with me to Bhopal. Here you would only pine, and father may also get annoyed some day and get angry with you. When you are away things would be managed quietly by mother. As it is, the marriage cannot take place for at least a year. . . .'

So it was agreed that he would go to Bhopal with his sister, and he went to bed happy and at peace with the world. He now felt sorry for his behaviour with Bari and Mushtari Bai, and wished that he had stayed on longer there just to please her. But the thought of Bilqeece engulfed him in its joy, and he lay on his bed dreaming of happiness, building beautiful castles in the air. . . .

Begam Nihal went to see Begam Shahbaz and spoke to her about the proposal. Begam Shahbaz did not wish for anything better and willingly agreed.

As thanksgiving Begam Nihal and Begam Waheed decided to have a meelad read. The house was swept and a white sheet was spread over the wooden couches, sweets were sent for from the bazar, and soon after the evening prayers two big lamps were lighted and kept on either side of a small carpet which had been spread on the couches with a bolster cushion at the back. Incense and myrrh were burnt and kept on stands. Rose water was kept in long flasks, and fresh jasmine flowers were laid on a platter. The scented smoke rose and mingled with the aroma of the flowers and filled the house with its sacred smell and imbued the hearts with religious awe as the whole family sat waiting for Asghar to begin reading the meelad.

Asghar began with a recitation from the Koran, then he began telling them episodes from the life of Mohammad, dwelling on his merciful qualities and the miracles, punctuating his talk with the phrase: 'Glory be to the Prophet and his descendants.'

He spoke of his marriage to the merchant woman Khadeeja; and he described how Mohammad went in person to Paradise and came back to the earth in a moment. Asghar spoke with great feeling and brought tears to the eyes of the listeners. Then came the moment of reading the religious anthem. Everybody stood up, and Asghar began to sing and Shams and Masroor joined him in the chorus.

His voice rose on the silent breeze, struck against the four walls, and echoed back into the night. He closed his eyes and sang, swaying his body to and fro. The smell of incense and myrrh went into his nostrils and his heart was filled with the glory of God and the fervour of Islam. And he sang more beautifully than ever. The listeners stood with heads hung down, drinking the words in through their ears. As the word Mohammad sounded they folded their thumbs and kissed them, then touched their eyes with the portions they had kissed, feeling a great love for the Creator and His Beloved, dreaming of Paradise and the promised rewards after death.

When the meelad was over Asghar sat singing hymns addressed to Mohammad. He began with a hymn asking the Prophet to help him in his need:

> O saviour, come to my aid,
> I am helpless in defeat.
> O saviour of men and faith,
> Come in my need to me.

Asghar sang and the women sat listening to him, swaying to and fro under the influence of religious emotion. A little breeze blew and the date palm leaves rustled, adding their own hallelujahs to those of man. Asghar ended up with a prayer to the Prophet just as Nisar Ahmad's golden voice rang in the night:

> It is my heart-felt wish
> To sit upon the trees
> On your tomb when from its cage
> The bird of my soul is released.

As the voice of Nisar Ahmad rose and fell, spreading far and wide, they all sat silent listening until his voice gradually died away into the night out of which it was born. Then they raised their hands in prayer, and stood up blowing their breaths, made holy by repeating the names of God, inside their shirts. The sweets were distributed; and they busied themselves with preparations for dinner....

13

BEGAM WAHEED began to make preparations to go back to Bhopal. Everyone became gloomy at the thought of parting. A sadness descended upon the house as if the departing guests were going away for ever and will never come back again; and everyone seemed plunged in mourning.

But Asghar was happy and filled with hope. He could not have lived in Delhi without feeling sad and unhappy, being in the same city and yet so far away from his sweetheart. There would be no reminders of her in Bhopal; and the distant clouds would look beautiful with a silver lining, and he would have leisure to dream in peace.

The heat had been oppressive. The loo blew throughout the day, and at night the pillows were unbearable. Dust floated in the air; and in the evenings the sun hung like an aluminium disc behind the sand.

On the day previous to Asghar's departure, however, the wind changed and an easterly breeze struck up. White masses of clouds floated in the sky, and the sun rested his head on their massive backs, and the world heaved a sigh of relief. At night the moon peeped from behind the sailing clouds; and the breeze remained cool.

Early in the morning the rain came suddenly pattering down. It rained for half an hour; the pleasant smell of the earth rose all around; and everything looked washed and soothing to the eyes. The sky was covered with dark collyrium black clouds. A cool easterly wind blew bringing peace and a message of beauty to the soul. The twitter of the sparrows, the screeching of the mainas, the cawing of the crows, so dull and heartrending otherwise, sounded so pleasing and intimate.

Asghar went about doing things with a light heart. It seemed to him that the whole wide world was revelling in a dream of love. The pigeon-fliers flew their pigeons with louder enthusiasm; and the vendors in the streets redoubled their cries. As the day advanced women were heard singing from the nearby houses the song of Saavan, the beautiful Indian rainy season with its associations of birth and spring:

> Who has put the swing on the tree?
> Come, let's swing, my friend.

Innumerable men, women and children came out of their houses and went for picnics to Okhla or Qutab Minar. Hundreds of hearts hungry for love and a little rest from the worries of life, went out of their dingy houses to enjoy the beauties of the earth just awakened by the healing touch of the rain. They carried delicacies wrapped up in cloths, in baskets, out in search of the open. The women dragged their dingy burqas like wet hens fluttering their wings. And a chatter and ceaseless babble of talk, the shouts of happy children and the noise of men shouting orders, filled the atmosphere.

As this was going on in the city Asghar and Begam Waheed said goodbye to the family. The parting of the women was full of tears. As they embraced they wept, and parted with heavy hearts, entrusting each other into the safe keeping of God.

As Asghar sat in the train there was a stir in his heart. The birds flew with more ease and the kites swam in the air. The trees waved their heads to and fro in an ectasy; and the heart of the world was filled to the brim with kindness and love. Far and wide wherever the eye could reach a rare loveliness seemed to reign supreme. In the subdued rumbling of distant thunder, like muffled drums heard from somewhere far away, there was not the anger of the gods, but a message of Birth and Life; and the hand of nature seemed to be stretched out in blessing and peace. . . .

PART II

My despair does not know
The turnings of the wheel of Time;
The day turned disastrous
Knows neither dusk nor dawn.

GHALIB

1

IT was the terrible summer of nineteen hundred and eleven. No one had experienced such heat for many years. Begam Jamal complained that she had never known such heat in all her life. Begam Nihal said she had never experienced such a summer ever since 1857, the year of the 'Mutiny'. The temperature rose higher and higher until it reached one hundred and fifteen in the shade. From seven in the morning the loo began to moan, blowing drearily through the hopeless streets. The leaves of the henna tree became sered and wan, and the branches of the date palm became coated with sand. The dust blew through the unending noon; and men went out with their heads well-covered and protected. The pigeons flew for a while and opened their beaks for heat. The crows cawed and the kites cried and their voices sounded so dull.

The sky lost its colour and became dirty and bronzed. The loo did not stop even at night. The stars flickered in the sky behind the covering layer of dust. The sand rained down all night, came between the teeth, covered the beds, and sleep did not come near parched humanity.

Tempers rose and from all around came the loud voices of women quarrelling, husbands beating their wives, mothers their children, and there seemed no rest for man.

Fires broke out every now and then. At such times the sky was made red with the flames that shot up from the burning earth. Men died of sunstroke; and even birds were not immune from the destructive influence of the sun, and many pigeons died.

Outside the city, beyond the Fort and beyond the Mori Gate, workmen were digging away in the scorching heat of May levelling or raising the earth, beautifying the ground in preparation for the Coronation of a new and foreign king. But that was still far off and no one seemed to be concerned.

Inside the city the wind blew free through the length and breadth of Chandni Chowk, raised dust in the streets and by-lanes, lashed the stalwart trees that stood in rows in the middle of the bazar from Fatehpuri to the Fountain and beyond. Men shut themselves up inside the houses or in shops. At noon the city seemed deserted and dead but

for the grating noise of tram cars that plied throughout the day, though
very few people used them. In the evenings men came out when the sun
had gone down and the water had been sprinkled, and the city
hummed with noise. . . .

*   *   *

Mir Nihal, wearing a muslin coat so made that one of his breasts
showed naked through it, and red shoes with flowers embroidered in
white on the toes, walked out of the shop of Haji Noor Elahi & Sons,
Lace Dealers. As he set foot in the street a hot gust of wind blew, and
Mir Nihal put a bandanna on his neck to protect it from the sun. From
a house-top nearby a pigeon-flier shouted excitedly: 'Aao, aao.' Auto-
matically Mir Nihal looked up. Although it was very hot yet the sky
was full of pigeons. Suddenly Mir Nihal remembered that he had forgotten to leave water inside the loft of his pigeons, and he quickened his
pace.

He would have liked to go home via Babban Jan's for she had been
ill; but his pigeons worried him. So he came straight down Chandni
Chowk towards the Clock Tower to go through Balli Maran, the
nearest way home. As he passed the Clock Tower he saw a number of
camel carts wind their way, creaking, groaning, moving slowly like
snails, from the Company Gardens to Khari Baoli, the grain market. He
felt thirsty and at the turn of Balli Maran he stopped to drink water
from the sabeel. Men had started going about and the shopkeepers
were sprinkling water in front of their shops.

As he passed through Balli Maran his nostrils were filled with the
smell of drugs and medicines. This was the street of druggists and
Hakims. With the smell the thought of death came into his mind.
There was an aroma of camphor in the air; and for some unknown
reason he began to think of Babban Jan. Her thought was sad and
sweet, like the memory of some dear one dead, coming from somewhere far away, ripping open the veils of the unconscious, saddening
the heart.

A wave of self-pity surged in his breast. He felt he was getting
old—he was sixty-two. He tried to suppress the feeling. But a peculiar
heaviness appeared in his head, a pressure of blood which wants to
burst out of its restricting channels of veins and arteries. For a moment
everything went black in front of his eyes. He thought it was the result
of his constipation. Or was it heatstroke? This seemed more plausible
to Mir Nihal.

So, when he reached the Kucha Pandit, he bought a pice worth of
unripe mangoes to have them roasted in the oven and have fresh
sherbet made. The fruit and vegetable seller, a fat young woman with
expansive thighs and breasts that could feed the whole of Hindustan,
with a face disfigured with deep pock marks, a sharp tongue and a loud
throat, started telling him that her melons were extra fine. She had just
received a parcel from Lucknow, she said. Or would he care to have
some mulberries? Mir Nihal said 'no'. 'Then take some pomegranates.
My man has just brought them from Qandahar.'

Mir Nihal was in no mood to buy anything; and he went along,
receiving greetings from the people of the mohallah and replying to
them. As he was going through Jangli Kuan he saw Nisar Ahmad
hurrying to the mosque. He was a tall, well-built man, somewhere on
the other side of fifty. He wore a shirt and paijama of homespun, a cane
cap brownish in colour and dirty at the edges, and a bandanna over his
shoulder. His head was close-cropped and made his forehead look
broad. His expansive fan-shaped beard was dyed red with henna, and
his moustaches were shaved on the upper lip in accordance with Islamic
laws. His nose was big, jutting out on his face like a rock, and a callosity
had formed on his forehead on account of constantly rubbing it on the
ground at prayer, and shone ashy grey from a distance on his dark face.
He was called Balal Habshi (the Negro companion of Mohammad who
was renowned for his azaan); and they had many things in common—
their dark complexions and their golden voices. Nisar Ahmad sold ghee
for a living, but it was said that he was a shady businessman and his
ghee was not pure.

But his azaan compensated for his faults; and everyone blessed him
and said he would go straight to heaven for calling the faithful to prayer.
There is no doubt that when he called the evening azaan he filled the
hearts with reverence and awe. Just as the sun had set his golden voice
would rise gradually in the air, and, rippling with the glory of Islam,
would unfold its message to the Mussalmans, bringing with it a sense of
the impermanence of life and the transience of the world. His voice
could be heard far and wide in several mohallahs, rising above the din
and noise of the town, leaping to the stars. Then slowly it would come
to an end bringing with it peace and silence, acting as a lullaby to the
tired hearts of men.

Mir Nihal wished to overtake him to ask him to send some ghee for
the pigeons. He did not take the ghee from home for fear of Begam
Nihal, who would have shouted at him and complained. But Nisar

Ahmad was ahead of him, and at the turn of Mohallah Niyaryan he was lost to sight:

Just then Sheikh Mohammad Sadiq peeped out of his shop and, seeing Mir Nihal, came to greet him. He made gold thread, and on his right leg he wore a short leather legging over his paijama on which he used to roll his cone-shaped bobbin. The thread would be hanging from the ceiling and Sheikhji would catch the long point of the bobbin and roll it on his leg, and the bobbin would go dancing and spinning for a while until the thread was spun. Then he would wind it up, draw more thread from the reel, and the whole process would be repeated once again.

Slowly Sheikh Mohammad Sadiq walked towards Mir Nihal. His beard was conical and small, and his bobbed hair was dyed red with henna and presented a funny contrast to his half-black and half-grey beard. As he came forward his red paijama-string dangled in front of him, trailing right down to the ground, and as he walked it moved to and fro.

'Assalaam-alaikum, Mir Saheb,' he said from a distance. 'How are you?'

'Waalaikum-assalaam,' Mir Nihal replied. 'I am alive. How have *you* been keeping?'

'I am all right,' said Sheikh Mohammad Sadiq, and he started walking with Mir Nihal towards Mohallah Niyaryan.

'I have been thinking of coming to you, but I was so entangled in worries that I could not come.'

'Is everything all right?' Mir Nihal enquired.

'It's your kindness. Everything is all right otherwise, but there is a little matter about which I wanted to talk to you.'

They had come to the turn of the lane, and Mir Nihal stopped to listen to Sheikhji's story. From the other side came Fazal Khan, karkhandar, and as he came near he flung a greeting at Mir Nihal and inquired:

'Is everyone all right at home?'

'Allah be thanked,' Mir Nihal replied. '*You* are doing well?'

'Your graciousness—thanks.'

Fortunately he did not stop and went away.

Sheikh Mohammad Sadiq caught hold of his small beard in his right hand, shy and nervous at broaching the subject. A kite came dragging along, striking against the roofs and walls and was entangled in some wooden planks and tin sheets which were lying on a roof nearby. Sheikhji mustered courage and spoke out:

'I have a niece. Her parents have both died, and I am anxious about her marriage. You'll forgive my presumptuousness, but—'

Sheikhji hesitated for a moment. The kite got disentangled and the owner pulled it home.

'If you will give your consent,' Sheikhji continued, 'I shall marry her to your servant Ghafoor.'

Mir Nihal cleared his throat and asked:

'How old is the girl?'

'She is about thirteen or fourteen, but she is so healthy that she looks much older.'

Mir Nihal muttered 'Umph' and pondered.

'Don't you think she is too young for Ghafoor?' he said at last.

'What you are saying is but too true,' Sheikhji replied with humility and submission. 'But what I say is that it is so difficult to get a match for her. And my wife is worrying my life out of me with reminders about the girl's marriage. If you have no objection. . . .'

Mir Nihal did not seem to approve of the idea; but he was in a hurry to get home. The pigeon-fliers were shouting more loudly and in greater numbers, and were constant reminders of his own birds to Mir Nihal. That is why he summarily dismissed the affair by saying;

'You speak to Ghafoor about it. The matter concerns him, you know.'

'What you are saying is all right; but what I say is that he is your servant; and what is your idea?'

To which Mir Nihal replied by repeating the well-known saying:

'When husband and wife are willing, what can the Qazi do?'

Sheikhji took this to be the consent and, smiling broadly, he caught hold of Mir Nihal's hand in both of his and began to shake it warmly. From behind came Mast Qalandar, a mad faqir, almost naked but for a strip of cloth tied to a string round his waist hiding his private parts. His matted beard, full of dust and soup and dirt, was tousled, looking like a bulbul's nest. His nails were long and black with filth, and his bare feet were dirty. But his body, hairy like a bear's, looked plump and healthy; and from his bushy face his small eyes sparkled. There was a look of madness on his face, yet people considered him a divine, a faqir very high up in the mystical order, as the name given to him, Qalandar, signified. He was a favourite with the gamblers who always consulted him for lucky numbers. Most of the time he sat near the tombs of Haray Bharay (the evergreen one) and Sarmad at the foot of Jama Masjid, and seldom came into the city. He constantly cried the same mysterious saying:

'When there is such pleasure in throwing it out how great would be the bliss in keeping it.'

His cries came from a distance; and as he came near Mir Nihal said goodbye to Sheikh Mohammad Sadiq and went home.

From a small, dilapidated house came the voice of a woman sharply reprimanding a girl:

'O thou, Fatto, may God's wrath fall upon thee. Where hast thou died?'

And a dog ran after a cat, chasing her away.

Mir Nihal was worried, feeling heavy in the head, anxious about the birds. The thought of Babban Jan came back to his mind again and with it a Rubai of Sarmad, the mystic faqir and Persian poet who was beheaded by Aurangzeb:

> I've lost religion in quite a novel way,
> Throwing faith for drunken eyes away:
> And all my life in piety spent I've flung
> At the altar for that idol-worshipper's joy. . . .

2

WHEN he reached home Nisar Ahmad was coming to the end of the afternoon azaan. The sky was covered with paper kites and pigeons, and Ghafoor sat smoking his hookah. Mir Nihal went inside the zenana and gave the green mangoes to Dilchain to roast them and make sherbet. From the kotha came the voice of Begam Jamal moaning and growling:

'Hai, hai! I am dying.'

'Is everything all right?' Mir Nihal asked Dilchain.

'She has got fever,' Dilchain told him.

Mir Nihal went upstairs. In her neat room Begam Jamal lay on a bed, groaning; and Begam Nihal and the whole family sat by her side, cutting areca nut and talking. Mehro was tacking a silver lace with loose gold threads for edges on a red silk head-cloth. Preparations for Asghar's marriage were going on, and the bride's clothes were being sewn. But while their hands were busy their tongues were free to talk on endlessly; and they did not pay much heed to Begam Jamal's unending 'hai hais'. When Mir Nihal cleared his throat in the staircase to announce that he was coming, they stopped talking and covered their heads not to be seen in déshabille.

Mir Nihal took off his shoes at the door and walked to Begam Jamal's side and, sitting on the edge of the bed, felt her pulse. As he did so everyone turned towards him and became attentive.

'Since when have you got the fever?' he inquired.

'Ever since the morning,' Begam Jamal replied covering her head. Then she began to groan and complain:

'Oh, my head! It's bursting. . . . Would someone give me a little water? My throat is parched. . . .'

Mir Nihal suggested that Hakim Ajmal Khan should be sent for.

'I had sent for Hakim Bhooray Khan, but he has gone out somewhere,' Begam Nihal said. 'And Masroor who had gone to call him also came back burning with fever. It is heatstroke. I have given both of them green mango sherbet and have sprinkled the mango-water on them. And *you* better take some mango sherbet yourself. Such terrible loo is blowing.' Mir Nihal muttered 'Humph,' cleared his throat, and said casually:

'Yes, I have brought some green mangoes and Dilchain is making the sherbet. . . .'

Then he came downstairs and went to see Masroor who was lying on the floor in the room all by himself. As Mir Nihal walked in Masroor muttered: 'Water, water,' and closed his eyes. Mir Nihal shouted at Dilchain:

'Everyone has left the poor boy alone. Give him some water.'

Putting his hand on Masroor's forehead he felt his temperature, and consoled him:

'Don't worry. The fever shall leave you soon.'

And asking Dilchain to give the boy more sherbet he went to see his pigeons.

*   *   *

Hot gusts of wind were blowing. The leaves of the date palm flapped with a dreary sound; and the glare of the sun hurt the eyes. But the pigeon-fliers shouted with gusto, beat corrugated iron sheets, and whistled loudly and long. The vendors cried their brazen cries in singsong voices:

'Sweeter than honey, two pice for a quarter.'

'Eat these mulberries, cool and sweet.'

And a hopeless dreariness was in the atmosphere.

Mir Nihal opened the door of the loft. The pigeons fluttered and rushed out and began to peck small pieces of lime and earth impatiently. Most of them rushed towards the water-pot, but it was empty. As Mir Nihal went towards the loft the birds followed him in the expectation of getting something to eat.

Three pigeons came out with difficulty, reeling as if they were giddy. Heatstroke. And four were lying dead inside the loft. Mir Nihal's heart sank. They were fine young birds and it would be difficult to replace them. He picked them up and put them in a corner to be thrown away. He filled the pot with water, and the birds rushed at it madly, crowding about it, getting one on top of the other in their impatience to reach the water. There were about forty birds, and the ill ones could not get to the pot. The moment they tried to climb its edge the others pushed them aside and they fell down limply and rolled on the ground. Mir Nihal put them inside the loft and gave them water in another pot.

He had already lost three birds two days ago—killed by sunstroke. And these seven made the number of dead ones ten, for the three ill ones were as good as dead. He had fifty of the best and most well-trained pigeons in Delhi; and the loss of these ten, therefore, was irretrievable. It took three or four months to train them well. Mir Nihal was so dejected that he did not fly the pigeons that day.

Khwaja Ashraf Ali peeped over his wall, wondering as to what had happened to Mir Saheb. He himself flew his pigeons, but did not let them go far away from the roof for fear of Mir Nihal's birds. The moment his pigeons made a slight detour he would shout to them and call them home. Then he would peep over the wall to see if Mir Nihal was going to release his birds. But Mir Saheb's pigeons sat on the roof picking grain. After a while Khwaja Ashraf Ali became bold and began to fly his pigeons with impunity, allowing them to go far away from home, shouting more loudly than before. But Mir Nihal was not impressed by these amateurish pranks of the Khwaja.

The loss of his pigeons had made him sad. For they were to him the precious toys which a child loves so much, whose loss leaves him brokenhearted. He had tended his pigeons for years, had taken great care of them, and their death filled him with grief. In his dejection he thought of giving up his hobby altogether. He felt really old now and was afraid of further disappointments. . . .

But he grew reconciled to the loss and wished to give himself another chance. It was not so easy to give up the pigeons altogether. The next

day being a Friday he went to the Chowk to buy some good young birds
and replenish his depleted stock.

* * *

A noble flight of steps led to the platform in front of the eastern, the
Shahi gate, of the Jama Masjid, steps going up from three sides, the
north, the east and the south. On the western side is the huge gate itself,
always kept barred and locked with just a small postern leading into the
courtyard of the mosque. In front is a great open space about forty feet
above the level of the road, paved with red sandstone. It is here that the
pigeon market is held every evening. But Friday being the Muslim
holiday there is always a bigger crowd on this day, and one can always
select the best pigeons.

Saluting people or acknowledging their greetings Mir Nihal walked
up the steps. On his right he saw the fat ice-cream seller sitting on a low
round and armless chair made of reeds. He was so fat that through his
home-made half-sleeved and small under shirt of muslin the folds of his
pulpy paunch were visible. He had a dirty Turkish cap on his head, and
his bloated cheeks were half hidden behind his long and thick moustaches and grisly beard, as if he had not shaved for a week. He wore a
tahmat with loud squares in red and blue printed on it.

He sat there satisfied and opulent like a Chinese Buddha, and
around him on chairs, similar to that on which he himself was sitting,
sat a few young men looking rakish in their gaudy clothes. A huge
round earthen pot was placed in front of him and, as someone asked for
kulfi ice-cream, he dipped his hand inside the pot and took out a
conical ice-cream case, flat at the bottom with the lid on top stuck with
dough. Then with the help of a black and dirty-looking knife he
removed the frozen dough and took off the lid which displayed a
beautiful white surface with finely cut pistachio nuts supplying colour
to the frozen milk. Then inserting a tin spoon inside it he passed it to
the customer.

Mir Nihal would not have noticed him at all, but he saw Khwaja
Ashraf Ali sitting there enjoying the ice-cream. He was rather plump,
and his beard, close-cropped on the cheeks, terminated in a slightly
pointed end of half-black and half-grey hair. He was wearing a drab-
coloured sherwani and a Turkish cap. As he saw Mir Nihal going up he
began to dip his spoon inside the ice-cream case more hurriedly, and in
his impatience a little ice-cream fell on his beard and his clothes. As he
ate he looked at Mir Nihal, and when he turned to look the tassel of his

cap hopped about, dancing in the breeze. By the time he finished the
ice-cream Mir Nihal had reached the top. Hurriedly Khwaja Ashraf Ali
paid the man, and began to climb the long flight of steps.

There was a jostling crowd on the platform, and hundreds of pigeon-
fliers had collected to sell and buy birds. Elbowing his way forward Mir
Nihal plunged into the crowd, casting his eyes at cages to look for
pigeons. Once or twice he detained persons who held pigeons in their
hands, and, taking them in his own, felt their necks, and opened out
their wings to examine the feathers. Then he caught hold of them by
the breast and made them flutter their wings and, not approving of
them, gave them back to their owners. Those he did like he gave to
Nazir, a professional pigeon-flier who served as Mir Nihal's agent, and
paid the price.

Khwaja Ashraf Ali also came along, looking at Mir Nihal through the
corners of his eyes. Mir Saheb had caught two of Khwaja Saheb's
pigeons a day or two ago, and they were also kept inside Nazir's cage.
As Khwaja Saheb came near he cast a glance at the cage and as he
recognized the birds he went a little pale. But he did not wish to buy
back his pigeons in front of Mir Nihal. He saluted Mir Nihal and
inquired:

'How are you keeping?'

'Your graciousness, thanks. How are you?'

'I am all right, Allah be thanked,' he replied. Then after a pause he
added: 'I was surprised that you did not fly your pigeons yesterday. Is
everything all right?'

'Oh yes, thanks,' Mir Nihal said. 'I was not very well, and some four
or five of my pigeons had died of heatstroke.'

A happy smile appeared on Khwaja Saheb's face, and a merry
twinkle danced in his eyes. But suppressing his happiness he said:

'Oh yes, such terrible loo is blowing this year that, not to talk of the
poor birds, human beings are dying of it. . . .'

They had come to a corner near the flight of steps. Below, across the
road, were the tombs of Haray Bharay and Sarmad, and beyond across
the grey and barren ground the red walls of the Fort stretched far away.
Below them on the eastern steps sat men selling quails and canaries,
bulbuls and nightingales, and many other small and colourful birds.
Still below near the level of the road sat shopkeepers selling all sorts of
second-hand nick-nacks and bric-à-brac from old china to bedsteads.
On the northern steps and on the ground in front of them sat the
quacks and druggists plying as usual a great trade in lizards' oil and

aquatic birds' oil, live lizards of various kinds and species, snakes, herbs and rare plants. In one corner stood a man shouting in a dramatic tone, selling his medicines to people who had flocked around him. He was describing the qualities of some medicine. Then he began to show it to the curious audience. When he had finished with it he began to sing loudly the evils of piles in verse:

> This damned disease of piles is so inconvenient:
> It shoots an arrow of death at the fundament.

Other noises came from all around. Crows and kites wheeled and cawed and cried and perched on the tall turrets of the mosque. Flocks of wild pigeons rose from the domes and the roofs of the Jama Masjid and flew away, or others came and descended inside the courtyard to quench their thirst at the tank in the middle of the courtyard. One could hardly hear anything in the midst of the din and the noise of a Delhi evening.

As Mir Nihal and Khwaja Ashraf Ali stood talking people came in and went out of the crowd, rubbing shoulders with each other. Mir Nihal bought a few good young pigeons and gave them to Nazir. In the meantime they were joined by Hakim Bashir. He was a man in his forties, and kept a long, flowing beard. He was also fond of pigeons. But he did not like the sort of pigeons Mir Nihal and Khwaja Saheb were fond of, called 'golay'. These pigeons flew low over the roofs in one straight line and required a great deal of hullabaloo to fly them. Hakimji was fond of Kabuli pigeons which flew high up in the sky and became invisible in the ether. They flew just above the house, going up and up into the heavens in a spiral ascent. They had just to be released early in the morning and up they went on their aerial tour. One did not have to shout at them or call them home. They went up of their own accord, and, when tired, came back home in two or four or six hours. And the longer they remained in the air the better birds they were. The eyes of these pigeons are white in contrast to those of the 'golays', whose eyes are red or muddy and dark. One can know their quality by looking at the fine grains in their eyes, and the colour of the whites.

Perhaps because Hakim Bashir was more sedate he liked this kind of pigeons. It was, perhaps, the strong mystical trend in his character which was responsible for his preference for high-flying pigeons; and the flight of the birds high up in the sky made him feel a certain nearness to God. In all probability, however, it was his non-Delhi origin which was responsible for it—he came from Meerut. Whatever it was, the Kabuli pigeons were a novelty in Delhi and had not been recognized. It did not require any skill to train them, nor was it exciting to fly them, for they just went up until they were lost to sight. They entered into a discussion about the merits of the various birds. Khwaja Ashraf Ali suggested contemptuously that the Kabuli pigeons were no better than the 'nisavray'. The latter are rather slow birds although they fly higher up than the 'golays'. They have heavy, fan-like tails and feathers on their legs, and are mostly flown by poor people. They are not made to sit on the roofs but on square-shaped structures jutting up towards the sky, hanging in mid-air like open umbrellas made of bamboo with squares left open to catch the birds with the help of nooses attached to long bamboo poles. It is on such structures that the Kabuli pigeons are also trained to sit.

'It requires no art or skill to catch these birds,' said Khwaja Saheb, 'or to train them to fly.'

'There you are mistaken,' Hakim Bashir replied. 'I grant that the "nisavray" pigeons are slow, and they cannot fly very high nor for very long. They are poor specimens of pigeons. But the Kabuli pigeons are very quick and noble. It is entirely wrong to think that it requires no skill to train them.'

'How?' Khwaja Saheb retorted. 'How do they require any skill to train them? You just fly them. That's all. Whereas our pigeons have to be trained to fly in flocks, to shoot like arrows, to mingle with other flocks and bring other people's pigeons home with them. They have to be very quick and learn the signs of the flag and recognize the sound of the whistle and the voice of the master. To train them, thus, is not an easy job. Is it? . . .'

As he said this he turned round to Mir Nihal for approval. Mir Saheb stood listening amusedly to the discussion; and in response to Khwaja Saheb he smiled sedately. A few other persons had collected round them and were listening interested. As Khwaja Saheb turned round they raised their voices in assent. This encouraged him, and he continued:

'There was Mir Jamal, our Mir Saheb's brother. He was a perfect artist in this line. His pigeons used to move at a sign from their master. If he pointed his flag in one direction no one could make them go in another. During the Darbar [the Coronation of 1903] they had arranged pigeon-flying matches. People trained their pigeons to fly from and descend upon the roofs of carriages which had been painted in different colours. Mir Jamal was also invited to take part in the matches, but he refused to get mixed up with the low crowd of sycophants and professionals. When people pressed him, however, he agreed. But he refused to train his pigeons to fly from the roof of a carriage. He said his pigeons would fly from his own roof, and at the appointed hour would take part in the matches which were being held beyond the Red Fort, a distance of about four or five miles from his house. Well, he trained his pigeons to fly so far away as that. On the day of the match, at the appointed hour, his pigeons came rushing like an arrow. A shout went up from the spectators: "There they come. There they come." And they came, mixed with the other pigeons, flew for a long time, circling over the grounds, played havoc with the other flocks, and went back home carrying thrice their number along with them.' Here Khwaja Saheb tapped his stick for effect and asked: 'What do you say to that?'

Then he turned to the people for appreciation, looking so proud and important.

Mir Nihal was smiling in a complacent manner; and other people were gazing at Khwaja Saheb with envy and admiration. Even Hakim Bashir looked amused. He felt that he could not hold his own in this atmosphere, and thought it better to keep silent. Just then the moazzin began to call the evening azaan; and one by one people began to go inside the mosque to offer prayers. They all crowded in front of the gate. They took off their shoes, took them in their hands, and bending low walked in through the small postern. In a few moments the chowk was empty and deserted while the faithful said their prayers and remembered their God. . . .

After the prayers Mir Nihal came out of the southern gate to go home. At this hour of the day the great mosque presented a sight like a fair. Just below its southern verandas sat the kababis inside their booths or on the pavement, roasting meat on their fire. And the smell of ghee, fat, oil and burning meat filled the air. As someone asked for kabab the vendor turned the skewers round to warm the spicy minced meat which had been wrapped round them, held together by means of thread and grilled into delicious kababs. As he took them off the skewers with a quick movement he broke them into two, put them in leaf-pots and, adding finely-cut onions, green mango and ginger and chillies on top, wrapped the whole into a neat hot parcel and passed it to the customer. Some of the shopkeepers sold big, flat, round loaves also, baked in the oven; and many bought them too, or, too hungry to take them home, sat inside the shops and filled their bellies.

Other vendors were selling small round kababs fried in oil, and

others still fried fish or meat cutlets, pulao or vegetable cutlets soaked
in curds. Many sold sherbet, plain or with jelly, which was drunk out of
coloured and painted china cups broad at the brim and narrow at the
base. There were others selling all kinds of victuals, ice-cream and
jellies. Men came and bought them, satisfied their thirst or hunger, and
walked away.

The tram cars came and stopped for a while. Children began a search
for used tickets; and beggars, blind, disabled or healthy, came and
began to beg from the passengers, cajoling them, blessing them, praying for the health and safety of their wives and children. The passengers
took out pice from their pockets, or undid the knots at the corners of
their handkerchiefs where they had tied their cash, and gave the pice to
the beggars; but many turned deaf ears to their cries.

Unconcerned, Mir Nihal walked past the vendors and the tram cars.
Many were going home from the chowk with pigeons in their hands or
carrying baskets full of birds. Often from the crowd someone shouted a
greeting to Mir Nihal. He replied and walked on, lost in thought. . . .

*   *   *

When he had finished his dinner Nazir brought the pigeons. Mir Nihal
took them upstairs to put them in the loft. Their feathers had to be tied
together with thread lest they flew away. Mir Nihal sat down and began
to tie the feathers of the pigeons by the dim light of a lantern.

As he had put the last bird inside the loft he stood for a while with
one hand on the door, thinking of the pigeons he had bought. An owlet
came and perched on the roof and, moving its head forward and back,
began to hoot. Mir Nihal looked up at the owlet and went to frighten it
away. A shooting star leapt from the dirty sky and, leaving a dim line of
incandescence behind it, was seen falling towards the earth. As Mir
Nihal was coming back to close the door of the loft he saw Ghafoor
walk in hurriedly.

'What's the matter?' he inquired.

'A man has come from Babban Jan Begam, and he says her condition
has become very critical. . . .'

For hours Mir Nihal had had premonitions of death; and at this news
he missed a heart beat. Intuitively he felt that the worst had come, and
with this thought the earth seemed to slip from under his feet. He went
downstairs hurriedly, forgetting to close the door of the loft, and went
to Babban Jan's.

3

WHEN Mir Nihal started for Babban Jan's it was past ten o'clock. Delhi was still awake; but the bustle and activity of the day had died down. People went about leisurely, as if they were just enjoying themselves or finding relief on the roads from the stuffy atmosphere of small homes bounded on all sides by imprisoning walls. Some laughed and chatted as they walked or stood in front of shops. And one man burst into song as he plunged into a dark and narrow by-lane, afraid of his loneliness, perhaps, or of the dark. His voice came from far away:

> Out of pity someone had put
> A lamp upon my grave at night;
> But oh, the wind was envious
> And with one gust put out the light.

Mir Nihal heard it and he was filled with anxiety as he thought that she might die. Who would care for him when she had gone? His wife was there, no doubt; and so were the children. But the world they lived in was a domestic world. There was no beauty in it and no love. Here, at Babban Jan's, he had built a quiet corner for himself where he could always retire and forget his sorrows in its secluded peace.

It was now over five years that he had kept her as his mistress; and a bond of love had grown between them. He felt it more deeply perhaps because he was old, conscious of the lengthened shadows of life. . . .

As he took the turn into the by-lane in which Babban Jan lived he heard one man quote these lines to another:

> In the winking of the eye my friend
> Has been snatched away from me.
> We had hardly seen the face of the rose
> When Spring walked out in its beauty.

He had a premonition that the worst had happened; and a sinking sensation came upon him. A cat passed across his way miaowing meekly as if she was lonely and wanted love. And a child, rudely awakened from sleep, began to whimper and call to his mother. Then all became silent once again. . . .

*   *   *

When he reached the house he found Babban Jan's mother crying silently. His heart sank, and he muttered with parched lips in Arabic:

'We belong to God, and unto Him shall we return.'
Then he asked her:
'When did she pass away?'
Babban Jan's mother began to sob hysterically.
'Half an hour ago,' she replied in a broken voice. 'She was my only
prop in old age. What will I do now? I have been ruined.'
Mir Nihal tried to soothe her by saying: 'Patience is the only virtue in
the face of the ills of Time. No one outruns his Doom by a single span,
and escape from the decrees of God there is none. . . .' But she still
whimpered, and the tears flowed down her wrinkled cheeks.
'I, a trembly old woman, am still alive to suffer the vagaries of life,'
she said between her sobs; 'and she has gone. . . .'
Mir Nihal went towards the veranda in which Babban Jan lay on a
bed, covered from head to foot with a sheet. He took up the lantern and
uncovered her face. Even in death she looked beautiful. Even death had
not taken away the charm from her face. Her eyebrows were arched and
her lips were gently closed as in a wayward smile, and her eyes seemed
to be closed in sleep and not in death. On her face there was a serenity
and calm, the realization of perfect peace which is not in this world.
Overcome with emotion Mir Nihal lowered the lantern and, covering up her face again, walked into the courtyard. The mother's sobs had
ceased and she sat on the bed holding her head between her hands,
staring with dazed eyes in front of her. Mir Nihal also sat down. He had
suddenly become weak and old, and there seemed no strength in his
limbs. He sat there for some time, lost in a world of memories and
regrets. Then he turned round to her and asked:
'Have you informed your people?'
'Yes, the servant has gone to inform them,' she said. 'They will come.
Then they will take her away from me and bury her. And I shall be left
all alone in the world with no one even to care for me. . . .'
And she began to cry again.
Mir Nihal tried to soothe her, but it was useless. Grief must have its
way. At last she became silent; and, thinking that the people would be
coming soon, Mir Nihal got up with a heavy heart and, giving the old
woman some money, cast a last lingering glance at the dead body and
walked away. She who was Babban Jan had gone. She who brought him
here had walked the way of death, and nothing could bring her back to
life again. . . .

*   *   *

In the morning when he woke the first thought that came to his mind was of Babban Jan. He sat on the bed with a pained look on his face, feeling heavy like lead, as if he himself had died. But he got up at last to attend to the duties of the world.

As he went upstairs to release his pigeons he saw feathers on the stairs, and many more on the roof. When he looked inside the loft he found that there had been a massacre. He had forgotten to close the door last night, and the cats had found their opportunity.

Some of the birds had managed to escape by flying out. They had been afraid of coming down from the roof for the feathers lay all over the place. But when they saw their master they came down and perched on his shoulder in the hope of getting something to eat, and began to peck at his beard. There was something so loving and tender in this action of the birds that a storm of self-pity welled up within his breast. His heart contracted into a point with pain, then expanded as if wanting to burst out of its sides. And he stood there lost in an engulfing sense of futility.

The pigeon-fliers were shouting, and now and then a flutter of wings came into his ears as some flock swished past just above his head, flying low over the roof. And Khwaja Ashraf Ali's voice could be heard louder than the rest. But what did Khwaja Ashraf Ali matter now or the pigeons or the shouts? Everything comes to an end one day, soon, too soon, alas. . . .

Some pigeons which were kept in another loft had escaped death. Mir Nihal put the birds which were outside with them, and threw them two handfuls of grain. As he was closing the door he heard a sudden noise, a thud of something jumping down inside the loft. He turned to look. It was a ferocious cat. She had fed herself to satiety on the birds and, too sluggish to go away after her rich feast, had gone to sleep on the upper compartment of the loft.

As she jumped down Mir Nihal's protective instinct was aroused. Quickly he closed the door of the loft and the staircase and picked up the stick to which the flying flag was tied. It was a strong and serviceable weapon, and he got ready to take his revenge.

The cat was trying to find a way out. In her vain attempts to escape she climbed up the bamboo-structure wall in front of the loft and was struggling to make a way for herself. Mir Nihal opened the door of the loft and frightened the cat down. Seeing that the door was open the cat jumped and made for the open. Just as she was half across the threshold Mir Nihal struck her one hard blow. The cat fell, but steadying herself rushed towards the wall to climb up and run away. She took a jump, but missed and began to crawl up. Her forefeet had already caught hold of the edge of the wall when Mir Nihal overtook her and with one blow brought her down. The cat gave a piercing howl, and instinctively rushed to the door of the staircase. Finding that it was closed she turned back; but before she could go elsewhere the stick fell on her. She was hit on the head and fell down. Then one, two, three, the blows fell on her in quick succession. Mir Nihal clenched his teeth and hit her everywhere. That was his only chance of revenge. He beat her until he was tired and the cat looked dead. . . .

This outburst calmed him down a little, and established his relation with the world which had been severed for a while. But something within him had died; and he did not go to the shop. She for whom he had worked was there no more. What did it matter now if he earned much or little? His elder sons had been insisting that he was old and needed rest. They were earning enough to support their father in old age. But still he had worked on, to cheat Time, perhaps, or to avoid the feeling of dependence even though on his sons. For when he earned the money he was master of it, and could spend it in any way he liked. He did not give much out of his share to Begam Nihal except a little for extra expenses. The rent from the houses and the land was enough to keep them clothed and fed. Most of his business was his own, and was spent on running the establishment of Babban Jan.

Now she was dead; and he did not care. What mattered it if he was dependent on his sons or anybody else? And he decided to give up his work. . . .

4

WHEN he went inside the house Dilchain asked him: 'Are your pigeons safe? Last night a cat brought a pigeon from somewhere and ate it under the wooden couch. I looked at the birds here in the loft, but they were safe.'

'It must have been one of mine,' Mir Nihal replied in a subdued way from behind his mood. Then he added in a tearful voice as self-pity surged in his breast once again: 'The cats devoured them last night.'

'Hai, hai,' Begam Nihal said in a shocked voice. 'These cats have become a dreadful nuisance. God knows where so many of them have come from into Delhi. But how did they get in?'

'I must have forgotten to lock the door last night.'

'Poor birds,' said Mehro, and looked at her father with concern.

Mir Nihal heaved a sigh and remarked:

'What is done cannot be undone. . . .'

When he was taking his food the thought of Babban Jan and his grief filled his mind. He thought of his callousness and the indifference of the world. There she was, dead, beneath the all-embracing earth; and here he was, taking his food, enjoying himself. Already under the earth the worms must have set upon her lovely body, already she was in the land of the dead. And here he was, thinking of other things, of other and lesser sorrows than her death.

As he thought of this the food stuck in his throat. Tears rushed to his eyes, and he looked away, outside. The wind blew dragging along the floor of the courtyard, carrying with it bits of paper, dry leaves and twigs of the henna tree along the gutters. His eyes fell on the lower leaves of the date palm which were sered and burnt up with the heat and the sun, and fluttered heavily with a deathly sound. Old age, he said to himself, and heaved a sigh.

Begam Nihal, who sat opposite, looked at his face. It was drawn and pale, and there was a look of sadness in his eyes. She thought that it was the death of his pigeons which had affected him so deeply. He was very fond of them, and they had often had quarrels over them. But now that he had lost them she was really sorry. 'Well, if they have died it does not matter,' she said. 'The world itself is impermanent. You can buy more.'

Mir Nihal looked at her with reproachful eyes which seemed to say: 'That's not it, that's not it at all. What do you know of my grief?' But he merely said to her:

'No. That's all right. I won't keep the pigeons any more. . . .'

And he called Nazir and gave the pigeons to be sold. Nazir was shocked and he could hardly believe Mir Nihal. He tried to dissuade him, but Mir Nihal was adamant, and the pigeons were taken away. . . .

* * *

The cat had been thrown into the by-lane, and when Mir Nihal went out in the evening he saw that she was not dead after all. She had licked the water from the gutter and had come back to life. So does life inflict wounds on men, thought Mir Nihal, but, looking grey for some time, they become whole and hale again. Fate treats human beings with cruelty and is unconcerned. Death takes lives, parts lovers, bereaves mothers and children, husbands and wives, and, with callous indifference, goes about her ravages with the hard-hearted grace of a fell beloved who prides herself on breaking both hearts and homes.

As Mir Nihal looked at the cat he was reminded of his pigeons and of Babban Jan. But what did it matter now? They were gone. Yet Death was alive and would come to him too and free him from misery and care. He turned his eyes away from the cat. She did not fill him with anger or hate. He was indifferent now. And he went to his friend Nawab Puttan in the hope of forgetting his grief.

*   *   *

Life went on as before. A crowd flowed on the road, vendors shouted, men laughed, and tram cars went rattling past. Nothing had affected the heart of the world. His grief was his and his alone.

A prey to his own thoughts, lost in his futility, he reached the house of Nawab Puttan. Some people were sitting there and among them Nawab Sirajuddin Khan Saael, the poet, wearing his four-cornered cap, his well-starched and fine clothes, and his impressive flowing beard. A discussion was going on regarding the merits of Zauq and Daagh as poets. Mir Nihal saluted everybody and took his seat. Nawab Puttan saw that all was not well with Mir Nihal, and he enquired: 'Is everything all right? Why are you looking sad?'

'Yes, all is well, thanks,' Mir Nihal replied. 'I am just tired.'

And the discussion continued, and Mir Nihal was also gradually dragged into it. His own favourite poet was Mir who belonged to an older generation and tradition, with a school of his own. But Zauq was the court poet of Bahadur Shah, and Daagh was the most talked-of poet in those days.

They talked of their distinctive merits, especially of their language and diction. From this point of view the palm went to Mir and Daagh, and the others were not considered so great. Saael always took the side of Daagh not because Daagh, the youngest of these poets, was still alive, a grey old man who had retired from the world and poetry and lived a quiet life alone, but especially because he was Daagh's son-in-law. When from a general discussion of their poetry they started discussing the superiority of these poets in the use of their pen-names in the last line of each ghazal, Saael established his father-in-law's

superiority by quoting the closing lines of the discussion in a resonant
and nasal tone:

> If someone asks for me, perchance,
> Then tell him this, O messenger:
> My pseudonym is Daagh and I
> Reside in the hearts of lovers.

The beauty of a maqta, the last line of a ghazal, lies in the use of the
pseudonym in a double sense, so that it could give the stamp of the
name to the poem as also suggest a different and poetic meaning. Here,
of course, in these lines, and elsewhere, Daagh was great, as he was in
his use of standard and most chaste Urdu and the idiom. Saael won the
day for his father-in law and looked very pleased and flattered. . . .

As the shadows lengthened the guests departed one by one, leaving
Mir Nihal and Nawab Puttan alone. A weary sun was setting behind the
earth, tired after the sore day's labour, in search of peace and rest and
other lands more beautiful than Hindustan. The dust and sand were in
the air and the sky looked passionless. But as the sun sank down a pale
red glow crept over the horizon and enlivened the heart of the world for
a while.

'How is Babban Jan?' Nawab Puttan asked. 'You had told me she
was ill when you were here last.'

'She passed away last night,' Mir Nihal said sadly.

'I am so sorry to hear it,' Nawab Puttan condoled. 'What was she
suffering from?'

'Typhoid,' Mir Nihal replied.

'She was a nice woman. I am really sorry.'

They were silent for a while, looking back into the past. Somewhere
in the lane a child was crying pathetically, and a man was shouting at
the child. This world is a house of many mirrors. Wherever you turn
you see your own images in the glass. They multiply and become
innumerable until you begin to feel frightened of your own self. To Mir
Nihal it seemed that it was not the child but he himself who was crying;
and a peculiar feeling of anxiety, almost akin to madness, took possession of him. He did not know what to do, whether to tear his clothes or
to cry.

Nawab Puttan broke the silence with the remark: 'You can have
another mistress. There is God's plenty on the earth.'

No. That was not it at all. Nawab Puttan did not know. Wealth and
opulence had made him callous. He did not know, perhaps, that even

the death of a bawd can go deep home to a man. Mir Nihal resented this remark. But Nawab Puttan was his friend, after all, and he replied: 'Do you think I am still young? Look at my condition and my age. It is time I retired and passed my life in quiet and the meditation of God. . . .'

In response to the statement, as it were, the moazzin began to call the evening azaan. The rooks cawed and flew away; and flocks of wild pigeons descended on roofs and trees to find rest for the night. And Nawab Puttan and Mir Nihal began to get ready for the prayer.

*   *   *

When they had finished their prayers the servant brought Nawab Saheb's hookah with its long and elastic tube, its water pot of black and white enamel, and its fire pot of nickel with a trellised lid from which silver chains hung all around. Near the silver mouthpiece a garland of fresh jasmines had been wrapped round the stick. Nawab Saheb began to smoke with an air of satisfaction and joy.

'Oh, yes,' Nawab Puttan said pulling at his hookah, 'I hear you are marrying your son to Mirza Shahbaz Beg's daughter. You did not tell me anything about it.'

Mir Nihal had not thought about Asghar for some time. He had gone out of his mind as if he did not exist. Asghar had gone to Bhopal and had found a good job. Mir Nihal knew that preparations for his marriage were going on the sly. Since he was not consulted (and he had refused to give his consent) he did not think about it. When Nawab Puttan asked him this question he did not know what to reply. He was surprised that the news had gone abroad, and a denial would not be right. A contradiction would mean that either he was telling a lie or Mirza Shahbaz Beg, by whom surely Nawab Puttan must have been informed. And then, however angry he might have been with Asghar he was, after all, his son; and he did not wish to let him down before a stranger, a friend of his, no doubt, but not a member of the family. Therefore he replied:

'The marriage is still far off. You would surely have been informed. Only I was worried and did not think of it. . . .'

And he said to himself: Why withhold consent? It mattered little whether Asghar married a low-born or a girl with blue blood in her veins. He would not be in it, anyway. He had lived his life, good or bad, done all he could for the children and the purity of his stock. Now it was their look-out whether they flourished or decayed. If Asghar refused to see his point of view he could go his own way and ruin himself. He did not care. Life had not treated him well; and if a son was also lost it must be borne. Besides, if Asghar got married without his consent it would be worse. Why heap disgraces unnecessarily on his old and hoary head? Why not die with a grace?

And when he went home he gave his consent to Asghar's marriage with Bilqeece. . . .

5

IN spite of griefs and sorrows a man gets used to life, for its flow must always go on. Soon Mir Nihal resumed his normal life and became reconciled to his fate. There is no doubt that he did not go to work, nor did he fly the pigeons now. They were all of the past and were left behind. The road of Life grew dim in the hazy distance, but he got ready to continue the journey all alone.

In idleness his old hobbies of medicine and alchemy revived. He looked up his old notebooks and interested himself in herbs and plants, and prepared pills and powders for the stomach-ache and other ailments. His faqir and alchemist friends began to come more often now that he had time. For hours they would sit comparing notes and relating anecdotes about faqirs and herbs, remnants of an alchemic life.

Many people frequented his house, many interesting persons. One of them was Mir Sangi. He was bald and the small white hair, soft like down, which still grew on his dark pate looked like bat's fur. He had been extremely rich once, but he had wasted all his wealth on alchemy, without having succeeded at all.

Another was called Red Beard because of his beard which was dyed red with henna. He had a big nose and small eyes, and his great horse teeth were yellow. Many of them had gone but the front ones were intact, and were always filled with pieces of flesh and bread which could be seen sticking in the cavities. He was so dark that here and there black patches showed on his skin as if they were the result of some disease. He always wore a small skull cap of white material; and on his dark complexion his red beard and the white cap presented a funny contrast.

One day they sat talking. Mir Sangi had brought Molvi Dulhan with him. The latter belonged to that order of mystics who dedicate their lives to God, without leaving the world. He wore a red sari, bangles on his arms, kept long hair like a woman, put collyrium in his eyes, and scented oil in his hair. For he had become the bride of God, as his name Dulhan signified. Mir Nihal had seen him once or twice, but he did not know that he was interested in alchemy. Mir Sangi had discovered his interest in the subject and had brought him to meet Mir Nihal.

'Do you know that prescription which is written on the southern gate of the Jama Masjid?' Molvi Dulhan asked.

'Yes,' said Red Beard. 'I have wasted years over finding out the name of that something which has not been given—that "half a pice worth of *that*."'

'If that could be discovered,' said Mir Nihal, 'the whole mystery would be solved.'

'Once a faqir did show me something,' said Molvi Dulhan, 'which, he said, was that very thing which is missing from the Jama Masjid prescription.'

'What was it?' asked Red Beard with curiosity and interest.

'It was a small golden flower with red circles and dots on the petals.'

'What was it called?' Mir Nihal inquired as he was reminded of a similar flower which was called 'the lamp of the night'.

'I forget exactly what it was called, something like "essence of gold". I was very young then and had never even dreamt that I would take interest in alchemy. I was living with an uncle in a village. One day this faqir came to the village in the course of his wanderings, and stayed in the village mosque. I was always drawn towards faqirs and sufis. I went and sat with him for hours, and did things for him, gave him food and massaged his legs. He was so pleased with me that he told me about the Jama Masjid prescription and showed me the flower and said that if ever I was in need of it I could make gold with its help.'

'Do you know where it is found?' Mir Nihal asked.

'On the Rajputana hills, the faqir told me. I made many attempts after that at finding it but failed. I found other flowers similar to it, but not one like that which the faqir had shown me.'

'It must be the same flower,' Mir Nihal said to his friend Mir Sangi, 'which the ironsmith showed me.'

And he began to relate the story of his uncle, Mir Iqbal, who had become a faqir and possessed the secret of making gold. He had retired to a small village in Rajputana and lived a life of meditation. It was by chance that Mir Nihal learnt that his uncle knew the secret of alchemy.

Some twenty years after the death of his uncle, Mir Nihal had gone to the village where his uncle used to live. There was an old ironsmith in that place who had become his uncle's mureed. When he learnt who Mir Nihal was he told him this fact. The ironsmith also knew the secret, and had shown him that flower, 'the lamp of the night'.

'The ironsmith took me to the hill one night,' Mir Nihal related. 'It was a moonless night, and when we reached the slope of the hill he asked me to crawl on my hands and knees, and he himself crawled up the slope in the same fashion. He had wrapped a handkerchief round his hand, and moved very slowly like a cat after its prey. The flowers were growing there, he had said. Among them there were some which gave out a quick sudden glow now and then, like fireflies or the twinkling of stars. These flowers were to be plucked. The smith advanced cautiously with one hand raised in the air. As something glowed he pounced upon it and kept it in the handkerchief, and brought it home. He was going to mix it with other ingredients and prepare gold. But I had to come away home, and did not see its preparation.'

'It was the greatest mistake,' said Red Beard with sadness, 'that you have committed in your life, Mir Saheb.'

Mir Sangi also heaved a sigh and began to relate the story of a cousin who had actually made silver once. As a child she was playing with some of her friends on the roof of a house. They were trying to make ornaments for their dolls out of tin. She heated the tin in a frying-pan, and when it liquefied she did not know how to cool it down. There were some herbs growing on the roof. She crushed them up and poured their juice on the liquid tin. There was a sudden noise and the whole thing became solid. She was frightened, the more so because the tin stuck to the frying-pan and she was afraid that her mother would shout at her for having spoilt it. Quietly she brought it and put it in the corner. When it was needed by her father to carry fire outside for his hookah he discovered the substance sticking to the pan and found that it was silver. When he inquired he learnt that she had made it and how. He went to the roof to see which herbs they were. But they had been crushed out of shape and he could not make out what they were.

He had hardly finished the story when Kambal Shah came in. He had a long, shaggy beard and a hairy chest. He wore just a tahmat, and was always wrapped up in a patchy blanket which he never took off, not even during the summer months. He never wore shoes, and they said that he was such a great divine that even though he walked through mud he never left a mark on the ground. He was tall and well-built and

spoke Urdu with a foreign accent, for he came from Afghanistan. He
was said to be high up in the mystical order although no one knew his
hidden spiritual powers, for such faqirs never reveal themselves to
human beings. He had known Mir Nihal for a great number of years,
ever since he had come from Afghanistan and had stayed with a cousin
of Mir Nihal's. He often came to see him; but he was not only not
interested in alchemy, but discouraged the hobby. He said that it took
man away from God. Yet Mir Nihal's alchemist friends said that he
knew its secret; and one day he had told Mir Nihal that he knew it. But
he would not divulge it, although Mir Nihal's friends hoped that some
day when he was pleased he might tell them. For only faqirs possessed
the secret of making gold.

He sat down, and the conversation continued regarding alchemy.
Molvi Dulhan related how his father had been given some liquid by a
faqir and he had turned a copper pice into gold with its help. Red Beard
related how someone else had made gold by chance. Kambal Shah
listened quietly, but when Red Beard had finished his story he said:

'Yes, it is in this mysterious way that God reveals Himself. But we are
blind, and fail to recognize Him. If all of us knew the secret of making
gold there would be no rich and no poor. We would all be proud, and
in our vanity we would forget God. That is why it is never good to
meddle in His affairs and try to know the mysteries of life. It is best to
accept things and be content. . . .'

No one answered and soon after they went away. When Kambal
Shah had also left Mir Nihal sat thinking about what he had said. It was
the rainy season. The sun was setting and the clouds had formed
exquisite patterns of gold and brown and red against the dark background of restful clouds, transporting the mind to blissful lands of
fabulous gold and untold happiness.

What Kambal Shah had said was true, perhaps, thought Mir Nihal.
His uncle had said the same thing to the ironsmith, and had forbidden
him the use of the knowledge unless he was badly in need of money.
His uncle himself, the ironsmith had told him, made it only when he had
used up all he had, and had no more food to eat. When he made gold he
asked the smith to sell it. With the cash thus obtained he gave a feast to
the poor, and the little that was left served for his own fare. When that
was finished he made a little more. But all the time he sat in the village
mosque, and passed a life of meditation, or went away on a pilgrimage.

Mir Nihal had doubted the statement of the ironsmith at the time.
But when he had told it to some of his friends they had said what a fool

he had been. Soon after he was himself interested in it, and went to that place to meet the smith and get the prescription. But the man had died; and the long and most arduous journey there was in vain.

Since then he had been in search of new prescriptions and herbs, and had tried to discover the secret. He had made many preparations, had burnt stones and metals, but always there had been something wrong. If it was over-heated once at another time it had been heated just a little too little, and he had never succeeded. Many faqirs came, but they never gave him the right prescription or the clue. They would tell him he had to reduce mercury or some other thing to powder, but they would never tell him the right way of doing it; and the whole experiment would fail. He often thought it was just a mirage. But then, there were the faqirs telling him that it was all so true and could be done. Yet no one really did it. Still, Mir Nihal believed in its truth and went on hoping against hope.

For if it were not for Hope men would commit suicide by the scores, and the world would remain a barren desert in which no oasis exists. On this tortuous road of Life man goes on hoping that the next turn of the road will bring him in sight of the goal. But when he takes the turn and still there is no sign of the promised land he still says that at the next turning he will come to it. Thus from turn to turn he goes on hoping, believing in the will-o'-the-wisp that is Hope. And Mir Nihal went on believing in disbelief. Days and weeks passed, as the years had flown before; and Life held sway as of yore over the empires of the world. . . .

6

THEN came the month of Ramazan, and the faithful began to fast. The days without food or water seemed unending and long. But the rains came, and it was not so difficult to fast.

Early in the morning, much before the crack of dawn, the faqirs came shouting and woke everyone up. The whole family then took a light meal to get ready for the day. Just as Nisar Ahmad called the morning azaan the fast began. Until evening no one could eat or drink or smoke. And as Nisar Ahmad called the evening azaan the fast was broken.

Then the beggars came, whining, singing, begging in set and doleful voices, blessing even before they had got something, in the anticipation of getting alms. Begam Nihal or Mir Nihal asked Masroor to go and give them something, bread or flour or pice. Or Dilchain was sent and went mumbling to the door. The beggars came throughout the day, but more after sunset and at dinner-time. Many thrived and did a good business. One, for instance, had asked Shams once to write a money order for him, and had sent fifty rupees home.

Whatever their faults, they always came regularly at their usual time, almost punctually by the clock. Everyone had so got used to their voices, especially of one who always came at dinner-time, that they all missed them if they did not come.

'What has happened to the poor faqir?' Begam Nihal would remark. 'He must have fallen ill.'

Other beggars came at different times of the day.

There was Iron Shah. He wore heavy iron chains round his neck and on his arms, fetters on his feet, and carried a heavy iron rod in his hand. There must have been at least twenty seers of iron on his body, if not more. It was said that as a boy he had become a disciple of some divine who had ordered him to wear iron all his life; and he was carrying out his master's instructions to the full. He was tall and well-built and was very fond of doing exercise and of drinking bhang. Behind him walked a fat and greasy goat, so well-trained that she followed the master wherever he went. He did not have any cry, but sang the Noor Naama, a semi-religious poem dealing with the seven skies. He had a very rich voice and in his tune there was resilience and pathos. His voice came from a distance, growing louder and richer as it neared:

> The sixth is made of rubies red,
> The seventh of emerald green, 'tis said.

He made his round after ten o'clock in the night and went away, leaving the world more lonely and silent than before. . . .

There were others who came at different times of the year, in different months and during various festivals. They would come, make their rounds, and then disappear to come back the next year again, perhaps when they had finished their previous year's earnings, or to earn enough for the coming year.

One of these was Shah Maqbul. He came in the month of Ramazan, and disappeared a few days after Eed. He would come in the morning, crying loudly in a singsong voice his half-verse, half-prose cries:

> Here is Shah Maqbul,
> He will take a pice
> And a yard of tulle.
> Give today or tomorrow
> But you must give on the day of Eed.

Every day he would come, make his round and go away, without stopping in front of doors unless some God-fearing person detained him. He never accepted anything but pice or his yard of tulle, if there was someone to give him that. If anyone gave him bread or flour he flatly refused. He had his own pride and dignity.

To children he was a constant reminder of the coming Eed; and the elders too were pleased. As Shah Maqbul arrived they all began to look forward to Eed, which was not far away, nor was Asghar's marriage. It had originally been fixed for the month of Eed, but had to be postponed till December as Mir Nihal's elder sons could not get long leave. They were busy making preparations for the Coronation of George V, which was to take place in December; and they had to send things and men for the event from their various districts to Delhi.

The preparations for the marriage, however, were going on. Everyone in the house was kept busy, some sewing, others tucking, others still cutting areca nut into small bits. For many guests were to come and everyone ate paan, and areca nut had to be got ready.

To facilitate the work Begam Nihal sent for her two daughters-in-law. The elder had many children and could not come to Delhi just yet. The second one arrived with her mother Begam Kalim who was Begam Nihal's sister-in-law and her four-year-old son.

A few days before Eed Begam Waheed came with Asghar. As the guests arrived they all embraced and felt happy at meeting after a long time, and the house began to hum with laughter and activity. It took on a gala appearance, and everyone looked joyous.

*　　*　　*

In the midst of this atmosphere and bustle Eed arrived. The children were full of excitement and were asking every day if their new clothes were ready, or whether new caps had been bought for them or not, or that they wanted shoes. It was a job keeping them quiet and pleased.

Asghar was very happy and went about doing odd jobs, feeling proud and very important. He had saved about a thousand rupees from his pay; and he went and offered them to his father. When he had first seen Asghar, Mir Nihal had been unconsciously filled with anger and resentment. But this act of Asghar's pleased him, and he forgave him. . . .

On the day of Eed Mir Nihal's second son, Habibuddin, arrived. Everyone flocked round him. He was the favourite of the family, not only with his parents but with all the relations, big and small. He was a handsome man, with kind and expressive eyes, and a fine oval beard on his face. He had a generous soul, and possessed a great capacity for genuine friendship. In life his principle, derived from the Persian mystics, was, as expressed by Saadi:

> He who makes my woes for me
> Will think about my woes.
> My brooding over them would be
> A greater woe than those.

Guided by this principle his life was really happy, full of love and affection, as he himself was full of sympathy and understanding. With his arrival it seemed that the central pivot had come, and everyone hung around him.

Then all the men and children dressed themselves in new and fine clothes and went for the Eed prayers. In the midst of his sons and grandchildren Mir Nihal felt happy. He had put on a turban with the tightly tied folds covering part of one eye. And in his muslin coat, tight-fitting paijamas, his fine shoes and his white majestic beard he looked magnificent. As the children flocked round him the skin on his cheeks quivered and his eyes sparkled with joy.

At the Eed-gah there were thousands and thousands of people, all elated and happy, with attar on their bodies and collyrium in their eyes. The noise of people talking, vendors shouting, children crying, filled the air. All along the roads and in the open ground near the Eed-gah toy-sellers had coloured the earth with bright earthen toys. Vendors went about selling delicacies, and many sold whistles and bugles and trumpets, and deafened the ears with their noises and cries.

Then the prayer began. They all stood in rows, one behind the other. There were so many people that they had to form rows outside the enclosure of the Eed-gah. As the shout of Allah-o-akbar went up a sudden quiet descended upon the earth. Everyone became silent as if no one was there at all. Only now and then a child began to cry, frightened by the sudden silence, perhaps, or at being lonely in the midst of that huge crowd. One could hear a horse neighing or a kite shrilly crying as it flew in the sky.

When the prayer ended they all began to embrace, falling on each other's necks, pressing the chests together warmly. All those who knew one another went through this show and expression of affection. And the lovers found the opportunity of their lives. A middle-aged man quoted these lines to a young man with arms open for an embrace, just where the whole family of Mir Nihal were embracing and waiting for the crowd to thin so that they could go out:

> It is the day of Eed, my dear,
> Ah come, let me embrace thee.
> It is the custom and besides
> There's time and opportunity. . . .

Before they started for home Mir Nihal and Habibuddin bought the children toys and things; and took sweets and other delicacies home. At home Eed presents in the form of cash were distributed. All the elders gave to the younger people, except unmarried girls and boys who were not earning yet, rupees or eight-anna bits. Even old Begam Jamal, and Begam Waheed, gave presents to all the children and they could hardly contain themselves for joy. The women had all dressed up in fine clothes, and everywhere happiness reigned supreme. . . .

Masroor had started flying kites already, and when Habibuddin came back he sent for kites and string worth five rupees and made Asghar fly them, and he himself looked on and watched the fun. Even Shams was with them all the time. Habibuddin had infused life and spirit into him too, and he was also tempted to fly a few kites. But Asghar was the man. He did not believe in forming a painch at less than two hundred and twenty yards' distance, nor did Habibuddin like it. There was more fun if the kite was higher and farther away. One of Asghar's kites succeeded in cutting nine others one after another without being cut itself. Then it was brought down, and on it was written in bold letters: 'Nausherwan', which has killed nine lions. Then it was flown again; but after another painch it got cut at last.

About two-thirty in the afternoon came Munawwar, the ice-cream vendor, and Habibuddin stood the whole family a treat. The men ate outside, in the mardana, and the children rushed in and out carrying ice-cream cases inside for the women. Soon Munawwar had exhausted his stock; and he emptied the water from the pot in the by-lane and the

children took the salted ice from him and enjoyed it to their hearts'
content. . . .

*   *   *

The days flew past, and it was now the beginning of September, and the
family was busy again with the preparations for the marriage. Luckily
during Eed the sky had been clear; but the rains came again slightly out
of time, and the roads and by-lanes became muddy, and the house was
damp and wet. Yet things went on as before.

The sky was overcast with black and grey clouds, filling the earth
with a beauty peculiar to India, bringing its associations of joy and
love and spring. In the nearby houses the women sang the sad but
beautiful songs of Saavan:

> He had said that he would come,
> That he would come.
> The clouds have come at last,
> But oh, he has not come,
> Full one year has passed.

> The thatch is old, my heart is sore,
> My heart is sore,
> And lightning is flashing fast.
> But oh, he has not come,
> Full one year has passed.

Against this sad and symbolic background of the Indian woman's
lament in the absence of her lover, preparations were going on for
Asghar's marriage. In all this bustle and activity the time passed quickly, and winter set in with its short days and long nights. With small
braziers in front of them the women would sit at night and talk, of the
future and the past, waxing reminiscent and sad, and often would be
heard the heart-rending voice of the blind beggar bringing with it
sadness and gloom. It came from far away on the winter nights com-
municating a sense of hopelessness:

> Blames were all that we received,
> What we'd come for we never achieved.

But he came very seldom for he mostly begged at the Jama Masjid
and sang to the passengers in the tram cars.

There came another beggar, commonly known as Bahadur Shah, for
he sang only the Mughal king's poems. He was old and short in stature,
and looked insignificant and futile like a swarm of flies over a dust heap

or the skeleton of a dead cat. But a sadder voice than his was hardly known. Bahadur Shah's poem which he sang brought back the memory of the olden days when Hindustan had not been shackled in its new sorrows. His voice did not merely convey the grief of Bahadur Shah, but in it was heard the plaint of India's slavery:

I'm the light of no one's eye,
The rest of no one's heart am I.
That which can be of use to none
—Just a handful of dust am I.

Why should they come to visit my grave
And waste upon my dust a wreath?
Why should they light a lamp at night?
The grave of helplessness am I.

I am not a soulful tune,
Why should anyone listen to it?
I'm the cry of a stricken soul,
The pain of a broken heart am I. . . .

And the months dragged on, and it was the month of December. Many activities were going on in Delhi, for the English king was going to hold his Coronation Darbar in this ancient seat of the mighty kings of Hindustan. The Delhi people were agog and stared in wonder at this bustle, many happy in the hope of gain, others raging within their hearts at the thought of subjection to a foreign race. . . .

7

MANY days before the Coronation people began to pour into Delhi from all parts of India and beyond. The roads were washed; oil was sprinkled to keep the dust down; and the city looked spick and span. Motor cars which had hardly ever been seen before came into Delhi and raced on the roads; and horses and elephants were seen everywhere. Queer-looking carriages passed through the Chandni Chowk and the Chaori Bazar, and strange faces were visible all around.

Most fantastic and colourful dresses rustled in the streets of Delhi from long robes to short coats and gowns to waistcoats, and headgears

of a hundred kinds. In and out of this holiday crowd walked the
Tommies in their drab uniforms, or Englishmen in their plain clothes.

Near the Fort the glacis was levelled into terraces, and the slope
leading upwards towards the road was turned into hundreds of stands
which encircled the whole of the Jama Masjid, and along the Esplanade
Road. From end to end of the Chandni Chowk divided down the
middle by a row of noble and expansive peepal trees, the central
causeway was turned into one long line of wooden stands. In front of
the Town Hall and around the statue of the English Queen one enor-
mous stand was erected; and the ugliness of the Clock Tower had been
concealed. The stands continued through the Fatehpuri Bazar with its
majestic mosque and grateful shadows, and continued to the Mori Gate
and beyond. All this made Delhi look more like an exhibition ground
than the city which was once the greatest in Hindustan.

As this was going on in the heart of the city guests began to arrive at
Mir Nihal's. His two sons and other relations came for Asghar's mar-
riage and to attend the Coronation; and the house was turned into a
Serai.

The women heard of the preparations for the Darbar and made sour
faces and passed bitter remarks.

'What would these beaten-with-the-broom Farangis do?' said Begam
Jamal; and Begam Nihal remarked:

'When the Mughal kings used to go out rupees and gold mohurs
were showered by the handfuls. What will these good-as-dead Farangis
give? Dust and stones! . . .'

The children, however, were happy. It was all a big fair, such as they
had never seen in their lives. At the shop of Mirza, the milk-seller, the
kababi and the barber, the bania and the carpenter, gathered and
talked of all that was going on in their city.

'I say, you seem to have all your five fingers in ghee these days,' said
the kababi to the barber. 'From morning till night you are running from
house to house shearing people. What about giving us a feast?'

'Yes, you must give us a damn good treat,' said Kallan, the carpenter,
slapping the barber on the back. 'You shouldn't forget us in your
prosperity.'

'Allah is kind,' the barber replied happily. 'I am not badly off. But
what about you, Kallan? You are out every day making those stands.
You must be earning a great deal too.'

'I thank God for His mercy,' Kallan replied. 'I earn about twelve
annas per day and bring the wood peelings home. God is kind.'

'You should thank the Angrezi Sarkar for this,' said Siddiq, the bania. 'For it is through it that we are getting all this.'

'What has the Angrezi Sarkar to do with this?' said Mirza, the milk-seller, who sat with his legs arched up in front of him. 'God alone gives us our daily bread; and Him alone should men thank.'

'But suppose the King had not held his Darbar here, what would you have done?' said Siddiq loudly. 'You couldn't have forced him to come here, could you? He is a very gracious Emperor to think of his subjects and of our Dilli which will now become the capital of India. Soon we shall all be rich and roll in wealth all our lives.'

'Yes,' remarked the barber, 'things do seem to be prospering. And our kababi is doing good business and Mirza too. So many thousands of people have come to Dilli. Will it be always like this, I wonder?'

'Of course,' Siddiq replied with enthusiasm. 'We will all be prosperous and happy.'

'I am not so sure,' said Mirza as he moved a big flat iron spoon up and down inside the milk in the huge iron cauldron to keep it from forming a residue. 'All this show and prosperity is temporary. It will all vanish one day, soon. I am not abusing God's graciousness. He is always good. But I do believe that the rule of the Farangis can never be good for us. See how they imprisoned Bahadur Shah, banished him, killed his sons and looted Dilli. All this does not betoken any good. . . .'

'You are always calling the English bad names,' said Siddiq, feeling hurt as if he himself had been abused. 'You are never contented with your lot. Wait and see what show and splendour there will be on the seventh of December. I am just dying to see my gracious English King. . . .'

Mirza heaved a sigh and remained silent. But Kallan and others became enthusiastic at the prospect of watching the procession of the King. A real king they had never seen; and the stories they had heard about royal processions from their elders seemed to be coming true at last. They were dying to see the big fair. For the residents of Delhi never miss an opportunity of enjoying themselves, and this quality is peculiar to Delhi-ites alone of all the peoples of India. Even during the terrible days of 1857, when the guns were spitting fire, they used to climb up on the roofs to watch the fun of cannon balls shooting red hot out of the cannons' mouths, and compared the firing to fireworks during the festival of Shab-barat.

But the older residents, who had seen a glimpse of the glamour of the

Mughals and had many relations killed during the great destruction and plunder of Delhi in 1857, were stricken dumb, or cursed the Farangis at home. . . .

*   *   *

Two days before the Coronation, Shams, who had been posted in the Fort, brought the news that the pavilion was burnt down.

'Last night,' he related, 'the beautiful pavilion was burnt down. The Punjab Governor had furnished it with his own expensive furniture, and other Sahebs gave their valuable carpets and other things to decorate it. But a mysterious fire broke out. No one yet knows how it all happened; and the loss is immense.'

Other fires had broken out, and the petrol depot had caught fire. Mir Nihal and Habibuddin felt secretly happy; but Kabiruddin kept quiet out of loyalty to those from whom he got his 'salt'. Begam Nihal, however, cursed the English, feeling happy at the news.

'It's God's vengeance falling on these good-as-dead Farangis,' she said. 'May they be destroyed for what they have done to Hindustan. May God's scourge fall on them.'

And she began to relate how ruthlessly Delhi had been looted by them at the time of the 'Mutiny', and the Mussalmans had been turned out of the city, their houses demolished and destroyed and their property looted and usurped by the 'Prize Agency'; and the city was dyed red with the blood of princes and nobles, poor and rich alike who had happened to be Mussalmans. . . .

All this, and more, had not been forgotten by Mir Nihal and his wife and the others; and they all burned with rage and impotent anger, for they could do nothing. . . .

*   *   *

In Delhi to this day there were innumerable princes and princesses alive, daughters and grand-daughters of Bahadur Shah. Many cut grass for a living, others drove bullock carts to keep body and soul together. The princesses had married cooks and kahars, their own servants, or served as cooks and maids. Many of them had become beggars and went about begging in the streets. Some were given five or ten rupees as pension by those who had usurped their kingdom. But there were many others who were not given even this much of help.

One of these was Gul Bano, a grand-daughter of Bahadur Shah. She was about seven years of age when the 'Mutiny' took place. She had escaped with her mother and a few others. But they had all died of cholera. She herself suffered many hardships, and when she returned to Delhi there was no one to give her even bread. She then married a cook who treated her badly; but eventually he died. And she was reduced to begging from house to house.

One day before the Coronation of the English king she happened to come to Mir Nihal's, for she often came. She was beautiful even in her old age with a broad forehead, fair complexion, and most beautiful eyes. She never begged directly, but sang Bahadur Shah's poems which he had written in his banishment and which had been banned. But people knew them by heart, and they were sung with reverence and tragic memories.

'You must have seen the preparations which are going on for the Darbar?' Mehro asked Gul Bano. 'What are they like? Are they better than what used to be in your time?'

Gul Bano misunderstood Mehro's intention and, heaving a deep sigh, she said with bitterness:

'Our days are done, daughter. We have been rendered poor by Fate. But we have still some self-respect. What does it matter if we are rulers no longer? We are still the descendants of the greatest kings of the world. Why should you pain us and laugh at our miserable plight?'

'I did not mean to laugh at you,' Mehro said, sorry for having hurt her feelings. 'I really wanted to know.'

'What is there to know?' Gul Bano said, looking ill and sad with memory. 'We are beggars and the Farangis are kings. For us there is only a bed of thorns, and they sleep on the beds of roses. But God gives to whomsoever He pleases, and takes away from others as it pleases Him. Yesterday we were the owners of horses and elephants, slaves and territories. But *they* usurped our throne, banished the king, killed hundreds of princes before these unfortunate eyes which could not even go blind, drank their blood, and we could do nothing. They are happy for they are dead; but I am still alive to suffer the bludgeon blows of Time. But all the things that pass, all the joys and sorrows of life, are false and unreal, mere shadows across the face of Time. . . .'

Tears streamed down her wrinkled face, and it became distorted with grief. Begam Jamal and Begam Kalim, who sat listening to her, heaved sighs, sorry for Gul Bano, as if her sorrows were their own, and remembered the good old days. Begam Nihal dried two teardrops from her eyes, and gave Gul Bano a paan. She accepted the paan, and sat silent, lost in thought, gazing into vacancy, thinking of some distant

world more beautiful and more happy than Hindustan. Then she began
to hum a tune, and of her own accord began to sing a poem of Bahadur
Shah in a trembling voice:

> Suddenly the wind has changed, my soul
> Is restless constantly.
> How shall I tell the tale of woe,
> My heart is rent with agony.
>
> Delhi was once a paradise,
> Such peace had abided here.
> But *they* have ravished its name and pride,
> Remain now only ruins and care.
>
> Ravished were the people of Hind,
> Unenviable their fate.
> Whoever the ruler of the day
> Espied was ordered put to death.

Tears came into the eyes of Begam Nihal and Begam Kalim; and
Begam Jamal began to cry. And when Gul Bano sang these lines no one
could repress her sobs:

> They were not even given a shroud,
> Nor buried under the ground.
> No one performed their funeral rites,
> Their graves were not marked by even a mound.
>
> Yet not content with this alone
> They suspect every Muslim who says
> Even a word against them,
> And with his life the penalty pays. . . .

Her own voice failed her, and she covered her face with her head-
cloth. . . .

*   *   *

Outside, in the mardana, Mir Nihal and Habibuddin and Kambal Shah
discussed the causes of the downfall of the Mughals. Mir Nihal said that
it was the treachery of Zinat Mahal, the second wife of Bahadur Shah,
who wanted the throne for her son Jawan Bakht, which led her to
betray her own people to the British who had promised to give her son
the Indian throne. Habibuddin held that the English would have been
defeated if Mirza Mughal and Mirza Khizar Sultan had listened to

Bakht Khan, the Lord Governor of Bahadur Shah, who was a great general, but they did not pay any heed to him.

'The princes had no knowledge of strategy,' said Habibuddin, 'nor did the whole army obey them. Whenever Bakht Khan asked them to let him lead the attack they refused. This was a great blunder and tactical mistake. For the princes had no first-hand knowledge of modern warfare. Even then much would not have been lost if only Bahadur Shah had listened to his Lord Governor. Bakht Khan had asked the king to come away to the hills with him when Delhi had been captured by the English. The reason why they lost the battle, he had said, was that the English commanded the most strategic point in Delhi, the hill; and the Mughal soldiers were fighting from a lower level. His scheme was to go to the hills near Delhi and fight the English from there. He was confident that all the princes and rajahs and other Indian chiefs would flock round the person of Bahadur Shah, who was still considered the real Emperor of India, as the treachery of the East India Company had become too well known. Very soon they would have not only taken Delhi, but would have driven the British out of India. But Bahadur Shah had no political sense or judgement. He loved to be looked upon as a martyr, and was too fond of a sufistic and easy life. He allowed himself to be deceived by that traitor, Mirza Elahi Bakhsh, who was an English spy and had sold himself to them. He impressed upon the king the honourable intentions of the English which proved to be nothing else but imprisonment, murder and banishment. All this, in my humble opinion, resulted in the final over-throw of the Mughal Empire.'

Habibuddin stopped, feeling extremely sad and bitter. Mir Nihal looked convinced and heaved a sigh. But Kambal Shah, who had been listening to their talk silently, said with an air of conviction and finality, as if what he were going to say was the real truth and the last word on the subject.

'It is not that,' said Kambal Shah. 'These things just helped in the downfall of Bahadur Shah. The real causes of the loss of the Mughal Empire were some mistakes committed by the elders of that king, and the biggest of them all was that they had separated lover and beloved from each other by burying Mohammad Shah between the graves of Hazrat Mahboob Elahi and Hazrat Amir Khusro. The great love which existed between these two demanded that no curtain should be put between them. Because, Hazrat Mahboob Elahi used to say, that if the laws of Islam had not forbidden it he and Khusro would have been buried in the same grave. Thus they committed a very grave mistake by burying Mohammad Shah in between the two lovers. This led to the downfall of their Empire. . . .'

As they listened to Kambal Shah a peculiar sensation ran down their spines, and their hair seemed to stand on end; and father and son both were filled with religious awe. They believed that Kambal Shah was a great divine, a Qutab, in fact. And the Qutabs, who are faqirs, act as the naibs or assistants of God on earth, and are in charge of various provinces, like Governors. No one knows them for they do not reveal themselves to human beings, and guide the workings of the world unknown to men. They know the secrets of God, and carry out His instructions, and no one can meddle in their affairs. That is why they accepted Kambal Shah's explanation with reverence and awe. But what was done was done, and could not now be undone. . . .

8

DELHI awoke very early on the seventh of December, 1911. At four o'clock people were up and ready to go and take their places at the Jama Masjid to see the procession. Mir Nihal was loath to go, but his sons persuaded him to come. The boys dressed up in their best and warmest clothes and their pockets were filled with dried fruits. Even Nasim, Habibuddin's four-year-old son, insisted on accompanying them, for his elder cousins were going; and he was carried by Ghafoor on his shoulder. Asghar and Masroor were put in charge of the boys; and Mir Nihal was there to look after them.

People were already going to take their places in the stands. It was bitterly cold and they walked fast to keep themselves warm.

When they reached the Jama Masjid a pale green light was creeping over the horizon. They took their seats on the steps of the mosque overlooking the maidan and the Fort. Policemen went about and the Tommies paraded on roads, and a noise of talk and laughter filled the air. They made themselves comfortable on their stony seats; and Nasim fell asleep in the lap of Ghafoor who had besmeared himself with more attar and had put a greater quantity of oil in his hair for the occasion. Gradually a little light appeared in the east, but soon it was smothered by a fog which covered everything up in its grey mantle. When a shivering sun came out it displayed a unique sight of hundreds and thousands of people, dressed in bright and gaudy clothes, all around; and Tommies stood lining the roads, afraid, as it were, lest the crowds rush at their King when he passed.

At last when the sun had risen and the fog had lifted, a salute of guns announced the arrival of the English King. As they sounded, a shout went up from the crowds, as if the King had come right in their midst.

It was a long time until the procession emerged out of the main gate of the Fort through which once the Mughal kings used to come out. Slowly it crept forward with horses and its show of martial might; and people gazed with wondering eyes, trying to distinguish the King in the crowd. But most failed to see which was King and which the officials. The English looked all so alike with their white faces and their similar military uniforms. Behind were the carriages of native rajahs and nawabs. As Mir Nihal thought of their slavishness and their treacherous acceptance of the foreign yoke he was filled with shame and disgust.

Here it was, in this very Delhi, he thought, that kings once rode past, Indian kings, his kings, kings who have left a great and glorious name behind. But the Farangis came from across the seven seas, and gradually established their rule. By egging on Indian chiefs to fight each other and by giving them secret and open aid they won concessions for themselves; and established their 'empire'. . . .

The procession passed, one long unending line of generals and governors, the Tommies and the native chiefs with their retinues and soldiery, like a slow unending line of ants. In the background were the guns booming, threatening the subdued people of Hindustan. Right on the road, lining it on either side, and in the procession, were English soldiers, to show, as it seemed to Mir Nihal, that India had been conquered with the force of arms, and at the point of guns will she be retained.

Mir Nihal closed his eyes for a while, but painful thoughts were in his mind which did not allow him any peace. As he tried to forget them more and more of them swarmed upon him.

Right in front of him was the Red Fort built long ago by Shah Jahan, the greatest of artists in mortar and stone, but which was now being trampled by the ruthless feet of an alien race. On his right, beyond the city wall, was the Khooni Darwaza, the Bloody Gate; and beyond that still was the Old Fort built by Feroz Shah Tughlaq many more centuries ago. Still beyond stretched the remnants of the past Delhis and of the

ravished splendour of once mighty Hindustan—a Humayun's tomb or
a Qutab Minar. There it was that the Hindu kings had built the early
Delhis, Hastinapur or Dilli; and still in Mahroli stands the Iron Pillar as
a memory of Asoka; and other ruins of the days of India's golden age,
and dynasties greater than history has ever known. Today it was this
very Delhi which was being despoiled by a Western race who had no
sympathy with India or her sons, thought Mir Nihal. Already they had
put the iron chains of slavery round their once unbending necks.

The horses pranced on the road as they walked; and people gazed
with curious eyes at the cortege of native chiefs with its vainglorious
pomp and show and soldiers in armour and coats of mail and swords
and lances, weapons useless in the face of guns. The procession passed
by the Jama Masjid whose façade had been vulgarly decorated with a
garland of golden writing containing slavish greetings from the Indian
Mussalmans to the English King, displaying the treachery of the priestly
class to their people and Islam.

It was this very mosque, Mir Nihal remembered with blood in his
eyes, which the English had insisted on demolishing or turning into a
church during 1857. As he thought of this a most terrible and awe-
inspiring picture flashed before his mind. It was on the fourteenth day
of September, 1857, that most fateful day when Delhi fell into the
hands of the English, that this mosque had seen a different sight. Mir
Nihal was ten years of age then, and had seen everything with his own
eyes. It was a Friday and thousands of Mussalmans had gathered in the
mosque to say their prayers. The invaders had succeeded at last in
breaking through the city wall after a battle lasting for four months and
four days. Sir Thomas Metcalfe with his army had taken his stand by
the hospital on the Esplanade Road, and was contemplating the
destruction of the Jama Masjid. The Mussalmans came to know of this
fact, and they talked of making an attack on Metcalfe; but they had no
guns with them, only swords. One man got up and standing on the
pulpit shamed the people, saying that they would all die one day, but it
was better to die like men, fighting for their country and Islam. His
words still rang in Mir Nihal's ears:

'The time of your trial has come,' the man had shouted. 'I give you
the invitation to death. The enemy is standing there right in front of
you. Those who wish to prove their mettle should come with me to the
northern gate of the mosque. Those who hold life dear should go to the
southern gate, for the enemy is not there on that side. . . .'

When they had heard this speech the Mussalmans had cried in

unison 'Allah-o-akbar'; and there was not one soul who went to the southern gate of the mosque. They unsheathed their swords, broke the scabbards into two, and flashing them rushed out of the northern gate. In front stood Metcalfe with his men, and all around lay the corpses of the dead. Already the vultures had settled down to devour the carrion; and the dogs were tearing the flesh of the patriots who lay unburied and unmourned. As Metcalfe saw the people with the swords in their hands he opened fire. Hundreds fell down dead on the steps of the mosque and inside, colouring the stones a deeper red with their blood. But with a resolution to embrace death in the cause of the motherland, the Mussalmans made a sudden rally and before Metcalfe's men could fire a second volley of shots they were at their throats. They began to kill the soldiers, who turned their backs and ran for their lives. The Mussalmans chased them at their heels, killing many more until the English had reached the hill. On the hill was more of the English army and a battle ensued. The Mussalmans had no guns and most of them lost their lives, the rest came away. . . .

As this scene passed before his eyes Mir Nihal could not contain himself and his rage burst out of bounds. There were those men of 1857, and here were the men of 1911, chicken-hearted and happy in their disgrace. This thought filled him with pain, and he sat there, as it were, on the rack, weeping dry tears of blood, seeing the death of his world and of his birthplace. The past, which was his, had gone, and the future was not for him. He was filled with shame and grief, until the tears of helplessness came into his eyes and he wiped them from his cheeks. People were busy looking at the show, and the children were curious and shouted. They did not know yet what it all meant. It all seems a fair to them, thought Mir Nihal; but soon, when they have grown up Time will show them a new and quite a different sight, a peep into the mysteries of life, and give them a full glimpse of the sorrows of subjection. But happy are they who feel not, for they do not know, and miserable are those who see and suffer and can do nothing. A fire burns within their breasts; but the flames do not shoot up. Only the soul is consumed by the internal heat and they feel dead, so dead, alas. . . .

The procession had gone behind the Jama Masjid, and people began to talk loudly, guessing who was who. Nasim was bewildered and began to cry, feeling lonely without his mother, and wanted to go home. Other children were crying and shouting, some wanting to go home, others wanting to urinate. Since there was no place where they could relieve themselves people had brought bottles with them, and made the children urinate in the bottles. As Nasim persisted in crying Mir Nihal took him in his lap and began to console him.

'We shall go home soon,' he said to Nasim. 'See there go the horses and the Farangis,' and he pointed to the riders as the procession had already come out on the northern side and was on the Esplanade Road. 'Don't you see them? Those are the people who have been our undoing, and will be yours too.'

Nasim looked at the procession, unable to understand what his grandfather was telling him.

'But you will be brave, my child, and will fight them one day. Won't you?'

Nasim looked at the horses and the men; and two teardrops hung on his eyelashes and glistened in the sun.

'You will be brave,' Mir Nihal repeated as he wiped the child's tears with his fingers, 'and drive them out of the country. . . .'

*   *   *

People all around were talking:

'Is that the King on the horse?' said one.

'Don't be mad,' another ridiculed him. 'He is a mere soldier or officer. Kings wear fine and flowering robes.'

'That's all you know,' a third butted in. 'The English wear only those uniforms. Understand?'

Many passed caustic and humorous remarks on the dress and faces of the native chiefs, laughing at their retinues, calling them tin soldiers or made of straw. The children were excited by the sight, and gloated over liveries and uniforms and so many white faces as they had never seen before. They shouted and asked questions from people who either did not know the right answers or were too busy themselves watching the fun. . . .

All this was too much for Mir Nihal, and he felt he could not stand it any longer. He got up to go away and forget his woes. With difficulty he made way for himself. Everyone turned round to look at him. Nasim began to cry again, and he asked Ghafoor to take the child home.

There were police everywhere on the roads, and the Tommies still stood on duty. It was with difficulty that Mir Nihal could reach the road. He was not allowed to go through the Chaori Bazar, so he decided to go home via Chooriwalan. There it was all quiet, and he sent Ghafoor ahead with Nasim. The roads and by-lanes were deserted as all the men had gone to see the procession. Only here and there some shopkeeper sat in his shop; and dogs went about sniffing the gutters. Over a dust heap in front of a butcher's shop two dogs were quarrelling over a bone. But a kite swooped down and carried it away, and the dogs were left alone, growling and sniffing the spot. From the distance still came the hum of noise; but here in the heart of the city a silence as of death prevailed. The guns were still resounding, and Mir Nihal was reminded of those days of the slaughter of Indians when too the English guns had boomed far away, and the city had been deserted and dead, strewn all over with the corpses of the brave.

As he walked, lost in thought, he suddenly became conscious of a sound of something rubbing against the ground. He turned to look. A beggar emerged from a by-lane, lifting himself up on his hands and dragging his legs along the floor; and a bag was hanging round his neck. As the beggar drew near Mir Nihal he stopped and looked up at him with imploring and pathetic eyes. There was a look of nobility on his bearded face, and his features unmistakably proclaimed that he was a descendant of Changez. As he saw the beggar the skin on Mir Nihal's cheeks began to quiver with emotion. He took out a rupee from his pocket and put it in the beggar's bag, and asked him:

'Well, Mirza Saheb, are you also going to see the procession of the Farangi King?'

An expression of pain appeared on the beggar's face, and, heaving a deep sigh, he replied:

'No, brother, these things are not for us now. There was a day when we used to go out in state, and people flocked to see us pass. But Time has upturned the glass. And we, who had once never cared even for kings, are being dragged about in the streets. We, who had helped the poor once, are not even pitied by them today. We are in the direct line of Changez who was looked upon with dread and awe. We are the descendants of Timur Leng who was the king of kings. We are the progeny of Shah Jahan who showered the beauties of the world upon a tomb. But today we have no place on the earth, and everyone laughs at our poverty and plight....'

His name was Mirza Nasirul Mulk, and he was the youngest son of Bahadur Shah. His voice began to tremble as he said this, and his eyes filled with tears, and he lowered his face. A storm was raging in Mir Nihal's breast also, and he was about to break down with grief when the Prince said: 'I must be going now....'

It was with a heavy heart that Mir Nihal went home, full of a sense of the futility and transience of the world. But great are the ravages of Time, and no one can do anything against its indomitable might. Kings die and dynasties fall. Centuries and aeons pass. But never a smile lights up the inscrutable face of Time. Life goes on with a heartless continuity, trampling ideals and worlds under its ruthless feet, always in search of the new, destroying, building and demolishing once again with the meaningless petulance of a child who builds a house of sand only to raze it to the ground. . . .

PART III

In the world is love and beauty,
But there is only blame for me:
Along with the rivers I weep and cry,
The deserts are dreary, dead and dry.
                    MIR TAQI MIR

1

SOON after the Coronation the preparations for Asghar's marriage went on more hectically. There were only fifteen days left and everything had to be in order.

The guests began to arrive one by one, relations from near and far, and there was no room in the house. Begam Kalim's house was full. Another house which was connected with it was borrowed from the residents for the marriage. All the houses were packed full of guests, and the real atmosphere of marriage prevailed.

With the increase in the number of guests the food could not be cooked in the house. A neighbouring house was borrowed for the purpose where hired cooks cooked the food and baked bread in the oven. Sharfullah, a cousin of Begam Kalim's, was put in charge of the kitchen. When the food was ready he himself took it out of the huge pots to be served. At dinner time long food-cloths were spread, inside the zenana for the women, in the mardana for the men. The women laughed and talked at the same time, the children wept and cried, and a loud din filled the house where no one really listened to another and people shouted all in vain.

Women worked away, embroidering, tacking laces and borders, serving food and talking. Those sets of clothes which were ready were tucked with thread together and kept in huge wooden trunks. They were the clothes which are sent to the bride from the bridegroom's side.

'You know, at my marriage . . .' someone would recall the past. 'And at mine . . .' another would wax reminiscent.

They talked of clothes and clothes, admired someone's dress, criticized another's taste. They talked of what they had worn at a particular wedding, or what they should wear now.

They had so many things to do, and their own clothes to set in order. The children would not let them work, but in spite of their shouts and demonstrations of self-will the work continued and progressed. . . .

*　　*　　*

Three days before the wedding the bride's dress and things were sent to Bilqeece's house. There were seven suits of clothes of gorgeous silks and gold brocade of different colours and heavy with rich embroidery. They were tucked together and strewn over with parched fluffy rice as a good omen. Then there was the jewellery, so many ornaments for the whole body made of gold and silver. They were presents from Asghar's parents to the bride; and some pieces had been presented by the sisters-in-law and aunts and other near relations.

Attar, rose water and scents were kept in beautiful bottles of cut glass. In two conical red paper bags, painted gorgeously with silver and gold, was powdered henna. In two other similar bags was sugar. Another bag contained sandal and other scented herbs.

Besides these things there were dried fruits, copra and crystallized sugar in trays. There were two white earthen pots with beautiful designs painted on them, one containing curds, the other sherbet for good luck. All these things were kept in trays and covered with fine and expensive covers and were carried by Chamaris on their heads.

The near female relations of Asghar went in dolis to Mirza Shahbaz Beg's house. Bilqeece was made to wear red clothes and was brought out before the bridegroom's female relations who put on her body fresh flower jewellery which they had taken with them and then the gold and silver ornaments. They 'sweetened' her mouth with crystallized sugar and gave her a purse containing one hundred and one rupees. All this and other ceremonies were accompanied with different songs, one for each occasion, sung by domnis.

They returned after nine o'clock in the night and in loud and excited voices began to discuss things. Before they could sit down to have dinner the bride's people sent the bridegroom's bath and toilet things, before they came for the engagement ceremony. There were so many utensils made of brass and plated with tin to make them look silvery. Among them was a wooden bath stool covered with tin on which beautiful flowers had been embossed, for the bridegroom to sit on during the mayun, ceremony preliminary to the bath. From this day on the bridegroom is supposed to take complete rest and he is given a thorough massage every day with scented preparations.

'This bowl is very beautiful,' one lady appreciated. 'This soap-case is very fine,' another remarked. 'I will get one like this for my daughter too.'

They were all full of praises for the things that had come. But some had never seen a soap-case before, as no soap was used.

'Ooi, sister, just see what a funny thing it is,' one lady remarked. 'Can you tell me what it is?'

'Yes, you are right, sister,' another replied. 'I had not noticed it before.'

They began to surmise what it was. The lady who had admired the soap-case told them what it was, and the other ladies said angrily:

May these good-as-dead Farangis be destroyed! What funny things they have invented. One does not know where these evil ones would stop. . . .'

* * *

No one could have dinner before eleven o'clock, the time fixed for the bride's people to come and put the ring round Asghar's finger. But they knew that they never came before one or two in the morning. . . .

* * *

Ahmad Wazir, the family barber, with his sparse yet longish beard, his ugly teeth, and his wealth of witticisms, went about making himself busy. And Ghafoor was feeling very important. Sheikh Mohammad Sadiq had spoken to him about the proposed match for him and had given him the bait of a handsome dowry. Now in the general atmosphere of marriage he was also glad, dreaming of his own.

As he and Ahmad Wazir sat down to have a few putts at the hookah, Ahmad Wazir said to him:

'When are you getting married to your fourteen-year-old fairy?'

'Why, are you remembering your old woman to think of mine?'

'She is not old at all. She is my second wife, and the darling of my heart. When I went to her in the afternoon I found she had put on new clothes and had put oil in her hair. "You are out to kill," I said to her. "Now get away," she replies. "You are always joking, but you never bring any presents for me." I knew what she meant. She just wanted to be loved. . . . But tell me, what should I do, please the wife or please the belly? . . . She is still good to bear ten more children. But I am growing old and can't play up to her.'

'Pass her to me, then,' said Ghafoor jovially. 'I will manage her.'

'What!' said Ahmad Wazir. 'Will you drive a two-in-hand?'

'I can drive a four-in-hand. What do you take me for? Just send her to me and then ask her.'

'No. She is safer with me,' said Ahmad Wazir. 'I can manage her in my own way. You might go and bump into some obstacle, and I will have to mourn the loss of two.'

And both of them began to laugh heartily.

* * *

Inside the house old Dilchain was feeling merry. She was quite sixty and her teeth had all gone. She had a pointed chin and a long nose, and because her teeth had fallen the chin and the nose came very much together. When they had finished dinner and sat in the room she snatched away Masroor's Turkish cap from his head, put on somebody's sherwani, and dressed like a man. Everyone began to laugh and joke at her expense. Then she suddenly began to dance. With her toothless gums she made faces and went round and round, ogling and making eyes like bawds, and ended up every whirl with a lewd but funny gesture, her hands awry and her chin and nose meeting almost in a loop. She looked so ludicrous that they all laughed and laughed until their sides began to ache. But she went on, as if she were intoxicated or had gone mad. Then she too began to laugh and tears came into her small, half-closed myopic eyes.

*   *   *

And the domnis sang in loud and screeching voices to the accompaniment of the drum, their voices going one way and the tune quite another. It was not so much singing as making a big noise. And what with their singing and the children's shouts and the women's laughter, one could hardly hear anything. But all this had to be done, and no one could stop it. How would it be a marriage otherwise?

*   *   *

At last about one o'clock in the morning the bride's people arrived for the engagement ceremony. Mirza Shahbaz Beg did not come. The party consisted of younger people in charge of Ashfaq's elder brother Mir Ejaz Husain, a venerable old man with a very long beard. He was very religious and carried a rosary in his hand. Every now and then he cleared his throat; and on getting up and sitting down he muttered loudly:

'Ya Rasul Allah (O Messenger of God).'

They had brought a baddhi, a garland of fresh jasmine flowers, which was put round the bridegroom across the back and shoulders. Asghar sat looking shy, covering his face behind a handkerchief. They hung a jasmine tassel from his cap; and similar tassels were distributed to the others.

Mir Ejaz Husain put the engagement ring on Asghar's finger muttering verses from the Koran. Then he handed to him a purse containing one hundred and eleven rupees. It was the same money which had been sent to the bride, returned with the addition of ten rupees according to custom.

Then they began to give him paans and crystallized sugar which they had brought with them. Each one of the bride's party gave Asghar one paan and a piece of crystallized sugar. They did this in quick succession one after another, hardly allowing Asghar to chew either the paan or the sugar. This was done more or less out of fun. Asghar concealed the paans and the pieces of sugar in his handkerchief. But they persisted in pressing more and more of them upon him until his hand was full and some pieces of sugar fell down which were quietly taken away by Asghar's cousin, Nazrul Hasan, who sat by his side.

Habibuddin whispered to Sharfullah:

'Why are you all so glum? They should not be allowed to go away so easily. . . .'

When the bride's people were entertained with sherbet one glass was presented to Mir Ejaz Husain. As he had finished drinking the sherbet Sharfullah stood up to wipe his lips according to custom. He took a rough towel and began to rub Mir Ejaz Husain's lips. For a moment he did not say anything, thinking that Sharfullah would finish soon; but Sharfullah began to rub harder. Mir Ejaz Husain cleared his throat loudly once or twice and began to free himself with his hands. Sharfullah caught hold of his head with one hand, pushed it back, and began to rub with all his might. Mir Saheb's beard went all awry, his rosary fell out of his hand, his cap rolled away, and he cried aloud in a choking voice:

'O Messenger of God. God is true.'

The sight was so ludicrous that everyone began to laugh. The bride's people felt enraged at this outrage; and Mir Ejaz Husain's son Chunnoo boiled with rage to see his father maltreated like this. But they could not say anything. They were in the hands of the bridegroom's people whom custom had given licence to joke on this day.

Habibuddin realized that it was too much, and he shouted at Sharfullah, who let Mir Ejaz Husain go. Blood had already rushed to his lips, and his eyes were filled with tears of anger and shame.

Seeing his brother's plight Ashfaq could not contain himself and said angrily:

'This is not the way of gentlemen! Don't you know that my father-in-law can buy everyone of you up. . . .'

At which Shams got very angry and said:

'What do you think of yourselves! As if we cared two hoots for your gold and riches!'

Asghar felt very humiliated and did not know how to stop the quarrel. He felt very much for Bilqeece's people, but by ties of blood he felt a loyalty to his own.

Habibuddin, however, came to the rescue. He also felt very angry with Ashfaq. What did he mean by such an insult! But he knew that Sharfullah had really gone beyond the limit. So the whole matter was hushed up. The bride's people considered themselves the aggrieved party; but their turn would also come one day, soon. . . .

*   *   *

When Asghar went inside the house he was made to sit on the bath stool. All the near relations had collected, aunts and grandmothers of various kinds and descriptions, cousins and sisters, all those who did not observe purdah with Asghar, for it is only the near relations who come before a man. Gas lamps were lighted and the veranda in which the ceremony was going to be performed was packed full of guests. Mir Nihal was asked to put pindis on Asghar's outspread palms joined together. Begam Nihal sat feeling very important, and so did Begam Waheed. It was not an easy marriage after all, and had been settled after great difficulties.

When Mir Nihal had put the pindis on his palms the other elders put more on the heap taking the number to seven. Mir Nihal smiled, and though he tried to suppress his smile yet his lips parted and his face beamed with happiness. A marriage has its own mood of jollity and no one can escape being affected by it. Then Mir Nihal was asked to sweeten Asghar's mouth by giving him a bit of the pindi. After this he went away to give the younger people a chance of enjoying themselves.

Then the mother and the aunts and the sisters, everyone, began to give him small bits of the sweets to 'sweeten' his mouth. It was auspicious to do so as it betokened good relations between husband and wife and a happy married life. Asghar shivered in his thin clothes as it was very cold; but the skin on his face was cracking with gladness. He was marrying the girl he loved after all.

The cousins, naughty girls, began to give him big pieces of the sweets. He managed to hold them between his teeth for a while then dropped them down. Yet they pressed more and bigger pieces. They wanted a fat neg, money distributed to the sisters and cousins. They demanded one hundred rupees, but Asghar refused. They higgled and bargained and Asghar went on refusing. It was all part of the game. So long as he went on refusing they kept on pressing more and more impossible lumps of the sweets. Surayya, 'brother' Naseeruddin's daughter, even gave him a whole pindi, half a seer in weight.

'All right, we shall knock off ten rupees if you can eat it at one gulp,' she said in a screeching voice jocularly.

'No, no, that's not fair,' Asghar protested. 'One hundred is too much; I can give you only fifty rupees.'

At which a whole chorus of 'No's' rent the air.

'Don't be stingy on this day, and don't be mean,' said Mehro. 'You are not marrying a pretty girl for nothing. . . .'

They did not leave him until he had promised to give seventy-five rupees.

This over, the pindis were taken away from his outstretched hands. He was tired; but he had to hold on still. The aunts and relations, senior to him in age and relation, began to fill his hands with silver coins, and some gave gold mohurs. The bridegroom's hands were not supposed to remain empty. Every old lady came forward, congratulated him, and put a few coins, according to her position and status, in his hands. Some gave ten, some gave five, some only two. Even Dilchain gave one rupee. When they were counted there were three hundred and fifty-five.

Thus does the family help at marriage, everyone contributing his or her share, to get it back in the same way when one of their children gets married.

When this ceremony was over, the ubatna, a scented preparation of herbs and drugs good for the complexion, was brought out. It had come from the bride's house in the form of powder but had, in the meantime, been wetted with water and made into dough. There was a rush at it. They smeared it on Asghar's face and arms and body. Then they began to smear each other's faces with it. Quietly a young man would go behind a girl and smear it on her face. The moment the cold dough touched her face she would scream and run after him to take her revenge. Soon they were all running about all over the house, boys after girls, girls after boys, one after the other. The house was filled with screams and shouts and the laughter from the pursuers and the pursued, as they indulged in this amorous revel.

'For God's sake, don't spoil my clothes,' a girl shouted as a boy overtook her.

'You can change them and look prettier,' he replied and caught hold of her.

'Hai, hai, what has happened to you? It's so cold. Leave me!' she shouted, trying to free herself. Yet, realizing the futility of a struggle, she relaxed, and he smeared her face and neck, tickling her with ice-cold fingers. The girl liked it immensely, but she protested all the same.

'All right, I will take my revenge. You can't escape. . . .'

The older ladies frolicked among themselves.

'Don't do it to me, for God's sake,' Begam Nihal protested laughing. 'Leave me, an old woman, at least.'

'A son's marriage does not come every day,' Begam Jamal replied; and she was not spared. She went and besmeared Begam Kalim in her turn. All the other ladies frolicked and enjoyed; and the men did it among themselves. Many pretty girls had their cheeks pinched, and the boys too were pinched and slapped. Clothes were torn, hair was ruffled. But it was all such great fun. . . .

2

THE day of the wedding arrived at last. In the morning the bridegroom's clothes came from the bride's house, a sherwani of gold brocade, a silk shirt, a turban, silk handkerchiefs, a white paijama with a screaming red paijama-string, shoes with flowers embroidered on them in gold; and other things like buttons, attar, collyrium, etc. These clothes were strewn over with parched fluffy rice. There were also the sehra and baddhi in a separate tray.

Ahmad Wazir, the barber, felt very important as he helped Asghar to dress. And with attar on his clothes, collyrium in his eyes and the joyous expression on his face, Asghar looked handsome indeed. The turban was folded by Habibuddin, and put on Asghar's head; and the sehra was tied to the turban.

The time fixed for the marriage ceremony was ten o'clock; but by the time they started it was half-past eleven. For little details and things which had been overlooked were set right and done at the eleventh hour. And things do take long!

Asghar sat on a gaily caparisoned horse with a golden saddle and gold ornaments, and behind him sat Nasim. The procession started with the members of the marriage party, relations and friends, at least two hundred in all, walking behind. Other guests were to meet them at the bride's house. In front were flute players who played loudly on their instruments gay nuptial tunes, their cheeks bulging out with the strain of blowing the breath into the flutes. Asghar sat on the horse led by a syce, covering his face behind a red handkerchief, proud and bursting with happiness.

The marriage party was received by the bride's people at the turn of the lane in which their house was situated. When Asghar was getting down from the horse a scuffle arose between the bride's side and Asghar's as to who should sit on the back of the horse first which must be occupied the moment the bridegroom gets down.

Sharfullah was to represent Asghar's side, and Chunnoo, Mir Ejaz Husain's son, was representing the bride's. The moment Asghar got down Sharfullah put his foot in the stirrup and flung his leg in the air to sit in the saddle. Chunnoo, in the meantime, had done the same from the other stirrup, and he also flung his leg in the air at the same time. The legs of Sharfullah and Chunnoo collided with a bang in mid-air over the saddle and were flung back. The horse became restive and both the combatants were dragged about a little. But the syce managed the horse, and the two antagonists kept sticking to their stirrups and, quickly balancing themselves, tried to jump into the saddle. Chunnoo, however, was on the left of the horse and could balance more easily. The result was that, though both of them got into the saddle almost at the same time, Chunnoo was slightly quicker and sat in the front, and Sharfullah found a seat behind him. So the victory, in a way, was Chunnoo's. The bride's people laughed and felt proud and said that the bride would have an upper hand and Asghar would be under her thumb. Asghar's side said that the first time Sharfullah had been the first to cover the saddle, and even now he had got into the saddle at the same time as Chunnoo. So, they supposed, both of them would have an equal amount of influence over each other.

* * *

There were at least a thousand guests, and the marriage ceremony was performed by the venerable old Akhunji Saheb, a very learned and pious Molvi, and, they said, an equally great divine. He read the verses from the Koran relating to marriage; then he asked Asghar thrice if he was willing to accept Bilqeece Jahan Begam, daughter of Mirza Shahbaz Beg, aged eighteen years and four months, as his wife in lieu of 50,000 rupees as dowry to be paid on her death. Asghar willingly consented with a beating heart. At the brink of this decisive change in his life he felt a curious sadness gripping his heart. He was nervous, not knowing whether he should feel happy or cry.

At the time of giving his consent to the marriage old Mirza Shahbaz Beg shed tears and looked as if in mourning. After all, he was giving away his daughter for good, and the thought was so sad. When the ceremony was over everyone raised his hands in blessing and prayer wishing a long and happy married life to the couple.

The moment they had finished praying dry dates were flung at the guests and thrown in all directions; and children rushed to pick them up. The shohdays began to shout blessings and clamour for a tip. They were given ten rupees but would not accept them. Not until they received twenty rupees did they become quiet.

Sherbet was brought in a silver cup and Asghar was asked to drink a little out of it. The rest was taken inside to be drunk by the bride out of the same cup.

Then the guests began to depart one by one, and as they went to the door they were handed sweets in a tin-plated brass plate wrapped up in a handkerchief, and were offered paans. The sweets were from Asghar's side, and the bride's people gave them roasted areca nut, cardamom and other things in small coloured plates. They departed wearing gay and bright clothes, along with their children and grandchildren whom they had brought with them uninvited. In the rush it was found that some had lost their shoes, Sharfullah among them. But he took another pair which were better than his own.

*   *   *

Where Asghar sat a number of his friends read out Sehras, impossible verses comparing the bride to the moon and the bridegroom to the sun. Even Nawab Sirajuddin Khan Saael had composed one which was appreciated very much, not so much for its poetic beauties as for the style in which it was read.

*   *   *

After about two hours, when it was long past one o'clock and Habibud-din had been asking Ashfaq to hurry up, Asghar was called inside to be introduced to the bride. Right in the vestibule his cousins and sisters, who were waiting to receive him, put the corners of their head-cloths on his head—another way of demanding neg.

They wore beautiful and expensive clothes. Their head-cloths were of gold thread or the softest of silks with bright borders and laces. Their shirts dazzled the eyes with their brightness; and some wore only brassières instead of shirts, and they were made of beautiful and expensive embroidered cloths. Their paijamas were wide and loose and so heavy with rich embroidery that they had to be carried held by the hands or hanging over their arms. The riotous colours, red and purple and blue, green and orange and pink, in various glowing combinations, hurt and yet soothed the eyes with their brilliance. Expensive ornaments covered all parts of their bodies; and the scents filled the nostrils. As they walked the bangles clanked, bells tinkled, and gold made a musical sound as it touched silver or gold.

In the noise one could hardly hear anything. There were hundreds of women in a small courtyard and in the verandas and the rooms. The children howled, the women shouted orders and talked at the top of their voices, and the domnis sang louder than ever before.

Slowly the gay procession moved and Asghar was received by his mother-in-law and other near relations of Bilqeece who would not observe purdah with him now.

In the centre of the room sat the bride wearing red clothes, with the exception of the flowing paijama which was made of green sateen, clothes which had come from Asghar's house; and a sehra was tied to her head. Her face could not be seen as her head-cloth had been pulled low down over her face; and she sat bent low, and her sister, Begam Ashfaq, was supporting her head on her hand.

After some time the ceremony of seeing the bride's face took place. The bridegroom and the bride were made to sit opposite each other, and a copy of the Koran and a mirror were placed between them. Asghar was asked to see her face in the mirror first, and then it was the bride's turn.

The domnis began to sing loudly in screeching voices in a chorus, beating time with the drum:

> I shall give you a lakh of rupees,
> Two lakhs if you will show your face.
> Take off your veil, my sweet, my bride,
> Take off your veil.

Asghar was asked to say to the bride:
'Open your eyes, my wife, I am your slave.'
It was impossible to see her face in the mirror as it was dark inside the room and the head-cloth had been thrown over them. The domnis sang:

> Take off your veil, behold the groom's face,
> How lovely and bright and handsome is he.
> Take off your veil, O happy bride,
> Take off your veil.

Asghar was dying of impatience and wanted to see the face again which had caused him so much pain, the face he was madly in love with. But Bilqeece had not yet uncovered her face. She was naturally shy, and sadness was gnawing at her heart. Asghar raised her veil himself and looked at her face, and put a little sandal mark on her forehead as he had been asked to do. The domnis sang on with greater zest and louder enthusiasm as if they were getting married themselves and the joys and bliss of marriage were their own:

> With a balance whose rod is made of gold
> And pans of silver, she weighs her charms.
> Take off your veil, O mother's darling,
> Take off your veil.

With sad and beautiful eyes, collyrium-blacked and bedewed with tears, Bilqeece looked at Asghar. The moment their eyes met a spark seemed to flash in their hearts, and Asghar was filled with longing and disquiet. Bilqeece was also filled with desire; but she was shy. And Asghar wished for the night when she would be in his arms, his own, until death do them part. . . .

When the ceremony was over Asghar took permission to go and to take the bride away. When he reached the threshold where he had left his shoes he found that one of them was missing. This was done by the bride's sisters and cousins. And not until he had given one hundred rupees was his shoe returned.

This took some time and it was already past three o'clock. The ladies were requesting Begam Shahbaz to hurry up the vida, the sending of the bride away. The domnis began to sing the sad song of parting in the form of complaint of daughter to father:

> Over walls of fresh green bamboos
> Make a roof of green leaves, father,
> Make a roof of green.
>
> Put new sheets upon the floor,
> Call the wealthy bridegroom's folk,
> Call the nicest folk.

It was painful for Begam Shahbaz to part with her daughter, although otherwise she was one of those who did not believe in worrying herself. But the vida is a sad affair, and the sisters and the cousins were all grief-stricken. Because the girl was now going away to another house, and would be theirs no longer. As they realized, however, that the separation had to come, tears came into their eyes. Women are born and are brought up by their parents only to be given away to strangers, people who have never known them before, never felt any love or affection for them. Yet the girl is, as it were, in trust with the parents for them. And when the time had come to know her charms, to see her do things for the parents and lend them a helping hand, she is given away to others. She will serve them now, and they will call her their own, for to them she now belongs. She is brought up just to be banished from home, her parents and her kith and kin.

With these thoughts a sadness descended upon the relations of the bride. And the domnis sang, igniting the dormant fires of sorrow in their hearts.

> You gave palaces to my brother
> Only banishment to me,
> Only banishment.
> I left my dolls, I left my friends,
> I left your land, my loving father,
> O, I left your land.
>
> Over walls of towering bamboos
> Make a roof of green leaves, father,
> Make a roof of green.

Everyone in the house looked sorrowful, and all eyes were filled with tears. Even some of Asghar's relations were filled with sadness, for the occasion was such and the ballad was so touching. Begam Waheed, lost between the emotions of joy and grief, could not check herself and two teardrops fell down from her eyes.

When Begam Shahbaz and her elder daughter came and sat down by the side of Bilqeece to say good-bye, they embraced her and began to cry. All around the women were sobbing, and in a corner stood Chanbeli howling and yet drying her tears with the corner of her head-cloth. And the domnis sang in pathetic tones:

> As the palanquin passed a mango grove
> A koel began to sing and cry,
> A koel began to sing.

O, dost thou, koel, sing the song
Of mother-in-law and sister-in-law,
Of mother and sister-in-law?

Over walls of fresh green bamboos
Make a roof of green leaves, father,
Make a roof of green.

Mirza Shahbaz Beg and Bundoo had also come in and they looked so
pathetic with faces woebegone and dirtied with tears at the thought of
parting. Bilqeece was going away now, and they had no claim over her,
no right to call her their own. She would do the bidding of others,
behave and act as they would like her to do. Even if they asked her not
to see her brother and father, she would have to yield and they would
be able to do nothing. But God's will be done, they consoled themselves: The work of the world must go on, and Nature must fulfil herself.
Their fathers had brought other people's daughters; they had done the
same; so were others doing with their daughter; and others still shall do
the same with theirs. But it is easy to say a thing and so difficult when it
comes to parting with one who had spent eighteen years with them,
eighteen beautiful years full of the associations of love and tenderness.
And the song added to their grief, filling their hearts with self-pity and
love:

But from behind my father cried:
'O stop the palanquin awhile,
Stop the palanquin.

'My daughter is the slave of your house,
And I too am your slave for life,
I too am your slave.'

Over walls of towering bamboos
Make a roof of green leaves, father,
Make a roof of green.

It was getting late, and they must hurry. Asghar stood there waiting
to take the bride to the palanquin and home. The whole atmosphere
had made him feel sad also. Everyone around him was weeping; and
Bilqeece was also crying behind her veil, and her frame was shaking
with sobs. As he bent down to pick her up, his heart gave a sudden
leap as he felt her in his arms, and he was filled with impatient desire.
His heart cried out with joy, and yet there was grief mixed with it. For

at a certain stage both the emotions mingle, and their distinctions vanish. As he gently picked her up everyone in the room began to sob more loudly than before. But the domnis sang the soothing part of the song:

> But then my father-in-law replied:
> 'Be not sad and grieve for nothing,
> Be not sad and grieve.
>
> 'Your daughter is the queen of my house,
> And you the honoured king we love,
> And you the honoured king.'
>
> Over walls of fresh green bamboos
> Make a roof of green leaves, father,
> Make a roof of green.

Asghar took his lovely burden and slowly walked into the courtyard, followed by the ladies and his relations. A beautiful blue sky was above them; and a speck of white cloud floated in the sky. It seemed that Nature herself was filled with gladness at the sight and prospect of love. But the women were still crying, and the domnis were singing still the plaints of the unhappy bride:

> You gave me silver and gave me gold,
> You gave me expensive ornaments,
> Expensive ornaments.
>
> But you forgot to give me a comb
> To do my hair and comb it well,
> To do my hair and comb.
>
> My mother-in-law and sister-in-law
> Now call me all sorts of names for that,
> Call me names for that.
>
> Over walls of towering bamboos
> Make a roof of green leaves, father,
> Make a roof of green.

As Asghar put her inside the palanquin which was covered with gold cloth, two other ladies got in with her—Mehro and a cousin of Bilqeece. Asghar walked out to ride home on his horse, the proud husband of a beautiful bride with whom he was in love, with the echoes of the parting song still ringing in his ears:

And my heart breaks with grief to think
The happy joys of home, my father,
The happy joys of home. . . .

*   *   *

Outside Habibuddin had taken over charge of the trousseau, utensils of
all kinds, huge wooden trunks full of clothes, with beautiful flowers
painted on them in silver and gold; a big wedding bed with silver legs,
its curtains of red and gold silk; bedding, chairs and tables and carpets.
The smaller things and utensils were put in baskets which were carried
for show by men, women and children on their heads, each basket containing only one or two plates, or cups and spoons.

Then the procession started for home headed by the musicians,
followed by Asghar sitting proudly on the horse, surrounded by his
brothers and cousins. Behind him was the palanquin carried by eight
palanquin-bearers. The rear was formed by the long unending line of
coolies carrying the trousseau. Laughing, chatting, joking, the procession passed through the streets and bazars full of people looking at the
procession with envying eyes.

When they reached home Dilchain threw water at the feet of the
horse, and Asghar was received by his mother and sisters who had
already reached home. Amidst noise and shouts the palanquin was put
inside the vestibule. Begam Waheed pulled out the legs of the bride
from the palanquin and washed her feet with milk, then she put silver
bangles round her feet for good luck.

Habibuddin was asked to carry the bride across the threshold in his
arms. But he entrusted the task to Shams, who took her in his lap and
carried her to the room behind the veranda where she was deposited on
a red carpet; and the house was filled with shouts and noise.

In the hullabaloo of a wedding no one as yet had any food with the
exception of the men who had been entertained to a feast at Mirza
Shahbaz Beg's. This had supplied the bride's people with the opportunity of taking their revenge. When the feast was over and the guests
stood up to wash their hands they poured water on their hands which
had been freely mixed with kerosene oil. Mir Nihal had been the first to
wash his hands, and when he discovered the joke which had been played
upon him he got very annoyed. But he had to keep quiet for fear of a
quarrel. Sharfullah, however, suffered the most, for his beard was also
besmeared with the foul-smelling oil; and everyone had a hearty laugh
at him.

The bride's food had arrived from her parents' house in huge iron pots which were brought in dolis carried by kahars. The bride is never sent away without food. And it was at five o'clock that the ladies had their food.

*   *   *

The boys were sent for inside the zenana and Asghar was made to eat rice pudding from the palm of the bride who had not had any food all day. Begam Waheed sat holding Bilqeece's hand, and Mehro put some pudding on her palm. The boys were not to allow Asghar to eat the pudding, but eat it straight off the palm before Asghar could reach it. A real battle of mouths ensued. It was only once or twice that Asghar could get at her palm to lick the pudding off. Either Begam Waheed pulled Bilqeece's hand away when Asghar bent down, or some boy snatched away the pudding. . . .

*   *   *

The near relations and the women were all dying to see the bride's face. Although the real ceremony of seeing the bride's face was not to take place until the next morning, Begam Waheed proudly showed her face to the near relations. Bilqeece sat crumpled up, her eyes closed, a nose-ring in her nostril, a forehead ornament on her brow, her dark hair looking beautiful decorated with a fine head ornament of pearls. With all her charm and loveliness she sat like an exhibit in a museum. Admiring eyes fell on her glowing face; and Begam Nihal felt proud of her beautiful daughter-in-law. With pride she showed everyone the trousseau which had been kept in Shams's room. . . .

*   *   *

Asghar was caught hold of by Shams and Saeed Hasan, who had not been able to come until this morning, and others, who began to initiate him into the mysteries of sex and married life. It was not until one o'clock in the morning that he could go to his wife who had been put in the bridal room. The house was quiet now as everyone was tired after the whole day's strain and had gone to sleep. The sky was heavy with millions of twinkling stars; a cold wind was blowing. And with a fast beating heart Asghar went to his bride. . . .

*   *   *

The next morning the ceremony of seeing the bride's face took place.

Bilqeece's clothes had been changed and she now wore light blue. In the midst of noise they all came, saw her face and put some money in her hands. All the relations, near and distant, gave money according to their status and position. And over six hundred rupees were collected. Then she went to her people to come back in the evening.

Everyone was in the merry mood of marriage which found expression in colour-throwing at each other. The whole thing was started by Habibuddin, who had asked Shams to get dyes from the bazar. They were mixed with water, and Habibuddin began to make a search for Saeed Hasan who was his own age and a great friend of his. But Saeed Hasan was in the house of Khwaja Ashraf Ali which had been borrowed for the wedding for the guests.

He was haranguing Nazrul Hasan who had been refusing to get married, although he was older than Asghar and had also got a job.

'There was a farmer and his daughter,' Saeed Hasan was trying to convince Nazrul Hasan by telling him a story. 'They once went out to the hills. There was a cave in the side of the mountain which was full of small red stones. Seeing them the girl shouted: "Rubies." "You are mad," her father said to her. "They are stones and not rubies." . . .

'Now, in their village there was a bania. He too went to that mountain and saw those stones lying there. He brought two of them with him and, tying them to a string, hung them in the shop as a mascot, and forgot all about them. One day the farmer and his daughter happened to go to the bania's shop to buy some salt and mustard oil. The girl's eyes fell on the stones and she shouted: "Rubies." The bania looked up and saw the stones. They were really rubies. He asked the girl where she had seen them and she told him. The bania asked the farmer to give his daughter to him in marriage. Because, you see,' Saeed Hasan concluded, 'it is always a woman's luck, and the bania was not a fool. . . .'

He had hardly finished the story when Habibuddin threw the coloured water over him. Saeed Hasan was taken aback. When he saw, however, that it was Habibuddin who had done it he got up to take his revenge.

Soon they were all rushing about throwing coloured water on one another. Not satisfied with this they poured the dyes in a small tank in the centre of the courtyard, and one by one they began to throw each other into the water. Asghar was brought perforce and given a ducking. But Sharfullah was missing. They looked for him everywhere, but he was not to be found. At last Shams discovered him fast asleep inside the house. They all came running and it was decided to carry him asleep on the bed to Khwaja Ashraf Ali's house. Four persons caught hold of the bed and carried him through the by-lanes. Sharfullah slept so well that he did not even feel the jerks and kept on snoring loudly. It was not until they were entering Khwaja Saheb's house that he seemed to stir. But they had reached their goal. Sharfullah woke up and shouted:

'I will fall down. Leave me.'

There was a splash as they threw him in the coloured water which was icy on account of the cold, and a good deal of it went inside his mouth and nose and ears. A great shout of merriment rose from all around as in his excitement he fell into the water again and again.

Then the contagion spread and even Mir Nihal was not spared. He protested in the beginning, but he began to smile in the end. No one had had the courage to approach the old gentleman, but Sharfullah did the trick.

The ladies threw coloured water over each other, and the children too were gay. The mothers were worried lest the children should catch pneumonia. It was so cold. But luckily it was noon and the sun shone bright and warm. And then, there was no stopping the children when the grown-ups were behaving in that fashion.

They all went even to Mirza Shahbaz Beg's house and coloured him too, although he got angry and abused Sharfullah. But in the meantime a pot full of coloured water had been thrown over him which cooled him down. Ashfaq got furious and shouted:

'Now shut up, all of you! Do you want to kill one of us? . . .'

At which tempers rose a little; and Sharfullah said:

'That's what you think of yourself! Wait and see!'

The result was that Ashfaq was besmeared with the stinking mud from the gutters and all sorts of rubbish and filth they could lay their hands on. Poor Bundoo was a sight with clothes all wet and his face all dirty with muck and filth.

It was not until they were completely tired out that they changed their clothes. No one had been spared, and even Ghafoor and Ahmad Wazir had gone mad with joy and had dragged even the mohallah people into throwing coloured water. And the wedding was rounded off with happy fun and merriment. . . .

*   *   *

The guests stayed on for a week after the wedding for other ceremonies, and to talk and talk, and share in the happy aftermath of an Indian marriage. Then one by one they departed, leaving the house more lonely and quiet. . . .

3

AFTER the marriage Asghar was happy, and went about with a light and rejoicing heart. In the daytime Bilqeece was very shy. She sat doing things with her head-cloth pulled low down in front of her face, and walked with slow and gentle steps. She never asked anyone for anything, not even for a glass of water. Begam Waheed always said to her: 'This is your home now; don't be so shy.'

But Bilqeece could not help it. Whenever she wanted anything she quietly asked Chanbeli, who had been sent with her by her mother. It was only when she went home that she really felt free. In her new home she only threw off her shyness when she retired with Asghar for the night to their room upstairs. Then they would talk of things and of persons, relations of Bilqeece and Asghar.

Sometimes, when they were alone, Asghar would put his hand round her waist, but this annoyed Bilqeece. She did not say anything to Asghar, but she felt constrained, and would become silent.

'Why are you so quiet?' Asghar would ask her.

She would sit gazing in front of her and say:

'I do not know what to say.'

He would have liked to hear her talk of love and happiness, her voice flowing like a sweet murmuring stream, talking of sad and beautiful things. He wanted her to kiss him and caress him, put her arms around his neck and whisper: 'I love you, I love you. . . .' But she was a simple Indian girl, and did not know the ways of love. . . .

When he told her how he had loved her and had burned to have her in his arms, she only smiled. He told her how he had seen her for the first time.

'There was such beauty and desire in your eyes,' he said. 'Didn't you love me?'

But she replied:

'I was bewildered when I saw you, and did not know where to hide myself for shame.'

Asghar was disappointed. He had always loved to imagine that she was madly in love with him, was dying with grief in his absence. He had imagined himself a Rajput knight or a chivalrous Mughal prince rescuing a love-lorn maiden. He had burned with a passion greater than Jahangir's for Nur Jehan. To him Bilqeece was lovelier than Mumtaz Mahal over whose tomb Shah Jahan had showered the beauties of the world.

Now and then Bilqeece looked at him with beautiful, furtive eyes. At such moments Asghar loved her more than anything in the world, and smothered her with kisses. But she was not romantic at all. This damped Asghar's feelings. He thought of his Mushtari Bai and other sweethearts. He remembered the warmth of their passion and their loving ways. By contrast Bilqeece looked so dull and insipid. But she was young and beautiful; and Asghar had built most beautiful castles around her lovely frame. He ascribed her coldness to shyness and to the atmosphere of restraint which prevails in Indian homes, and went on loving her with an intensity which she did not understand. Yet he was not so much in love with her as with his own self, his own dreams and illusions which she had created in his mind. . . .

*   *   *

Though her mother was not so cold and averse to the pleasures of the world, Bilqeece was quite differently made. She had been brought up by an aunt, her father's sister, an old and religious person. Till the age of fourteen she had lived in the atmosphere of an Indian home where women are not supposed to have desires and passions.

She had been taught to read and write letters, but she had not read many books except on religion. She had mostly passed her time in looking after the house. The only pleasure which she had been allowed was playing with dolls. Or she had played the innocent game of pachisi now and then.

Even in her childhood she had not been allowed to keep her head uncovered. She had been constantly told that one day she would have to go away to someone else's house, and that she must always behave properly. She was taught the arts of cooking and sewing and behaving like a perfect housewife generally.

In the world of an Indian home, where the woman is relegated to a subordinate place, love enters very rarely. An unmarried girl is not allowed to chew paan or wear flowers in her ear-rings or her hair. She is not even allowed to wear fine and expensive clothes or to use attar. She lives under the threat of going away to strangers when she grows up, who may turn out to be rich or poor or nice or bad. In this atmosphere the idea of love does not take root in the heart. Even if the girl falls in love with a cousin she cannot speak of it for fear of being punished and looked down upon as an evil thing. By education and hearsay she is made to believe that passion is the worst kind of sin.

That is why it was no wonder that Bilqeece was unromantic. She did not deny Asghar any pleasure, but she did not know how to make those wonderful conversations which Asghar yearned for. Still, love begets its own pleasures and imparts an education of its own. She adored her husband, whom she had been taught to look upon as her lord and master. And now and then she nestled up to Asghar, who loved her with all his heart at such moments.

She had no discomfort in the house of her parents-in-law; but she had no feeling of freedom as she was a stranger in the house, and because of a sense of respect for her parents-in-law. She felt more free with Begam Jamal, for she was related to Ashfaq and was, thus, equally related to her.

She often felt the desire of having a home of her own where she could do whatever she liked, and serve her husband in her own fashion. But she could not say anything to Asghar. She did not know how he would take it. She was so new to the place. . . .

Everyone in the house treated her with kindness and affection. Even Begam Nihal became very fond of her when she came to know her well. As weeks passed by Bilqeece began to take part in the household duties more freely. Preparations were now going on for Mehro's marriage. Saeed Hasan was rejected finally; and Begam Waheed had stayed on.

Bilqeece did a good deal of needlework. She even cooked some dishes now and then. But one thing gnawed at her heart secretly. Mir Nihal did not talk to her. She knew that he had been opposed to their marriage and thought that he was angry with her.

'He doesn't like me, perhaps,' she confided to Dilchain who had taken to her like a mother.

'He will, daughter,' Dilchain assured her. 'Only give him time. He is not such a bad person.'

Bilqeece heaved a sigh and kept quiet.

In the evening she prepared a special dish for dinner. When Mir Nihal ate it he asked his wife:

'Who has cooked this dish today?'

'Asghar Dulhan (bride). Why, is it badly cooked?'

'No, not bad,' he said, 'not bad at all.' And he smiled and looked pleased and stroked his beard.

One evening he brought fine green sateen and gave it to Bilqeece. 'I have brought this for you,' he said.

Her face beamed with happiness and, as she fingered the cloth, she said to herself: 'He is pleased with me.' Mir Nihal also smiled and came away.

'She is not a bad sort,' he said to his wife. 'She will keep our son happy. . . . But her mother is a whore.'

'Hai, hai, what has happened to you!' Begam Nihal said harshly. 'You have grown old, but you have not given up the habit of calling others bad names!'

Mir Nihal got up, a little ashamed, and went out. . . .

*   *   *

One exquisite evening in March, Bilqeece and Asghar sat in their room. A cool and pleasant breeze was blowing; and the rich fragrance of the henna tree, which was in bloom, created a stir in the heart. The sun was hiding his flushed face behind the hills far away, exhausted after a long day of love-making and dreams. There were thin clouds on the sky; and the glow of the setting sun fell on them and dyed them the most passionate red the eye of man has seen. A sadness was in the air and hearts were filled with yearning and pain. Bilqeece sat lost in thought looking at the sky. Asghar came and sat by her and put an arm around her shoulders in a loving and protective way.

'Why are you sad?' he gently asked.

And as gently she replied:

'I was thinking.'

'What about? Tell me,' he said playfully.

'I was just wondering,' she said softly and looked at him with beautiful eyes full of an expression of worship and love. 'You know, you also look sad sometimes. Perhaps because you haven't got a job. But you should put your trust in God and something will surely come your way. . . .'

She said this with so much affection and tenderness that Asghar was filled with love for her. He pressed her to his side and kissed her on the cheeks, and she relaxed in his embrace. The beauty and sadness of the Indian spring added to their passion and their dreams. They sat there arm in arm, cheek on cheek, dreaming of far-away, happy things. The shadows deepened and gradually the darkness increased around them.

The stars appeared one by one, silent stars, shining like glow-worms in the sky. And he thought how wonderful it would be to live with her in a small house all alone. . . .

4

BILQEECE had become pregnant, and was nearly always ill. Her appetite deserted her, and she only ate dried mangoes or tamarinds. She felt sick all the time and was confined to bed. Her complexion lost its glow and became sallow; and hollows appeared under her eyes. Now and then she looked up at the date palm whose leaves had become thin, for the lower ones had sered and fallen; and it seemed to her drab and full of hopelessness.

But now and then she became conscious of the new life within her. As the child moved inside her womb her heart was filled with a rare joy, and everything looked to her beautiful. The henna tree which had shed its old leaves and had put on new ones, the sparrows twittering on the walls, the breeze that blew, everything brought to her a message of Beauty and sang the pæans of Birth. She covered herself up with a sheet in a protective way, and gently, very tenderly stroked her belly as if caressing the child inside her.

Everyone became more gentle with her, and asked her to take care of herself, and not to walk fast or climb the stairs too often. Asghar was also happy, full of pride and vanity at the prospect of having a son who would not only carry on his father's name, but would be his support in old age. He would give his son a good education and bring him up according to his own ideas; and he would make good his father's failings, realize his frustrated ambitions. They talked a great deal of this son of theirs, made schemes for him together, and even gave him a name.

At these moments Bilqeece looked at Asghar with passionate and loving eyes which seemed to express gratitude and indebtedness for having given her that which she most desired, fulfilment of all her dreams. She even put her hand round his neck one day and caressed his hair; and his heart came well nigh to bursting with love and happiness. He often brought presents for her and gave her a pair of English shoes which, he said, she should wear at Mehro's wedding. All this made her happy beyond measure, and her heart went out to her husband. She just wanted to fall down at his feet and worship him like a god. And Asghar was more than satisfied. . . .

*　　*　　*

In this mood the date of Mehro's marriage drew near. Bilqeece was better now, and her nausea had almost left her. With happiness she sewed and helped preparing Mehro's trousseau. She went to her parents off and on, because her father had fallen ill. But she came back to get busy with the preparations for the marriage.

The guests arrived again, though not so many as at Asghar's wedding. After the mayun ceremony Mehro was kept inside a room for a week, and was massaged with scented preparations every day.

The marriage party arrived from Bhopal one day before the wedding. On the day of the wedding Mehro was dressed as a bride. Masroor, who had gone to see the bridegroom, came and said to her in a whisper: 'Your bridegroom is ugly, positively ugly.'

'Shut up,' she said to him. 'Don't crack jokes with me.' But in her heart she was filled with dread, and began to weep behind her veil.

The marriage was going to be performed in the evening. When the bridegroom and his party arrived Mir Nihal saw Meraj for the first time. He was really ugly, with a black bushy beard and the ferocious eyes of a madman. One part of his face was disfigured, and one ear was missing. Meraj was very fond of shooting, and one day his gun had gone off by accident and had disfigured him for life. The bullet had not been extracted from his brain as there was the risk of his losing his life, and this had affected his mind.

Nazrul Hasan had been sent from Delhi to see the bridegroom. They had, however, kept him out of Nazrul Hasan's way, and he came away without seeing him. But it was thought that he had no defect.

When Mir Nihal saw his future son-in-law, he was filled with disgust and said that he would not give his daughter away to a madman. Everyone was shocked at this news. They persuaded him to agree, but he refused to listen to them. Habibuddin was also filled with loathing at the sight of his future brother-in-law. But he had foresight and wisdom.

'What are you doing, father?' he argued with Mir Nihal. 'If the marriage is cancelled it would mean a bad name for our family. . . .'

'I can't give my daughter away to a man who looks like a kazzaq. There is no dearth of boys.'

'But don't you see, if they go away without the marriage taking place, no one will blame them. They will all say that there is some defect in the girl. We shall then have no face to show to anyone. . . .'

It was with difficulty that Habibuddin made his father see the point and persuaded him to agree to Mehro's marriage. It was with trepidation and tears streaming down his face that he gave his consent.

Masroor went and informed Mehro of all the developments. She sat there frightened and mortified, the tears flowing down her cheeks. But she could not say anything. The girls were never consulted about their own marriages and were given away to any men their parents selected.

When after the vida she saw Meraj she felt like a cow under the butcher's knife. But she could not alter her fate, and had to accept it with as much courage as she could muster. . . .

*   *   *

Inside the zenana the women guests did not know much about these difficulties. They had come to attend a marriage and displayed their finest clothes and talked and laughed and made merry. Bilqeece wore her fine bridal clothes and looked charming. Many ladies saw her English shoes and were outraged.

'Hai, hai, sister, have you seen those dirty shoes Asghar's wife is wearing?' said one of the guests. 'We have never seen such a thing before!'

'She looks like a good-as-dead Farangan', another replied.

'Yes, what else could you expect from Mirza Shahbaz Beg's daughter? They seem to have eaten some Farangi's shit. . . .'

Thus the women whispered to one another. Bilqeece heard these remarks, for they had been said in her hearing, and were meant for her to hear. She felt ashamed and tears rushed to her eyes. But she had to keep her mouth shut, although the insults were obvious and pointed. Had they been directed towards her alone it would not have been so difficult. They were insulting her father; and this cut her to the quick.

When the rush of marriage was over and she was able to see Asghar alone, she told him of all the insults which had been heaped upon her, and burst into tears. Asghar was filled with anger when he heard this. He felt so sorry for her that all the insults seemed to have been showered upon him. He took Bilqeece in his arms and kissed her and said: 'You should forget all about it. I shall take a separate house and we shall live alone as soon as I have got a job. . . .'

5

'THE Deputy Commissioner is very pleased with me,' Habibuddin had said to Asghar. 'If you like I can speak to him about you. Or, if you prefer the police, I am on very good terms with the superintendent of police, and you can get a good job in that Department.'

Asghar had refused, saying that he had no desire to enter Government service. In the first place he would be posted to small districts where he would have no company; and then, he would have no settled life. Habibuddin had said that he would rue his decision one day; but Asghar was adamant. He wanted to go into business.

His friend Bari had suggested to Asghar that they should start some business of their own. They thought of various avenues and discussed which business they should select. Asghar had always loved well-tailored clothes and he suggested a tailoring shop.

'But we are not tailors,' Bari said. 'Who will cut the clothes?'

'That is true,' Asghar agreed. 'Let us think of something else. What do you think about shoes? . . .'

In this way they made plans and schemes which, however, remained confined to themselves. Everyone they consulted about it discouraged them. They had really no experience of business. So they gave up all thought of it.

But Asghar managed to get a good job in a big Indian firm through Mirza Shahbaz Beg's influence. He was given a good start and was very happy. Bilqeece was happy too for she could now have a home of her own.

She was in the ninth month of her pregnancy, and her mother insisted that she should come to her house for the delivery. Begam Nihal did not like the idea, but since Asghar wished it she allowed Bilqeece to go to her parents' house for the confinement.

Some days before the delivery panjiri was made and distributed to the near relations to inform them of the happy event. It turned out to be very tasty, and they declared that the coming child would be a girl.

Bilqeece's delivery was prolonged and painful. She cried with pain; and Asghar also suffered on her account. At last a baby girl was born. Asghar was disappointed at the news; but it was such a relief to know that the suspense was over.

When Asghar was allowed to go into the room he saw Bilqeece lying on the bed covered with a sheet, white as death. A bright smile lit up her face as she saw him. Slowly she moved her hand and put it in his. As Asghar bent down to kiss her his heart gave a leap. It was so strange to be a father!

The baby was taken to Mirza Shahbaz Beg who lay very ill so that he might read the azaan in the child's ears. The little girl was swaddled in clothes, looking red like blood. Her eyes were closed, and so were her little fingers. After the azaan had been called Mirza Shahbaz Beg put a little honey on the child's tongue. She opened her mouth a little, then making a bad face began to scream.

Then came the eunuchs, wearing long hair and women's clothes, but with caps on their heads, the head-cloths lying on their shoulders. Outside the house they stood and sang congratulatory verses in loud, unmusical voices, beating time on the drum, clapping vulgarly. It was not until they had received a suitable bakshish that they went away.

In Bilqeece's room which had been closed from all sides, they burnt all sorts of herbs. She made the baby lie down by her side, feeling proud. As the child cried or moved her arms the mother's heart also cried or leapt with joy. When the baby's mouth touched her breast to feed, a fine sensation ran down her spine, and her life seemed to flow out into the child with the milk. She made her lie close, very close to her, and with one arm round the child went happily to sleep.

On the third day she was given soup and a little meat cooked in rice. On the tenth day she was given a bath. The doors of her room were opened and fresh air was allowed to come in. When she could walk about a little she went to her parents-in-law, the proud mother of a child, to receive congratulations.

*   *   *

When the baby, who had been named Jehan Ara, was a month and a half old came Bakr'id. Men went to pray earlier than on the day of Eed; and when they came back they sacrificed goats. Mirza Shahbaz Beg was not able to go to pray as his condition had worsened.

On the third day of Bakr'id he breathed his last. The whole house was plunged in mourning. But Begam Shahbaz did not give up her breakfast even for one day, and sent for fluffy cakes from the bazar and ate them secretly, although for show she wept and cried. Bilqeece, however, was half dead with grief. Asghar tried to console her, but in vain. . . .

*   *   *

Since Bilqeece had gone to her parents' house she had hardly been able to stay at her parents-in-law's for more than a week. Now her mother was left alone as Ashfaq had to look after Mirza Shahbaz Beg's business and had to go away to Calcutta, and Bundoo had got a job in Rampur. So Asghar took a house adjoining that of Begam Shahbaz, and began to live there with his wife. He fitted it up beautifully and bought more English furniture. All this kept Bilqeece very busy, and she forgot her grief a little.

When Asghar went to the office she went and spent the day with her mother and sister. She came back home in the evening to see to Asghar's food and comfort. The two houses were side by side, and for convenience they had a door built in the wall so that the houses were now joined to each other.

Bilqeece's nine-year-old sister Zohra spent most of her time with Bilqeece and helped her with the child. In the evenings other relations came to see them; and Nasim and Kabiruddin's children often came, for they had been put to school. Nasim was now over five years of age and had been put in a maktab to learn the Koran. When the children came Bilqeece stuffed them with sweets, and Asghar gave them beautiful pencils or fancy notebooks. And they all felt very happy.

One morning Saeed Hasan came to see Asghar. He had not taken his rejection to heart, and had already sent his proposal for Surayya, Mir Naseeruddin's daughter. For, he felt, he could not live without a wife.

It was a Sunday and Asghar had just had his bath and was wearing a gaudy dressing-gown. Saeed Hasan was taken aback as he saw the dressing-gown for it was a novelty. At home Asghar did not have much freedom because of his father; but in his own house he could indulge his tastes.

'Where did you get this fine chugha coat?' Saeed Hasan enquired.

'It is not a chugha, but a dressing-gown,' Asghar informed him as he led him into the room where a sofa, some chairs and tables were kept in the English fashion.

'You have became a fashionable gentleman,' Saeed Hasan said as he looked around with curiosity and bewilderment.

'How can a poor man like me become fashionable?' said Asghar. 'I just cover my body; and whether it's a shirt or dressing-gown is immaterial.'

But he seemed happy, none the less, at having attracted notice.

Saeed Hasan felt the chairs and bent down to have a good look at them. Then he stood up and looked long at Asghar with pity and grief on his face. 'What a pity'. He broke his embarrassing silence at last. 'Our people used to sit on the floor. It could be used to sleep on and for other purposes. But we are forgetting our own culture and are learning the ways of others. The virtue of constancy is dying from the world.' He heaved a deep sigh, and went on to relate the story of Mir Aashiq after whom the mohallah called Kucha Mir Aashiq is named.

'He was an old man,' said Saeed Hasan, 'and used to live in Chitli Qabar. Every day he used to go out for a walk via Jama Masjid and, making a round of the Chandni Chowk, came home via Lal Kuan and Chaori Bazar. He was always punctual to the minute, and never stopped anywhere against his custom. He saluted only those people on his way whom he used to salute, and stopped at his usual places for just a minute or two minutes or five minutes as his custom was. No one could detain him a second longer than his wont, and no one could get a response from him if he saluted him and was not known to him.

'Now, some loafers used to sit in a shop at Lal Kuan. One day one of them had a bet with the others that he could shake hands with Mir Aashiq. As he passed that way the loafer's friends challenged him to go and shake hands with him. He came forward, but the moment he came near Mir Aashiq, his courage failed him. His friends made fun of him, and he made a resolve to detain Mir Aashiq the next day. When he passed that way again the young loafer got down from the shop and coming near Mir Aashiq cried: "I cry a-mercy, Mir Aashiq." Hearing this unexpected cry he turned round. The young man went forward and, catching hold of his hand, began to shake it. Mir Aashiq did not like it. But now that he had shaken hands he could do nothing; and in response to the young man's salute he replied: "Waalaikum-assalaam," and went away. Since then every day when he passed that place he stopped for a while, turned round, and saying "Waalaikum-assalaam" went his way.

'One day the loafers got annoyed with this young man, and said that if he had any friend he could come and save him. This matter came to the knowledge of Mir Aashiq. He wrapped a winding sheet round his head, took his sword in his hand, and came to the place and said: "Here is his friend who will defend him. Who is there who wishes to fight? Let him come forward." Of course, not one of the loafers had the courage to fight, and Mir Aashiq told his young friend that he had no cause to fear. Once he had called himself his friend, his friend he will remain until he died. . . .

'Those were the people, so constant and true to their word,' Saeed Hasan concluded. 'But we are forgetting all the virtues of the past.'

As he said this he heaved a sigh; and Asghar felt ill at ease. But that was Saeed Hasan's way, and Asghar could not change himself. He said to himself that every new thing is looked upon with suspicion and ridicule. He had suffered on that account himself. . . .

6

THE months passed by, and 1912 gave place to 1913. During the December of the previous year a bomb had been thrown at Lord Hardinge when he had held the 'Imitation Darbar', as the Delhi people called it. But the Viceroy had escaped death. The 'iqbal' of the British Government had started asserting itself. Only the people had become disillusioned, and had started complaining about the hard days which were coming; and the Terrorist Movement was gaining ground all over the country. Already dissatisfaction with the foreign yoke had spread, and Bengal seemed to be taking the lead in this direction.

In Delhi itself many changes were being proposed. The gutters which were deep and underground from the times of the Mughals to this day were being dug and made shallow, and the dirty water flowed very near the level of the streets, and the stink was everywhere. The city walls were also going to be demolished. The residents of Delhi resented all this, for their city, in which they had been born and grew up, the city of their dreams and reality, which had seen them die and live, was going to be changed beyond recognition. They passed bitter remarks and denounced the Farangis.

Worse than all the changes which were felt so deeply by the people was the disfiguring of the Chandni Chowk whose central causeway was demolished and the expansive peepal trees which had given shelter to the residents and the poor from the scorching rays of the sun, were cut down. The road did look wide and broad, a real boulevard, but its uniqueness and oriental atmosphere were destroyed. This affected the people more deeply than anything else. For this was the bazar through which they had walked day in and day out throughout their lives. With these changes it looked something quite new, not the real Chandni Chowk with which so many memories were associated. Outside the city, far beyond the Delhi and Turkoman Gates, and opposite the Kotla of Feroz Shah, the Old Fort, a new Delhi was going to be built. The seventh Delhi had fallen along with its builder, Shah Jahan. Now the eighth was under construction, and the people predicted that the fall of its builders would follow soon. Its foundations had at least been laid. From that eventful year, 1911, which marked, in a way, the height of British splendour in India, its downfall began.

Though the residents of Delhi sometimes feel disgusted with their birthplace, and have often said out of a feeling of frustration:

> O Delhi, ho Delhi,
> To hell with you Delhi,

they love it too with all their hearts. Zauq, the court poet of Bahadur Shah, had expressed their love for Delhi in the following lines:

> Let it be granted that there is today
> A greater patronage and love of Art
> In Hyderabad; but, Zauq, who has the heart
> To leave the lanes of Delhi and go away?

They argued that once the new town was ready the old would be neglected and allowed to fall into ruins.

Besides, a new Delhi would mean new people, new ways, and a new world altogether. That may be nothing strange for the newcomers: for the old residents it would mean an intrusion. As it is, strange people had started coming into the city, people from other provinces of India, especially the Punjab. They brought with them new customs and new ways. The old culture, which had been preserved within the walls of the ancient town, was in danger of annihilation. Her language, on which Delhi had prided herself, would become adulterated and impure, and would lose its beauty and uniqueness of idiom. She would become the city of the dead, inhabited by people who would have no love for her nor any associations with her history and ancient splendour. But who could cry against the ravages of Time which has destroyed Nineveh and Babylon, Carthage as well as Rome?

*   *   *

Mir Nihal often talked of this to his friends, and they all felt grieved. But they were masters of their land no longer. They were in the hands of the foreigners who did as they pleased, and they had no command over their own destiny. That is why Mir Nihal began to live more and more at home, in his own world, and in the atmosphere of alchemy and medicine, a world which was still his own where no one could disturb him or order him about.

In his seclusion his grandchildren were a great source of delight. Nasim he was very fond of, and he liked Kabiruddin's two young boys, Hamid and Shahid, one about ten years of age, the other eight.

Nasim was a bright and imaginative boy, but a little too restless and spoilt. He played about and babbled meaningless verses which he had himself composed. He would sing them loudly and long in a monotonous tune, as if he were bored. Often he would sit and dream, of beautiful toys and princesses and fairies, and of birds and beasts.

He had been put in the maktab, but he found it so boring to go to the mistress day after day, month after month, and hated learning the Koran in Arabic, which was all Greek to him. Yet there was no rest or getting away from the lessons. When he came back from the maktab, Mir Nihal taught him how to read and write Urdu. He was, however, more kind; and Nasim and his cousins would sit outside in Mir Nihal's spacious room in the mardana. Hamid and Shahid used to go to school, and Mir Nihal asked them to read out their lessons to him. Nasim was made to write the alphabet on a wooden slate with a reed pen. Mir Nihal was usually gentle with them, but if they forgot their lessons he got very annoyed and shouted at them. . . .

On summer noons he would sometimes ask the children to press his legs and arms. In the afternoons, after the lessons, he would give them tea, the one thing he was addicted to. Ghafoor would bring the samovar and put it on the floor. When the water started singing Mir Nihal added tea leaves, cinnamon and cardamom to give it flavour. In the meantime Ghafoor had taken out beautiful cups and spoons of real china with blue flowers painted on them, from the almirah in the wall. The cups were beautiful, narrow at the base and broader near the brim, without handles; and the spoons were big and lovely, and matched the cups in colour and design. Mir Nihal added milk and sugar, poured out the tea in the cups, and gave fluffy biscuits to the children who dipped them in the tea and ate them with the spoons.

Mir Nihal looked happy and pleased as the children ate, as he did when Nasim came to him to ask for some tasty digestive powder.

Hamid and Shahid were shy and sent Nasim to ask for it. He would come and beg:

'Grandfather, please give me a little digestive powder.'

Mir Nihal would ask Ghafoor to bring out the bottle, and he would give Nasim a pinch, but he would beg for more.

'It is not good to take more of it,' Mir Nihal would say, but he would give a little more none the less.

The moment Nasim came outside in the lane, Hamid and Shahid would catch hold of him and they would distribute the powder among themselves and lick it off their palms.

Mir Nihal was always happy with the children around him and his eyes brimmed over with laughter. One day, however, he became very annoyed with them and lost his temper. It all happened like this.

Begam Kabiruddin had received a money order from her husband and had kept the money near her on the wooden couch where she sat sewing. As she stood up absent-mindedly she kicked the money with her foot, and a rupee rolled away under the couch. Shahid found it and told Hamid, and Nasim was taken into confidence. They conspired together and, instead of giving the rupee back, they went to Mirza's shop and bought some biscuits and milk sweets which were Mirza's speciality. They enjoyed these delicacies secretly, and hid the change in a hole in the wall of the vestibule. Dilchain came in from somewhere and discovered them hiding the change. She went and asked Begam Kabiruddin if she had given the children some money. This made her count her cash, which was found to be one rupee short. She began to shout at the children. Unfortunately for them Mir Nihal came in just then, and learnt what had happened. If he hated anything it was stealing or telling a lie.

'What!' he thundered at the mortified children. 'You have learnt how to steal! Bring my sword, Dilchain. I will teach them how to steal again.'

He went inside a small dark room and brought out his sword which was kept concealed inside a huge wooden trunk, and flashed it before the petrified eyes of Hamid, Shahid and Nasim, more to threaten them than anything else. They were already half dead with fright. At the sight of the naked sword they dirtied their paijamas. Gentlemen's children could not steal! . . .

But this was a rare incident. Mostly the children were happy, and played or quarrelled among themselves. In the evening would come Mir Nihal's friends, and sometimes the children would also be asked to sit there to listen to the conversation and learn how to behave. . . .

Ghafoor would sit inside his small room and smoke, not daring to do so before his master. He had been married last year, soon after Mehro's marriage, to Sheikh Mohammad Sadiq's niece. But the girl had died within six months of the marriage of ulcers in the womb. She was really too young for the strong and virile Ghafoor, and the strain had been too much for her. Sheikh Mohammad Sadiq had wished to get some compensation, but Mir Nihal had got rid of him. He had warned him that the girl was too young for Ghafoor. If he had persisted in his folly it was his lookout. After his wife's death Ghafoor had become a little quiet and subdued. . . .

* * *

Inside the zenana things went on almost as before. Mehro's absence, however, was felt by everyone. Otherwise there was no change. The four walls stood all around, shutting the women in, keeping all fresh air away from their dreary lives which, however, never seemed to them monotonous.

The wind blew, or it became warm and stuffy. The loo howled or the winter wind was unkind. The rains fell, the sun shone as if it would shine never more. The faqirs came, whined, begged in doleful voices, and at night the cats miaowed or caterwauled; and life went on. . . .

7

JEHAN ARA was about a year and a half old and could sit and crawl. She was a constant source of delight to her mother. But Asghar had become indifferent. His dreams had come to an end, and he did not find his wife so charming as he had done over a year ago. In the mornings he got up late, busied himself with the toilet, looked at himself in the mirror for long. At ten o'clock he went to the office and came back late. Bilqeece's younger sister Zohra spent the days with her, and Begam Shahbaz often came, so she did not feel lonely. But she remained sad and dejected at Asghar's coldness and lack of sympathy.

Jehan Ara was teething and was often ill. Asghar complained to his wife and shouted:

'There is no peace in the house. The child seems to be constantly ill, and you are always busy with the child. What is the use of a wife when you get no comfort and no love . . .?' Bilqeece felt hurt and cried silently.

Begam Shahbaz was a clever woman. She saw that Asghar was not so warm towards his wife as he used to be. She felt sorry for her daughter, and asked her:

'What is the matter with Asghar? It seems you two are not happy together. Have you annoyed him in any way?'

'I don't know,' Bilqeece replied sadly. 'I have not given him any cause to complain. Perhaps it is because he has to work hard in the office that he is like this.'

'No, daughter,' Begam Shahbaz replied with a sigh. 'You are young and do not understand men. I will get some charm from Pirji to soften his heart.'

When Begam Jamal came to see her one day she spoke to her about it, and complained:

'Before his marriage he was so loving and affectionate. But now he treats his wife so badly. My poor daughter is pining away, but he is callous and does not care.'

Begam Jamal also ran Asghar down, saying that he was selfish and interested only in himself, and sympathized with Bilqeece. . . .

All this made Bilqeece more sad. She was herself conscious of Asghar's coldness towards her. She had noticed that he was more interested in the maidservant than herself. And when her mother talked to her in this fashion her doubts were confirmed. She had really done something to annoy him, she thought. How could she make amends for what she had unwittingly done?

One evening she was sitting alone. It was one of those rare evenings in October when summer is departing and there is a feeling of autumn in the air. The sun was setting and had coloured the sky with passionate colours; and a gentle sadness was in the atmosphere like the memory of bygone love and happy dreams. The rooks cawed and wheeled and circled over towering trees, settled down on the branches, then rose again cawing loudly in a chorus. The pigeons flew in flocks, tame pigeons of the pigeon-fliers, and wild pigeons going to their nests and resting-places for the night. A beggar was whining in front of a door somewhere in the by-lane, blessing a newly married couple:

'May Allah keep the bridegroom and the bride happy and well. . . .'

Bilqeece was feeling broken-hearted, and as the beggar's voice came she put a hand on Jehan Ara who lay asleep by her on the bed. She felt sorry for the child and for herself, because Asghar had become so indifferent. He had been so full of love, had talked of nice and beautiful things, had doted on her even one year ago. What had happened to him now? What could she do to please him, and regain his lost love?

As she sat there, lost in thought, Asghar came in and, without paying any attention to her or the child, went into the room to change and wash, and called the maidservant to give him tea. Bilqeece at once got up and herself began to prepare the tea. When Asghar had finished his toilet he started having tea in silence. Bilqeece sat near him and looked at his face now and then. She was taut with a feeling of suspense, frightened like a child who has been reprimanded.

Two divergent feelings possessed her. She wished to speak to Asghar, ask his forgiveness for whatever she had done to displease him. At the same time she was afraid and did not know how he would take it. She could not muster courage to broach the subject. This suspense was killing, this wavering between two worlds. One part of her said that she should make a clean breast of it and fling all self-respect to the winds. The other said no, because it was not sure of the gain.

As she sat contemplating Asghar finished his tea and went out into the courtyard. The sun had almost set and the night, with its awakening cold, was spreading her dark and star-bejewelled wings over the earth. An aroma of smoke was in the air and produced a feeling of elation and sadness. Asghar saw Jehan Ara lying on the bed. The paternal feeling awoke within him and he bent down to kiss her. Bilqeece saw him do this and her heart leapt up with hope and a wistful joy.

She came and stood behind him watching him caress the child, and a bruised smile played on her lips. As Asghar saw her, however, he left off caressing the child, and looked far away. The house-tops stretched all around, dimly visible in the hazy light. On the sky the stars were beginning to shine. He remembered other stars, brighter and more beautiful than these, which had once brought to him a message of love and beauty. Now they seemed insipid and lustreless.

Bilqeece saw him, and felt as if the world were falling to pieces all around her, and in the midst of the debris she stood without a friend or sympathizer all alone.

She mustered courage and spoke softly like a child apologizing after a reprimand:

'I do not know what I have done to displease you that you do not even speak to me now. . . .'

Asghar's first feeling was that of resentment, and wrinkles of annoyance appeared on his brow. Bilqeece heard her own voice echoing and vibrating, hammering on her eardrums. In the silence that ensued she heard a beggar's voice coming loudly and clear:

'You who have eyes are fortunate, for sight is the greatest boon. . . .'

Asghar, perhaps, had no sight; and she herself was groping in the dark. . . .

'If you keep on loving me a little,' she said in a tearful voice as Asghar kept silent, 'life would not be so miserable.'

She could not say any more. A cracker burst somewhere making a loud report and filled her with dread. She sat down on the bed and two teardrops slid down her face.

Memory awoke in Asghar's heart, and the consciousness of old love revived for a while. Suddenly he was filled with pity for his wife, and he sat down by her side and put an arm around her, trying to console her a little.

'Why should you think that I am displeased with you?' he said in a reconciliatory tone. 'I have been up to my neck in work, and have been worried.'

Her innocent and simple heart was filled with joy, and she smiled behind her tears.

The night had spread out her charms and the bright October moon peeped over the wall and filled the earth with a cool and silvery light. Across the moon two bats flitted with joy, and a cicada chirped somewhere from a hole. A wintry silence spread all around, and a restful feeling was in the air. The broken ends of summer and winter seemed to be united by the pleasant autumn night which created a gentle sadness in the heart like the music of a Yogi playing upon his sitar on some mountainside or by a soft and murmuring stream far away from the selfish world of men. . . .

* * *

But once the heat of passion and love dies it becomes difficult to bring back warmth to the heart. The sensitive strings of its lyre snap and it becomes impossible to produce music upon it once again. Love is something spontaneous. It is that fire which once alight cannot be put out. But when it begins to smoulder and die, nothing on earth can revive it. The heart becomes hardened to its storms. It fails to respond to its once swaying melody. Asghar's passion had become dulled and

died. He no longer felt the same warmth towards Bilqeece. She did not
rouse the old emotions in him. A few days after this reunion he went
back to his mood of indifference.

Begam Shahbaz saw that he was cold towards his wife and towards
herself. She wanted all the attention to herself. In the beginning, when
he had been in love with Bilqeece, he had fawned on his mother-in-law
and had been very affectionate. Now he did not care.

Once she had an attack of fever and she started complaining:

'Once he used to sit near me for hours even if I had a little headache.
Now I am burning with fever and very much does he care if I live or
die. . . .'

She always complained at the least inconvenience or show of indifference. Asghar got more disgusted and annoyed, and treated his wife
even worse. He would come to the house and ask the maidservant to
give him his food or do things for him. If Bilqeece did it he always
found fault with it and said that it was not properly done, or the plates
were dirty, or the food was bad. Never did a smile light up his face.

Begam Shahbaz saw all this. There is a limit to one's forbearance.
Bilqeece suffered all these things in silence; but Begam Shahbaz could
not bear it any longer. One day she said to him:

'I have been noticing for months that you do not seem to have any
affection or love left for your wife. There are other husbands in the
world. See how much they love their wives and homes. But you seem to
hate your house and wife and everything which is connected with her.
Why, after all?'

'That is just what you think,' Asghar said in an angry voice, because
the thing was true and made him feel guilty. 'I don't know how else I
should care for her. I work and slave from morning till night in the
office. Can't I have a few moments of peace and loneliness?'

'That's most wonderful indeed,' she said with bitterness. 'If you
preferred to live alone, why did you marry at all? You have a certain
responsibility towards your wife and home.'

'Then please tell me how to fulfil my duties,' Asghar replied, losing
his temper. 'Tell me how many worries I should shoulder—that of the
office or of the wife and the home?'

'What is there to be annoyed about so much? Surely you did not
marry to starve your wife. You have got to provide for her.'

'When have I grudged giving her money?'

'Money is not all. You have to be kind and affectionate.'

'These qualities are missing from my character,' he said in a very loud voice. 'You knew what sort of a man I was when you married your daughter to me. You were not blind. I can't change my nature. . . .' It ended in a quarrel. Asghar went and shouted at his wife: 'How do I starve you?' he thundered.

'But who said so?' Bilqeece asked in a soft tone.

'Who said so?' he said in a sarcastic tone, livid with anger. 'Your mother, who else! You must have complained to her.'

'No. I can swear by God that I said nothing.'

'Then who else could have told her? If you have any complaint why can't you speak to me?'

'But I said nothing,' Bilqeece replied in a frightened voice.

'This is wonderful! The daughter says she said nothing. The mother complains and shouts at me. And my life has become a hell between you two. It is better to commit suicide than live such a miserable life. . . .'

Bilqeece felt as if she had dropped the looking-glass in which she had been looking and it was shattered to pieces, and her own image was broken into particles of glass. A storm of self-pity rose within her breast and tears began to stream down her face. Her days of happiness were over, she thought, gone for ever into the darkness of the night. A feeling of helplessness came upon her and she began to cry.

But her tears displeased him more. And this did not improve matters at all. He began to live more and more away from the house. Bilqeece consumed herself and suffered in silence, weeping when she was alone. Life for her became a living death.

8

THEN came the War; and the recruits marched past on the roads singing songs; and their voices filled the streets:

> Come and join the army,
> The recruits are standing by. . . .

They flooded the Chandni Chowk, and went about staring at things with wondering eyes, lost in the big city they had never seen before.

Those who had been conquered were going to fight for the conquerors, lay down their lives for twelve or eighteen rupees a month.

Mirza's shop became the centre of gossip, and the kababi, the barber and others collected there at night and talked of the War, how it progressed, and of new and deadly inventions.

'They have invented remarkable machines, you know,' said the kababi as he pulled at the hookah, 'which can conceal thousands of soldiers and carry them right into the midst of the enemy without being seen.'

'The Germans, they say,' said the barber, 'have invented small razors which are poisoned. They let them lie on the fields. Their beards grow grisly, and they scratch and scratch in pain. So, when they see the razors they pick them up. These razors are very convenient to use. They require no brush or soap to soften the beard first. You can use them straight away. But the moment the soldiers shave with them they are dead.'

'The most wonderful thing they have invented,' said Kallan, the carpenter, 'is a wooden cock which resembles a live one. It looks so real that you cannot think that it is artificial. They leave it in the enemy's camp at night. The soldiers who get no other food but gram to eat, rush to catch the cock. But before they can do so the cock crows and bullets shoot out of its mouth, and it farts out such poisonous gas that all of them die.'

'Yes, the Germans are very clever,' said the kababi as he listened to the others with his head bent a little to a side. 'They have made eggs. They leave them in the fields. When the soldiers see them they mistake them for the eggs of wild fowl and pick them up. But the moment they touch them the eggs burst with loud reports and kill them all....'

'It is all a trap to kill you, you fools,' Mirza, the milk-seller, said as he tossed milk for a customer from one bowl into another with a quick and rhythmic movement in order to cool it, and the milk made a swishing sound and frothed as it was tossed. 'They all make fine promises to you. They say there are beautiful women, there is so much to eat, there is so much gold to loot and plunder. But what I say is that they are all lies. All lies, I tell you.'

He stopped to cut a little cream off the milk in the huge cauldron with a big circular spoon, and adding it to the frothing milk passed it to the customer, who began to blow at it before drinking.

'They just want you to go there,' Mirza continued. 'But once you are across the seas you cannot come back. You are trapped. If you want me to tell you the truth, there is no food, no women, no gold, no anything there but hunger and bloodshed and death. DEATH. That's all there is, I tell you. They are all illegally begotten ones, these Farangis, and no good will come to you from them. Just see how we had hoped that prosperity would return after the Coronation. But there is only more starvation. The prices of things have gone up. We can't even get sugar. Ghee is now five chhatanks for a rupee whereas before 1911 it used to be one seer and over. And wheat is sold at eight seers to the rupee. What I say is: Have you ever heard of a worse famine than this? Tell me. Am I wrong? . . .'

As he said this his small red eyes seemed to bulge, and his conical white beard seemed to be pointed and sharp like a dagger. The others all listened to him with attention and mounting anger. Kallan, the carpenter, was so carried away that he held the stick of the hookah near his mouth, and his burning eyes glared at Mirza's face. And the barber and the kababi and the others were all engrossed in Mirza's speech. So much so that the customer had not finished his milk and was all tears, so touched was he by this spirited discourse.

When he finished they all said in unison: 'Yes, you are right. The Farangis are cheats and faithless swine.'

But Siddiq, the fat bania, with a huge and protruding paunch and small eyes that peeped from behind the fatty pouches under them, who had come during Mirza's speech and stood listening behind the dirty wooden bench on which they sat, raised a voice of dissent. Since the prices of grain and ghee had gone up he was making more profits, as he had stored up grain in his shop. Besides, he smuggled ghee into the city without paying octroi tax. So, it was not unnatural for him to stand up for the Government.

'What you say is all right,' he began, and everyone turned round to look at him, 'but my opinion is that it is not good to go against your king. . . .'

The light from Mirza's two-wicked kerosene lamp without a chimney fell on the bania's face and made it look grim and macabre like some fat and painted devil. The customer threw the earthen milk cup away which broke into pieces with a hollow sound. A mangy cat crept out from under the plank jutting out of Mirza's shop and began to lick the milk from the pieces of the broken cup.

'He will be your king, not ours,' Mirza said sarcastically. 'Our king is only God.'

'But God has made Jaraj (George) king, and you have to accept him as such. You eat his salt and are talking like this about him. . . .'

'Well, move on,' said Kallan, the carpenter. 'We do not eat his earnings but of the labour of our muscles. God did not make your Jaraj king, but our Prophet. . . .'

As he said this he made a grotesque and sour face. They all began to laugh, and Siddiq walked away feeling annoyed and ashamed at being made fun of. A strong gust of wind blew and the dim kerosene lamp which lighted the lane went out, and Siddiq was lost in the dark. . . .

9

ONE evening Mir Nihal was coming home from the house of Nawab Puttan. The roads were as busy as ever, and tongas and tram cars went noisily past; but there seemed to be few pigeons in the sky. The war had not much affected Delhi otherwise; but since the prices of grain had gone up fewer people could afford to keep and feed pigeons. Mostly poor people were fond of them, water-carriers and workers employed in small home industries, or those who made silver leaf or gold thread and laces for a living. The trade of the latter had been affected, as cheaper laces and gold threads had started coming into India from England and Germany. Besides, fewer people seemed to buy these things. All this plus the higher prices of grain forced them to economize. In fact, they could hardly afford to keep pigeons now. Only the more well-to-do among them could indulge their hobbies. And one of the most outstanding characteristics of Delhi was threatened with extinction and death. But still there were enough people who flew the pigeons and kicked up their usual tapage.

Unconsciously Mir Nihal felt this change as he looked up at the sky. The moment he did so he was overcome with a giddy feeling, and his head became heavy. He stopped for a while to regain his balance. His eyes fell on a dead pigeon lying in the gutter. Its wings were wet with the dirty water, its blue legs were sticking upwards, and one of its eyes had an ugly and sickening glare. He was unconsciously reminded of his pigeons, and with the memory his old love of the birds came back to his mind.

As he went forward he saw people bringing a dead body on their shoulders. Mir Nihal muttered to himself in Arabic: 'We belong to God

and unto Him shall we return.' He walked forty paces with the funeral,
and lent his shoulder in carrying the dead. The strong aroma of camphor filled his nostrils and made him feel sick. His head became more
heavy and his eyes seemed to be burning. He hurried home thinking
that he should prepare some good medicine for his constipation.
     When he reached home Nisar Ahmad began to call the evening
azaan. Mir Nihal performed the ablutions and, spreading a prayer-cloth
on the floor in the veranda, began to pray. In the middle of the prayer
he suddenly felt his body become heavier, and he found it difficult even
to keep standing. He thought it was nothing, and he concentrated on
prayer. But the heaviness increased; and as he bent down he could not
maintain his balance and toppled over. The strength had suddenly left
his body, and he felt lifeless and dead. He tried to call out to someone,
but he could not speak.
     Ghafoor saw his master fall down and rushed to his help. He asked
him what the matter was; but Mir Nihal could not speak. With difficulty Ghafoor put him on the bed and gave Dilchain the news to be
carried inside the zenana.
     Hakim Ajmal Khan was immediately sent for. He said that it was a
paralytic stroke, but since it was not accompanied with fever it was not
very dangerous. He prescribed medicines and went away without taking any fees, for the Hakims did not charge anything from the residents
of Delhi.
     The family sat near Mir Nihal worried and full of fear. They asked
him how he felt. Mir Nihal lay on the bed with his beard all awry, and
his eyes bulging. He made attempts at talking, but could not talk. He
tried to move his hands and legs. Only the left hand and leg could
move. The right side had become paralysed. . . .

                              *   *   *

After three days he felt slightly better, and could utter a few broken
words. But he felt that his tongue had become heavy like his limbs.
Hakim Ajmal Khan came once or twice and brought rare medicines with
him from home. Mir Nihal was given the soup of wild pigeons and
Ghafoor brought them from the Chowk, and Masroor caught the wild
pigeons who had nested in the cornices of the veranda.
     For a fortnight he did not regain the power of speech. Then the
medicines had their effect. It was such a relief to be able to talk. But his
arm and leg had been affected badly and he could not walk or even sit
up without another person's help.

His friends came and suggested various remedies. Kambal Shah suggested the oil of pelican, fabled to feed its young on its own blood. It was sent for, but could not be found. Habibuddin, however, succeeded in having one caught. Kambal Shah himself supervised the preparation of the oil.

Mir Nihal lay on the bed and watched the things all around. He had learnt to enjoy life from his bed. The children had found the bird a thing of great interest. They would come near it and put their hands very near its beak, and the bird opened and closed it with a noise. They did it the whole day long, so long as it was not killed. Mir Nihal saw them play and smiled now and then. He was getting reconciled to his perpetual imprisonment.

When the oil was prepared about three months had passed since Mir Nihal's attack. It was rubbed on his arm and leg which had been affected. The wrestler, Shammoo Khan, massaged Mir Nihal every day for an hour and gave him all hope of recovery saying that his massaging had cured many paralytics. But nothing did him good. He felt so hopeless and constrained. Every night he went to sleep hoping to wake up hale and hearty in the morning, but it was hoping all in vain. He had hated to be dependent on his sons for money. Now he had become dependent on others for everything. He would see the water kept near him, but if he was thirsty and no one was by he could not even drink.

*   *   *

As the months dragged on his condition improved to the extent that he could sit up of his own accord by catching hold of the wooden side of the bed, and he could drag himself a little on it. In the evenings he was made to sit in a chair. He could just stand up on one leg with the help of a stick and drag himself a few paces. The first day that he was able to do this he felt happy and hopeful.

But time hung heavy. The days were mountains high to climb, and life became a misery. At night the ladies came out to see him, for in the daytime there was the difficulty of purdah, and someone or the other was constantly dropping in to inquire after Mir Nihal's health or to chat. At night the door of the mardana was closed, Ghafoor was sent out, and no one could come in.

In the daytime, however, Mir Nihal felt so bored. During the long and unending summer noons he lay moping on the bed, with nothing to do, cursing life and wishing for death. The wind blew and dust got into his eyes, and the bed sheet became dirty with the sand. He felt like tearing his clothes and going mad, and the tears of helplessness very often streamed down his face.

To while away his time he started trapping rats which were as big as a small-sized hare. There was a trap in the house, but its catch did not work properly. So Mir Nihal tied a string to it, kept the trap near the gutter through which the rats came, and lay on the bed ready to pull the string. The first time he trapped a rat he felt so happy. The moment he had caught it he shouted to Ghafoor, and, with a broad smile wrinkling up his face, he showed him what he had caught. Ghafoor also smiled, but thought to himself that his master was growing childish. Masroor was sent for to kill the rat, and Dilchain also came to watch the fun.

The rats did not come so often in the day. At night Mir Nihal lay on his bed in wait for them, for he could not go to sleep till very late in the night as, to pass away the time, he slept in the day. As a rat got inside the trap he pulled the string. In the morning the rat was despatched by Ghafoor or Masroor. Shams was afraid of killing them and watched the fun from a distance.

One day Mir Nihal lay on his bed. It was about twelve o'clock of the day and a dusty wind was blowing. There was a heart-rending hopelessness in the atmosphere. The vendors shouted their dreary cries and added to the monotony of life. There were fewer pigeons on the sky, and fewer men were shouting at the birds. He watched the pigeons flying and mixing with other flocks, and he remembered the good old days. His eyes fell on the date palm. Most of its leaves had sered and fallen. Only a thin bunch of them at the top fluttered in the wind, and its bare trunk looked uglier and darker with scaly rings all around which looked blunted and dull—the years which had left their marks as they had come and gone.

The trap was set for the rats, but they had become more clever and avoided it. A mongoose came instead and sniffed about. By a rare trick of memory Mir Nihal was reminded of the snake he had killed on that night years ago. By contrast he felt so unhappy. There was a day when he could catch snakes with his hand. Now God had taken all strength away from him and had made him useless for all the pleasures of the world.

The mongoose was joined by its mate, and a game of love-making began. The male purred and produced an angry sound and rushed at the female and bit her on the neck. She escaped and went into the gutter. But she came out again, and their courting continued. Once as she was trying to run away from the male the female went inside the trap. But Mir Nihal did not pull the string. He was reminded of Babban Jan who too had been trapped by death at a time when she was young and of an age fit only to play the game of love. When the she-mongoose came out he pulled the string and closed the trap not to tempt them and himself. . . .

He lay there thinking of the ups and downs of life, and of the futility of things. Thinking, however, had become his only pastime, the hourly routine. There was no joy left now, no pleasure in anything. The day dawned, the evening came, and life went on. . . .

10

BEGAM NIHAL felt extremely sorry for her husband. She prepared his medicines herself and cooked some delicacy or other for him. His teeth were falling out one by one, and Begam Nihal had soft bread cooked for him with ghee mixed with the dough so that he could chew it easily. But her own eyesight was failing her. One day as she was getting down the platform she missed the steps and rolled down. Dilchain and Begam Jamal rushed to help her to her feet.

'Allah saved your life,' said Begam Jamal. 'You are not hurt, are you?'

Dilchain looked mortified and said:

'Shall I call Hakim Karimuddin Sight-giver? You must do something for your eyes.'

'Yes, call him tomorrow. It is really a hard life living blind.'

Hakim Karimuddin came and gave her some special collyrium and white pills which had to be rubbed on stone with water, and the unguent thus prepared was to be put in the eyes. But there was hardly any improvement.

For fear of falling down Begam Nihal started walking with the help of a stick. Most of the time she sat cutting areca nut into small bits, staring in front of her with dead eyes.

She did not go anywhere except to Asghar's now and then. Jehan Ara was now about five years old and had grown into a lovely child. Bilqeece had started running a temperature, and had become thin and weak.

Asghar was no more in love with his wife; but he did not behave so
callously as he had done some years ago. He had found other interests,
had relations with other women, and was just indifferent to his wife.
But he had become attached to Jehan Ara, and had accepted Bilqeece
as a thing for granted, who could neither be ignored nor done away with.

Begam Shahbaz was broken-hearted and got all sorts of charms and
amulets for her daughter, saying that it was the effect of magic which
was responsible for her poor condition. She said that Asghar had done
something to her so that she may die and he might become free to lead a
happy life once again.

Begam Nihal also realized that the relations between husband and
wife were strained. But she did not blame Asghar. She said that Bilqeece
was not treating her son well, and had become the bane of his life.
When she went to see her, however, she always suggested to her mother
that she should consult this hakim or that doctor.

Asghar often complained to his wife:

'Nothing is ever in order in the house. You never seem to take any
interest in the house. My life has become a misery, O God. I don't
know why I was born. I had married in the hope of getting some peace,
but there is none for me. . . . '

*   *   *

Bilqeece lay on the bed, staring at the ceiling. Pale and sickly looking
lizards crawled on the walls, and she felt frightened all alone in the
house. In the evenings the pale light of the setting sun came into the
room through the door, and fell on her face. As the day neared its end a
feeling of hopelessness filled her heart and made her think of death. She
thought of death very often now, for this seemed her only hope of freedom from the sorrows of the world.

But the thought of Jehan Ara filled her with dread. What would
happen to her if she died? Who would look after her? She would be
neglected and treated harshly. Perhaps Asghar would marry soon after
her death. What would his second wife be like? She would, none the
less, be a step-mother, and Jehan Ara would be left an orphan to suffer
the jealousy and anger of another. This thought ate constantly into her
mind.

She had herself known a little love, a little kindness. That was
something. The moments of joy which she had known in her early
married life came to her mind in her sorrow. Now and then a faint smile
flickered on her lips with the glow of memory. As she rummaged for

happy souvenirs, Asghar's kisses came back to her mind, and back of them still the love of her father.

She would lie on her bed dreaming. The sun would set and the night would come with her stars and silences. She would hug Jehan Ara to her breast, listening to a greater calm, a greater peace, which lies beyond the shores of Night. Happy faces would come to her in her sleep and talk to her of love and happiness. They would lead her by the arm into sequestered bowers and beautiful gardens, or glide along the banks of sweet-murmuring streams. She would wake up with a start and find herself all alone. She would throw her arms around her child and lie there listening to the night and the beating of her heart.

One night she had a terrible dream. She was bathing in a river with some companions whom she could not recognize. She stood on the bank and jumped in the water, laving her body and her face in the cool and pleasant stream. Then she felt that someone was calling her from behind. She turned round to look. There was a man beckoning her with his finger. As she went near him she seemed to recognize Asghar. As she looked, however, the face underwent a change and he looked old. There were wrinkles on his face and his skin looked brittle. His nose looked prominent and frightening. It jutted out straight on the face, big and ugly, and the nostrils were deep and black. He looked at her in a concentrated fashion and one of his eyes glared more ferociously than the other. There was such terror in his look that beads of perspiration appeared on her face. Frightened she opened her eyes. Silence rang in her ears and her heart beat fast. Instinctively she hugged Jehan Ara to her breast, and lay with her eyes wide open. But the picture of that man with his frightening nose and the glaring eye did not leave her. There was something so gruesome yet hypnotic in the image that she closed her eyes again and saw the face. With difficulty she opened her eyes and woke up her mother who slept near her. . . .

For days after she had dreamt of that face that nose and that glaring eye haunted her. She felt as if she had seen Death, the gruesome hag, thrusting forward her claws and dragging her into her lap.

Begam Shahbaz sent for Pirji, an old man with a goatee beard who always wore a blue tahmat and a blue turban on his head. He read verses from the Koran and blew his breath at Bilqeece. He blessed her and said that she had no cause for worry.

'There are evil spirits in the world,' he said. 'They sometimes come and disturb us in our dreams. You should not think of this and be anxious for nothing. The word of God is the best remedy for all ills.'

He gave her a charm which was to be washed in water and the water thus prepared was to be drunk for seven days every morning.

But Bilqeece knew that it was all useless, and she thought of death. For, she said, death was much better than such a life. In that other world there would at least be freedom from the fever and the fret, the consequential worries of life.

The thought of Jehan Ara saddened her the most. What would really happen to the child after her death? And, if at all, it was for her sake that she wished to keep alive.

'Why do you lie in bed all the time, Ammi?' Jehan Ara would sometimes ask her mother. 'Why don't you play with me?'

Tears would rush to Bilqeece's eyes and, kissing the child passionately, she would say:

'Ammi is not well, my moon. When she gets well she will play with you. . . . But be a good child and love your father.'

And she said to her mother:

'Promise me one thing, mother. You will take care of Jehan Ara when I am dead.'

'What has happened to you, daughter?' Begam Shahbaz replied in a shocked voice. 'Your enemies should die and not you.'

'No one is sure of life and everyone has to die one day,' Bilqeece said sadly. 'In case I die you will surely look after my child. Won't you, my own mother?'

The character of Begam Shahbaz was a strange mixture of opposites. She had an affection for her daughter, no doubt, but she did not believe in worrying herself too much. She was vain and egotistical. And though she had become a widow she had not given up wearing her fine clothes and jewellery. She loved herself more than anything else in the world. Whenever someone came to see her she talked only about her woes, and invented imaginary ailments to attract attention and win sympathy.

Yet with all this Begam Shahbaz did love Bilqeece, perhaps because Bilqeece loved her dearly. It pleased Begam Shahbaz to dote on someone and have someone constantly doting on her. Her elder daughter, who now lived in Calcutta, was not so loving and affectionate. That is why when Bilqeece said this about Jehan Ara, Begam Shahbaz felt sad and promised to do what her daughter had asked her. And a promise saved her so much worry . . .

11

ONE night in January Bilqeece lay on her bed in the room. It had rained and a cold wind was blowing. She was very weak and had become emaciated and thin. She lay staring at the ceiling, and her big eyes looked pale like narcissi. Her mother was praying in the adjoining room, and Jehan Ara had gone to sleep.

Somehow Asghar felt so affectionate towards his wife that he came and sat by her. There were fine masses of clouds on the washed and clear sky, and a young moon floated behind them. Here and there clusters of stars shone in between the clouds, and added to the lustre of the night. In the by-lane a boy went past singing a song which had become the craze in a droll and dragging tune.

> O save me from being indebted
> To Jesus for his healing breath.
> You have given me pain and you
> Alone can cure and save me from death.
>
> Someone comes upon my grave
> Veiled and hidden in the night.
> O breeze, I pray to thee alone,
> Blow out the lamp, put out the light.

His voice died away in the silence of the night, and Asghar felt a gentle pain in his heart. From somewhere the memory of his lost love came back to him, and he felt that he had been really callous with his wife. As he looked at her ill face he felt guilty of neglect. But love had died in his heart. Why had he been in love with her, he thought, and why had he become indifferent to her? She had loved him and adored him, perhaps. Why did he not feel anything for her? What is love, after all? Does the charm of a woman lie merely in her graceful ways, or in her confessions of love? Yet the moths hover round a candle flame, scorch their wings and are burnt to ashes and dust. They also love the light and sacrifice their lives for it. Wasn't Bilqeece sacrificing her life for him? Didn't she love him silently like the moths the candle flame? His conscience pricked him, and he thought that he should make good the past losses by taking care of her.

Bilqeece also heard the song and it somehow seemed to apply to her case. She felt a storm of self-pity well up within her breast. She moved

her hand slowly and catching hold of Asghar's hand said to him in a
thin voice as if from far away:
'Do not worry on my account, please. I will not survive and live for
long. You should marry again. I free you of the debt of my mehr. . . .'
As she said this she pressed his hand softly, and then as gently let it
go, and looked at him with worshipful eyes.
There was something so touching and sad in her words and her
gesture that Asghar was moved deeply, and tears came into his eyes.
'You should not be so dejected,' he said to her in a voice hoarse with
emotion. 'You will get well soon, and we shall live happily together. I
will call a doctor tomorrow.'
He looked away from Bilqeece as two hot tears slid down his cheeks.
Lightning flashed behind the clouds and lighted up the sky. Bilqeece
seemed to be lost in a reverie. As he looked at her face he realized how
fine and gentle she was, still lovely though ill; and he felt ashamed of
himself and his inhuman conduct. As he looked at her again he felt
suddenly that he loved her still. And a fear took possession of him that
she might die and leave him alone.
'Will you forgive me,' he said sincerely, 'for my indifference and
neglect of you? I am guilty of treating you badly.'
Bilqeece looked at him with her big and floating eyes and replied
tenderly:
'There was no fault of yours. It was all mine and mine alone. . . .'
It is surprising how a little love, a little kindness, can sometimes go
deep down into the soul. It seemed as if a new life had come into
Bilqeece. Her will to live returned all of a sudden; and she wanted to
fall down at her husband's feet and worship him. . . .

                              *   *   *

In the morning Asghar called Dr. Mitra. He examined the patient and
pulled a long face. Asghar was filled with fear, and asked the doctor
what she was suffering from. It was a clear case of TB, the doctor told
him, but there was every hope of her recovery provided proper care was
taken. He prescribed medicines and rest.
Begam Shahbaz became happy that the husband had at last softened
towards his wife, and said an extra prayer to God. She had been giving
Bilqeece medicines which had been prescribed by Hakim Saheb who
had said that it was ordinary fever. When Asghar told her of the serious
nature of the disease she became concerned. That very day she sent for

Pirji and got some amulets and charms for her daughter, and prayed to the various saints and to God to cure her for the love of His Beloved.

Other relations and ladies came to see Bilqeece and suggested all kinds of remedies. One said that Hakim so-and-so was a very good physician and had cured many persons who had despaired of recovering. Another said that a faqir had once given a dose of medicine to the cousin of her brother-in-law's father-in-law, and the effect of the medicine was that he had vomited, and the TB germ had come out and within a month he had started walking about.

Begam Shahbaz would have liked to try some of these medicines and give them to Bilqeece. Asghar told her not to meddle with the doctor's treatment. Charms and prayers were all right; but he did not allow any other medicine to be given to her besides that of the doctor.

The weather was fine during February and March. Asghar paid more attention to his wife, and sat with her every day talking or playing with Jehan Ara. This plus the proper treatment did a lot of good to Bilqeece; and they all hoped and prayed for the best. Happiness seemed to be returning to the home, and separated hearts seemed to be uniting once again. . . .

.

PART IV

No candle burns upon my grave
Nor blows a drooping rose;
And no moth burns its wings in the flame
Nor the bulbul sings his woes.

ZEBUN NISA

1

THE summer of 1918 was more terrible than the summers of the previous years. The sky was of a coppery hue throughout the day, and at night the stars were hidden behind the sand which rained down from the sky, and the loo did not stop. It howled more fiercely than before as the City Walls had been demolished and the wind could now blow free from the mountainous wastes outside the city. It howled through the empty streets and in the narrow by-lanes and bazars. The dogs moaned and wept at night as if afraid of death, and the cats, whose numbers had surprisingly decreased, were quiet and subdued.

Nature herself was rebellious and seemed angry with the people of Hindustan. Hundreds and thousands of Indians had been killed in the war, acting as fodder to the German guns. But not content with this and, as it were, filled with anger against the inhumanity of man, Nature wanted to demonstrate her own callousness and might. Influenza broke out in epidemic form, and from the houses in the mohallah all around heart-rending cries of lamentation and weeping began to rend the air. There was hardly any house where a death did not take place. Shams lost his wife, and in his grief became more mystical and religious than ever. Every evening he went to the cemetery and sat by his wife's grave for hours, seeing the day die and night spread her veil of darkness and gloom over the grief-stricken earth.

Men carried dead bodies on their shoulders by the score. There was not a single hour of the day when a few dead bodies were not carried outside the city to be buried. Soon the graveyards became full, and it was difficult to find even three yards of ground to put a person in his final resting-place. In life they had had no peace, and even in death there seemed no hope of rest.

A new cemetery was made outside the city where people buried relations by the score. The Hindus were lucky that way. They just went to the bank of the sacred Jamuna, cremated the dead, and threw away the ashes and unburned bones in the water. Many were thrown away without a shroud or cremation. They were mostly the poor. Yet in death it was immaterial whether you were naked or clothed or burnt or thrown away to be devoured by vultures and jackals.

For the Muslims it was worse. When they had been buried they were faced with another gruesome menace. Many shroud-thieves had appeared on the scene. The people had discovered new and newer ways of procuring bread.

This epidemic, outcome, perhaps, of the gases used in the European War, supplied them with an easy way of earning a livelihood. Many went to the graveyards at dead of night with spades and long iron hooks. It was not difficult to dig open the new graves, especially because they had been dug and filled up in a hurry. With the help of their iron hooks they pulled out the winding-sheets and got good money for them. Hyenas and jackals thus found their task made easier for them. They could enter the newly opened graves and fill their bellies to the full.

The grave-diggers made a good living and amassed fortunes. They raised their wages from two rupees to four and from four to eight, and even then grumbled and complained. They did not bother to see that the grave was properly dug or deep enough or not. They had so many more to dig. If someone protested they only said:

'Dig for yourself, then. This is the best that we can do.'

And the needy had, willy-nilly, to acquiesce. But this was not all. They supplied the poorest specimens of brittle slabs of stones to cover the grave with. When big holes and cracks were left in between, the grave-diggers did not even fill them up with mud and started throwing dry earth in which fell through inside and covered the corpse to the greater grief and sorrow of the bereaved. But there was no help. The grave-diggers had a ready excuse that no stones were available in the market, and that they were really obliging them by supplying even these for the fear of God.

They dug up old graves for the stones, and supplied them at very high rates. Worse than this, they opened up new graves whose corpses had already been finished by the beasts and the winding-sheets stolen by the thieves. If someone happened to recognize the place where he had buried a sister or a wife only the previous day and had now come to bury a brother or a son, he made loud moans and shouted at the grave-diggers. But they only replied:

'Are you in your senses? How could we commit such a sin! You must be mistaken.'

If he still protested they remarked:

'Are you going to bury your dead here or not? We have so many waiting still. . . .'

In the city a different, though similar, scene was being enacted. The cloth merchants, banias these, raised the price of line-cloth which was used for winding-sheets. No one could complain, and, if anyone did, the banias said that on account of the war the price of cloth had gone up; and if still the customer protested, they replied:

'One should not think of expense regarding a winding-sheet. After all, this is the last time that you are going to spend on the deceased. He must have given you so much comfort in life, and may have even spent on you. You should not really grudge him a decent burial. . . . But if you cannot afford, well, then buy a cheaper winding-sheet. . . .'

But, of course, the cheaper shroud would be so thin that one could see the naked body through it; and the person would starve, but spend a little more to give his dear one a decent shroud. . . .

And the ghassals also charged much more. They did a roaring business and kept all the time on their feet, running from house to house to wash the dead. But they hardly gave them a bath. They just laved the bodies with water, grabbed at the gold or silver rings which had not been taken off the fingers of the dead, and concealed them in inner pockets. They charged a high sum for having performed this virtuous deed, and departed for the next, from morning till night, from sunset till dawn, stroking their pious beards, feeling their deep purses that were filled with silver and gold, muttered the name of God, and massaged their bellies with satisfied yet greedy hands. . . .

Delhi became a city of the dead. But the people of Delhi, true to the traditions of the past, did not miss an opportunity of having a few digs at Fortune. They made songs and sang them; and the leaflets containing them were sold for a pice each:

> How deadly this fever is,
> Everyone is dying of it.
> Men become lame with it
> And go out in dolis.
> The hospitals are gay and bright,
> But sorry is men's plight.

Yet the songs did not improve matters; and there seemed no peace for the soul of man.

Azaans were called at all hours from the house-tops and the mosques. Prayers were said to God to mitigate the evil. But God did not exist, perhaps; or, perchance, their feeble voices did not reach the sound-proof gates of Heaven situated on the seventh sky, fortified by the lower six. For the azaans and prayers were of no avail. Death walked with hurried strides through towns and cities, devastating them, taking her fat and unending toll of lives, stalking among the dead. And Izrael, the angel of death, had not a moment to spare. From house to house he rushed, from door to door, snatching the souls away from human beings burning with fever yet hungry after life, wanting to live on in a world which did not care about them at all. . . .

2

SINCE that night in January Bilqeece had been happy, and her condition had improved. But as the summer months came she felt exhausted and run down. From all around came the sounds of lamentation as someone died, and Bilqeece's heart misgave her. Her will power had kept her alive; but the constant reminders of death filled her with dread.

It was now the month of June, and the epidemic was raging. One day Bilqeece, too, was caught by the fever. The doctor came and said that she would get well soon. The news of her fever reached Mir Nihal and Begam Nihal, and they became anxious. Begam Nihal went to see her and stayed with her for two days. But she had really become useless for everything on account of her eyesight which had almost failed her. Besides, she could not leave the house and Mir Nihal alone for long.

One evening Asghar came, looking woebegone. Bilqeece's fever had not gone down, and her condition had become worse. Begam Shahbaz had not been able to sleep for two days, and had kept Asghar also awake as she was afraid. Begam Nihal got ready to go with Asghar, but he said to her:

'No, Amma, why should you trouble? There is nothing to worry about. I shall take Masroor with me to sleep there.'

Begam Nihal sent Dilchain also to sleep at Asghar's. Asghar was very tired and soon went to sleep. Masroor slept in between Bilqeece and Begam Shahbaz; and Dilchain slept at the extreme end of the courtyard. The night was dark, and a strange silence as of death lay all around. Masroor dozed off. Begam Shahbaz was afraid lest the Angel of Death should come to her by mistake, and she pinched Masroor with her toe. Masroor woke up with a start, but he found everyone asleep. When he was about to doze off again she pinched him a second time. Masroor sat up on the bed and looked all around; but there was nothing wrong. He was rather surprised for he had definitely felt someone pinch his leg.

When Begam Shahbaz did the same thing a third time, Masroor called out:

'Who is there?'

There was no reply. Begam Shahbaz lay on the bed, as if fast asleep. Bilqeece breathed heavily, and an uncanny silence lay over the earth. Only somewhere a dog barked and began to moan; but there was nothing out of common in the house. . . .

At last Begam Shahbaz fell asleep. About four o'clock in the morning Bilqeece felt her breath sticking in her throat; and she called out:

'Is someone awake?'

She did not call anyone by name, and no one woke up. She called again, but there was no reply. The third time she called out a little louder than before. Masroor woke up and asked her:

'What is it, Sister-in-law?'

'Will you please call your Brother . . .'

Masroor felt there was something unearthly in her voice, and he woke Asghar up.

'What is the matter? Is everything all right?' he asked in a frightened voice.

'Yes,' Masroor replied. 'Sister-in-law wants you.'

Asghar got up hurriedly. The world lay hushed in silence which was deep and yet seemed to be filled with strange and distant sounds of whispering. An unnatural loneliness filled the house. Asghar came near Bilqeece and saw her face in the dim starlight. She looked ghastly and pale. The pallor of death was on her face, and a peculiar expression in her eyes. She had, perhaps, sensed the approach of death and felt the breath rattling in her throat, and when she spoke there was something uncanny in her voice. 'I am going,' she said calmly, as if she had overcome all sense of regret and loss. 'Goodbye. Forgive me my faults, and take care of Jehan Ara, please. . . .'

'What are you saying?' Asghar said in the desperation of sudden grief. 'Look at the dawn greying in the east. In the morning . . .'

But something within him snapped, and he seemed to hear a long-drawn sigh rise from the earth and reverberate in the air to pass into the sky. . . . The breath rattled in Bilqeece's throat, and her eyes seemed to be pulled up as if by some unknown force. Asghar caught hold of her hand which was trembling as if an electric current were passing through her frame. He began to read the prayer for the dying. But she had gone, gone into the world of eternal peace and calm. . . .

3

AFTER her death Asghar was grief-stricken. He went to the graveyard every day, and sat by his wife's grave for hours. After the fortieth day of her death the grave could be made permanent, and Asghar had it built at some expense, and had the borders painted green and red. He went there every evening and put flowers on the grave and had water sprinkled over it.

One evening it was hot and Asghar took a tonga to go to the graveyard. As they came to the lonely road leading to the cemetery, the tonga-driver began to sing in a hoarse voice the latest sad and melancholy tune:

> Go, my life, and may God be with you;
> The parted will meet one day if Fate will allow.
>
> Pain and sorrow and a cruel fate
> Have brought me well nigh to a lifeless state.
>
> But do not say that love is false, my dove:
> I have shown you how they die in love. . . .

The song reminded Asghar of his indifference towards Bilqeece, and of her deep and sincere love for him. His heart was saddened, and when he reached the grave he wept and prayed long for forgiveness of his sins.

There was such rest and calm in the cemetery that he did not wish to come away. Where he sat he did not hear the heart of the world beating far away. He did not feel its hectic pulse throb. He was transported into a distant land full of a rare contentment and joy.

He sat there until the sun set and a soft, sad silence crept over the earth. The stars appeared one by one in the green and transparent sky;

and his heart was filled with a gentle pain, the mystical sense of the
transience of the world. . . .

4

MIR NIHAL lay on the bed, day in, day out, yearning, remembering,
buried under a debris of dreams. He felt that he was useless, heavy lum-
ber, and was filled with a sense of the futility of his life. The world
around him moved on or frittered away. He remained where he was,
living in a constant twilight of velleities and regrets, watching the young
die one by one and gain their liberty from the sorrows of the world.

Mir Sangi had died and Red Beard had become too old to go about
anywhere and came to see him only now and then; and Kambal Shah
had disappeared. Thus, Mir Nihal was left the sole guardian of years
that had gone. Now and then he fished for pearls from the age-old sand
of Memory; and as he remembered how love-fires had kindled, raged
and died, he shed a few tears of self-pity and helplessness.

Memories of days and hours came swarming like flies upon him, and
he thought of his life from childhood to the present day. Delhi had
fallen, he reflected; India had been despoiled; all that he had stood for
had been destroyed. Only a year ago a new wave of freedom had surged
across the breast of Hindustan. People had become conscious and
wished to come back into their own. The Home Rule Movement was
started, and there were prophetic rumblings of distant thunder as the
Movement went sweeping over India. But, somehow, all this did not
affect Mir Nihal. It was not for him, the martyrdom and glory in the
cause of the Motherland. His days had gone, and a new era of hopes
and aspirations, which he neither understood nor sympathized with,
was beginning to dawn. His world had fallen. Let others build their
own. He was one of those who had believed in fighting with naked
swords in their hands. The young only agitated. Let them agitate. He
was unconcerned.

New ways and ideas had come into being. A hybrid culture which
had nothing in it of the past was forcing itself upon Hindustan, a
hodgepodge of Indian and Western ways which he failed to understand. The English had been beaten by the Turks at Gallipoli. Even this

had not affected his heart. He had become feelingless and was not
interested whether the Caravan stayed or moved on. The old had gone,
and the new was feeble and effete. At least it had nothing in common
with his ideals or his scheme of things. A hopeless weariness was in the atmosphere; and the dust blew more
often than before. The glory had gone, and only dreariness remained.
The richness of life had been looted and despoiled by the foreigners,
and vulgarity and cheapness had taken its place. That relation which
existed between the society and its poets and members was destroyed.
Perhaps the environment had changed. Society had moved forward,
and the people had been left behind in the race of Life. New modes had
forced themselves upon India. Perhaps that is why that unity of experience and form, which existed in Mir Nihal's youth, had vanished.
Whatever it was, a new world had come into being and, he felt, he was
not part of it.

Often as he lay on his bed he heard men sing in vulgar tunes new
verses cheaper than any that had ever been written before:

> In the absence of my well-belov'd
> I have drunk, O saqi, like wine my blood.
> And when my heart was roasted with grief,
> I ate it like kababs with relief.

> After the prayers for the dead
> My hangman laughed and laughing said:
> It was a damn' good riddance indeed,
> I have performed a virtuous deed. . . .

What had happened to the great poets of Hindustan? Where were
Mir and Ghalib and Insha? Where were Dard and Sauda or even Zauq?
Gone they were, and gone with them was the wealth of poetry. Only a
poverty of thought had come to stay, reflected Mir Nihal, and in place
of emotion and sentiments a vulgar sentimentality. Time had reversed
the order of things, and life had been replaced by a death-in-life. No
beauty seemed to remain anywhere and ugliness had blackened the face
of Hindustan. . . .

Asghar often came now wearing English clothes, but his father did
not say anything. He seemed to have forgotten that he had ever hated
them. Nisar Ahmad called his glorious azaan. His voice was still as
resilient as before. When Mir Nihal heard it he muttered to himself:
'Glory be to God'; but he did not pray. It was so difficult to sit up. How
could he perform the ablutions five times in the day and move up and

down? His body had become heavier than lead, and it was not easy for him to sit up for long. Ghafoor helped him with the least thing he wished to do. But he had become used to the indifference of the world. For Begam Nihal it had become difficult to come outside very often. She had become almost blind. Most of the time she sat cutting areca nut, or disentangling tangled thread. She would sit on the bed, her legs arched up in front of her, the tangled thread lying in a heap by her side. As she disentangled it she wound it round her legs. Then she made it into skeins of straightened thread.

Two deep furrows had formed on her cheeks running on either side of the nose coming right down to the chin; and her skin had become wrinkled and loose. She sat there moving her hands, her eyes sunk in hollows, a dead expression on her face, weaving and unweaving tangled memories. She had become dependent on Dilchain who was still hale although she walked with the help of a stick.

Begam Jamal was also feeling the effects of old age. Though she still grumbled and complained yet she had become more subdued. Masroor had failed two or three times in the matriculation examination, and had given up studies altogether. He was not much interested in them, anyway. Then he had got a job in an English motor firm, but he was very hot-tempered and vain and looked down upon the other clerks. One day he had a quarrel with the manager and had been turned out. Now he was preparing to go away to his aunt.

Shams often flirted with the young maidservant who had been engaged, although outwardly he was as pious and religious as before.

Begam Waheed wrote regularly home and seemed to be getting on well, as her children had grown up, and her daughter had been married and was herself a mother now. But Mehro was unhappy, although she herself did not write of her troubles and woes. She had been able to come to Delhi only twice ever since she was married seven years ago. Her husband was very suspicious and did not like her coming to Delhi.

Yet Life went on without any break or consciousness of change.

5

SINCE Bilqeece's death Asghar had started looking after Jehan Ara himself. He did things for her, washed her and dressed her, and even

sewed her torn clothes. When he went to the office she stayed with her
grandmother and came home in the evening. Zohra often came and
found him doing something for the child. She felt sorry for him and
wanted to help him.

'It is a woman's job,' she would say. 'Let me do it.'

But he would curse his fate and reply:

'It is my lot, and I have got to bear the burden of care. . . .'

She would make a fuss; he would be smitten with self-pity; and with
difficulty he would let her help him.

Zohra had grown into a beautiful girl of sixteen, and her charms
seemed to be greater than those of Bilqeece. She was conscious of her
sex, and there was an air of abandon about her. She looked at Asghar
with admiring eyes, and pitied him in his sorrow and loneliness. Asghar
had also become aware of her presence, and when she came his heart
was filled with a secret joy. . . .

One evening when she came she found Asghar sitting on the bed,
lost in thought, his head between his hands, his face a picture of misery.
She felt sorry for him, and sat down by his side.

'You always look so worried and sad,' she said tenderly. 'It makes me
also sad to see you thus. It is much better to speak of your sorrows than
to keep them to yourself.'

Asghar heaved a sigh and said in a voice full of self-pity:

'Who would care to hear my woes? I am the cry of some world-
forsaken soul; I am the pain of some broken heart.'

She was pained by his words, and she put her soft fingers in his hair
and, playing with it, said lovingly:

'No, you should never say that. You do not know how it pains me to
hear you talk like that.'

'But who cares for me? Who will ever do?'

Her heart was bursting with pity and love, and she said in a whisper:

'I . . .'

His heart gave a sudden leap as he heard her say that and he turned
to look at her. There was such a look of inebriety and tenderness in her
eyes as comes with great longing. The wave of love seemed to be
surging in her breast. A storm of emotion rose in him also; and his
sadness was changed into desire, his self-pity into love. He put an arm
around her and as it touched her ripe though tender breast a thrill ran
through his body and his flesh began to tingle with ecstasy.

Zohra's heart also gave a leap; but she was smitten with shame and a sense of guilt. Quickly she disentangled herself from his embrace and ran away, hugging her secret to her breast, afraid that it had been divulged....

* * *

After this incident she did not come for a few days. Asghar had found joy at last. But when she did not come he became impatient. He went to his mother-in-law, but Zohra avoided him. He sent Jehan Ara to call her, but instead of coming herself she detained the child. He sent a note. It remained unanswered. He did not know what to do. Zohra's absence made him think of her more and more. He was so obsessed with her that he could not think of anything else. Unconsciously, without realizing it, he went deeper into a thick forest, like a hunter after his quarry, and lost his way. Three days passed and he was frantic. Zohra herself wanted to come, but an overwhelming shyness kept her away. She did not know how to face him.

In the evening he was walking up and down the courtyard, full of a curious restlessness, trying to find some way of calling her. Jehan Ara was playing with a rubber ball. Some water had collected in a corner, and Jehan Ara's ball rolled away into it. As she went to get it she slipped and fell down. She was hurt and began to cry. Asghar quickly went to her and lifted her up. Her clothes were spoilt and he wanted to change them. Jehan Ara howled and wept and called for her aunt and would not let him change her clothes.

Begam Shahbaz heard her pathetic cries and sent Chanbeli to find out what had happened.

'What is the matter with the child? Why is she crying?' Chanbeli asked with anxiety.

Asghar was annoyed with Jehan Ara. He slapped his forehead loudly with his palm and began to complain:

'She will drive me crazy. She went and fell down in the mud and hurt herself, and now she wouldn't let me change her clothes. She doesn't allow anyone but her aunt to touch her. Hard is the lot of motherless children....'

Chanbeli heaved a sigh as she remembered Bilqeece and went to Jehan Ara to console her. But she cried for Zohra and would not let even Chanbeli touch her.

'I will take you to auntie, darling. Come,' Chanbeli consoled her. But Asghar said:

'Leave her alone. I will manage her somehow. She must get used to her motherless life. How long will poor Zohra go on doing things for her?'

Chanbeli was feeling sorry for Jehan Ara, especially because she was crying so pathetically, and she said:

'But she is just a child. I will send Zohra Begam.'

Zohra was extremely fond of Jehan Ara and came at once, forgetting her shyness in the face of her anxiety for the child. Jehan Ara was still sobbing and her cheeks were dirty with tears and her face looked miserable with grief. When she saw Zohra she was consoled and became quiet. Zohra changed her clothes and gave her toys and she began to play.

Asghar stood near her filled with a great desire to hold her in his arms. But Zohra was shy. It was in an unguarded moment that she had betrayed her subconscious love for Asghar out of pity for him. She had never realized that he would take it in that light. She was feeling guilty as if she had committed some great sin. Yet she was happy and full of an unknown joy which filled her mind and body and soul, a joy so great that she was jealous of it and wanted to keep it concealed within her bosom lest someone snatched it away from her.

When Jehan Ara had become quiet Zohra became conscious of Asghar's presence and avoided looking into his eyes. Then she rose to go. Asghar barred her way, and asked her wistfully, as if he was himself feeling guilty:

'Why did you run away like that, that day? And why did you not come even when I sent for you?'

'Let me go—please,' she said shyly.

'Having set my heart afire with the music of your presence,' he said passionately, 'having lighted the flame of love in the night of my life, you wish now to keep away from me.'

'I did not mean anything,' Zohra said looking at her feet.

'But you mean so much to me,' said Asghar with a lump in his throat. 'You cannot go away. You are the joy of my heart. You are the light of my soul . . .'

'Please, let me go. Mother will be waiting . . .'

She tried to pass. But Asghar caught hold of her in his arms. She struggled for a while, then relaxed in his embrace. . . .

*   *   *

Since that day love established its claims on their hearts, and swayed them with its enchanting melodies. Zohra was young and beautiful, and under the shadow of Love's tapering flame Asghar seemed to find happiness at last. Hardly six months had passed since Bilqeece's death. Yet he was thinking of marrying again. How cruel is the heart of man!

6

ON the thirtieth of March nineteen hundred and nineteen, Asghar was coming back from the office about five o'clock in the evening. The streets were deserted and empty as if some great calamity had befallen. Tommies stood on watch in the Chandni Chowk, and Indian policemen patrolled the streets. The Government had opened fire on Indian mobs that day. Asghar had heard the shouts and the sound of guns when he was in the office.

Troublous days had come for Hindustan. Since the Home Rule Movement had been started in 1917 a fire of anger and hate had been ignited in the hearts of Indians. Nineteen hundred and eleven was left behind when the people had hoped that the British rule might somehow prove beneficial and bring prosperity to unhappy Hindustan.

After the passing of the Rowlatt Bill, all over the country people went out in mammoth processions shouting slogans and protesting for the freedom of their Motherland. They had no weapons or arms; and in Delhi, the great city which had always fought for her own, the English army and the native police had opened fire on them.

As Asghar walked down he saw at many places written in bold letters the popular slogan of that day:

> The Rowlatt Bill has been passed,
> The English have gone out of their wits.

The inscription did not communicate anything deep or significant to him. He merely looked at it askance, felt a little frightened, and walked on. He had his own sorrows to think of, his own life to set right. He was unconcerned whether the country lived or died. The world might last or come to an end. He did not care. It had lived on in spite of revolutions and wars. How would it help him if he worried over these matters? They did not better his fate or make his life happier by any chance. Let those who cared bruise their fingers in attempting to pluck the rose. He lived in his own world where these things did not matter. For him only one thing was lasting, one thing which kept the heart of man alive. And it was love. Men come and men die, generations pass, and centuries drag on. But love does not die. It touches the heart to Beauty, brings unbounded joy in its train. And he who is not a devotee of this beautiful goddess is not worthy of being called a man.

Asghar was in love; its fire was raging in his breast, and he was thinking of winning his sweetheart. He had already decided to speak to his mother and father about it. . . .

As he walked lost in thought, weaving old dreams into new garbs, a few urchins passed by him. He was wearing English clothes and they began to mock him and shouted in his face:

'*Bol gai My Lord kukroo-koon .*'

Asghar quickly turned into a by-lane.

In the by-lane it was quiet. Life went on as calmly as before. A flower-vendor was singing in a dragging tune the latest popular song, as if nothing unusual had happened and he were quite unconcerned:

> When you go to see my sweetheart
> Ask for one,O messenger,
> With eyes of narcissi, swaying gait,
> And youthful charms attend her. . . .

The tune and the song created a soft stir in Asghar's heart and made him think of Zohra. The memory of her kisses began to burn his lips, and the warmth and intensity of her feelings seemed to course in his blood. He was filled with the desire of going home to her; but he decided to see his mother and speak to her about arranging his marriage with Zohra. An impatience and uncertainty were gnawing at his brain, and he began to walk faster.

As he came into Kucha Pandit he saw Mirza, the milk-seller, walking with a frantic look in his eyes, and his bobbed hair was dishevelled. His old wife, who often sat in the shop, was lamenting and rending the air with her cries:

'Oh God, may these Farangis die. They have snatched away my darling, my loved one from me. May they be destroyed. . . .'

Asghar was filled with curiosity and he stopped at the shop of Siddiq, the bania, to inquire what the matter was. Many customers were standing in front of the shop, and one of them was saying to Siddiq:

'I say, hurry up, or my wife will shout at me.'

There were many pots fixed in the wall so that they looked like dovecots. Siddiq put a round spoon inside a pot and taking out the cereal put it in the outspread handkerchief of the customer.

'What has happened to Mirza?' Asghar inquired.

'Happened? He has lost his son,' said Siddiq. 'He was a healthy young man, and had only this morning washed and rinsed the cauldron. But he went to non-co-operate and was shot down. And my opinion is that it served him right to go against the Government....'

Asghar felt sorry and turned to look at the receding figure of Mirza. He was going towards the alley, and looked frantic with pain. A strong gust of wind blew raising with it bits of paper and dust, and as the force of the wind died down they began to fall limply to the ground. Mirza turned into the by-lane, and Asghar walked away.

7

WHEN Asghar reached home he found that Habibuddin had come. He had not been keeping well for some time. A little work exhausted him. So he had come to consult some Hakims.

'What is the situation like in the city?' Habibuddin asked Asghar.

'The Chandni Chowk was deserted and looked dead,' he told him. 'There was not a soul about. When I came to Kucha Pandit I learnt that Mirza's son was one of those who had been shot dead.

'What! Mirza the milk-seller's son?' Habibuddin said in a grieved and shocked voice. 'That handsome youth who used to sit in the shop?'

'Yes. He had gone to non-co-operate and was killed.'

'It's so sad,' said Habibuddin. 'The English frankly say that they fear no one but Muslims in India and that if they crush the Mussalmans they shall rule with a care-free heart....'

Mir Nihal lay on the bed near them listening to the conversation. He did not seem to have anything to say. Still, a smile lit up his toothless and wrinkled face. . . . One or two other friends came in and they started talking of old times.

Nasim had also come with Habibuddin. He was quite twelve years of age, and had grown into a good-looking boy. He sat respectfully listening to his elders although he looked bored. The days of his childish babbling were over. Now, as he heard his father talk on with ease and grace he admired him and wondered as to what was the secret of talking so well. The conversation never seemed to end. One thing gave rise to another and, like thread from a reel, it moved on and on and never seemed to be exhausted.

He had become self-conscious and had also developed a sense of his own importance. Not only because he was the son of a Government official and his father's subordinates talked to him with respect, but at home also he was spoilt, being the only son.

One of Mir Nihal's friends asked him in which class he studied; and he replied that he read in the sixth class. The gentleman asked him other questions regarding his studies and Nasim replied appropriately.

As attention was paid to him Habibuddin felt proud of his son, and asked him to recite his favourite poem, a political song which was written soon after the Balkan War but had become popular again. Habibuddin liked it as it expressed the sentiments of Mussalmans. Nasim felt shy, yet he recited some of the verses.

> The wish for glory and martyrdom
> Has begun to sway our hearts again.
> We shall try his skill and see
> What strength is left in the enemy's hand.
>
> Let the time come we will show
> What courage there is in us still.
> Why should we tell you now what we
> Have in our hearts?—the power of will.
>
> But, traveller on the road of love,
> Tire and weary not in the way:
> The pleasure of tramping the desert is
> Greater the farther is the goal away.

Everyone showered praises on Nasim, not so much for his recitation, perhaps, as for the patriotic sentiments expressed in the poem itself. Habibuddin felt proud of his son, and tears of happiness came into Mir Nihal's eyes. The others patted Nasim on the back; and Asghar took out a rupee from his pocket and gave it to him. Nasim hesitated and looked at his father, doubtful whether he should accept it or not.

'Your uncle is giving you the rupee. Take it,' Habibuddin said, and Nasim accepted the money.

Of all persons Saeed Hasan came in just then. He and Habibuddin were great friends, and they embraced warmly. Saeed Hasan had got married to Surayya, and he had a son and was very happy.

'I never expected to find you here,' Saeed Hasan said with joy. 'It's wonderful to meet again. When did you come?'

'This morning.'

And they began to talk of various things, and soon came to the burning topic of the day. Habibuddin asked him what he thought of the Movement for freedom and the situation in the city.

Saeed Hasan did not much believe in patriotism. He had completely failed to sympathize with the Movement and was disinterested. He was one of those who accept an order of things and come to believe in it. For they did not wish to take any trouble to think for themselves. So long as a thing did not disturb the placidity of their lives they never said anything against it. The game of Politics was too difficult for Saeed Hasan to understand. Besides, British rule did not meddle with his life, although a foreign modernity and ways did go against the grain because they directly affected him. That is why, whereas he raved against English ways of living and thought, he never said anything against the foreign rule. Life went on peacefully for aught he cared; and that was all he was interested in, like most Indian fatalists. And when Habibuddin asked his opinion he replied:

'It's all God's gift. He gives position and glory to whomsoever He likes, and takes it away from whomever it pleases Him. It is not for us to judge.'

Once he had begun it was difficult to stop him, and he went on to illustrate his point with a story.

'You have perhaps heard the story of the barber who used to attend on the king,' he related. 'He had managed to amass two gold mohurs which he always kept in his bag. Every morning and evening he looked at them and felt happy. One day the king asked him: "What's the condition of my subjects?" "There is not one, your majesty," the barber made reply, "who hasn't got at least two gold mohurs by him." The vizir was sitting nearby, and the king beckoned to him to search the barber's bag. By way of looking for the nail-cutter the vizir searched the bag and found two gold mohurs in one of the pockets and stole them. When the barber went home in the evening he opened his bag to feed his eyes on the gold. But the gold mohurs were not there. He was heartbroken at the loss. He did not know where they had been stolen as he had been to many places. He was so grieved that he fell ill.

'When he did not go to attend on the king for a few days the king sent for him. "What was the matter with you that you did not come to clip our nails?" the king asked him. "I was ill, your majesty," the barber replied. "What is the condition of our subjects?" the king inquired, and the barber made reply: "The condition of the subjects, your majesty, is not very good. There is not one who has even two gold mohurs." The king smiled behind his beard and beckoned to the vizir, who looked in the barber's bag for the nail-cutter, and put the gold mohurs back. "But you have two gold mohurs here," said the vizir to him. The barber was overjoyed and said: "O, your majesty, I had put them in one of the pockets of the bag and forgotten in which of them they were."

'So, you see,' Saeed Hasan concluded. 'It is not for us to judge. For who can meddle in the affairs of God? . . .'

8

IT was not until a few days later, when Habibuddin had left, that Asghar was able to have a talk with his mother about his marriage. Begam Nihal was sitting in the veranda, as usual disentangling tangled thread. When she found it impossible to do anything with the jumbled mass of thread she broke it and tied the loose ends with knots, and encircled it round her knees. She was completely blind now and her back was bent.

'My life has become a misery,' Asghar said with pathos. 'I have to work in the day, and then look after the house and bring up Jehan Ara—'

'I know, my child,' Begam Nihal replied tenderly. 'God is my witness that I cannot sleep at night peacefully, and thoughts of you worry me more than anything in the world.'

Asghar heaved a sigh and looked out. The courtyard was strewn with torn paper, bits of stones, vegetable peelings and all sorts of rubbish, and everything seemed to be in a state of neglect. The sweeper woman had left off coming regularly, and when she came she always avoided sweeping the courtyard. Dilchain had left the water tap running, which had been installed in the middle of the courtyard under the henna tree. And life seemed to be falling to pieces.

'You know, Amma,' Asghar said with a sigh, 'it does not matter so much about me. But the poor child, her life is in a mess. There is no one to give her food or change her clothes. It is, sometimes, because of her that I think it would be better for me to marry again. There is no doubt that it would mean a step-mother, but she will at least take care of the child.'

'Yes, do marry, my son, and God bless you. I had thought of it myself many a time, but I did not say it lest you took it amiss. I am glad that you have decided to take this step. A man can never look after the home or children. . . . Have you any girl in view?'

'Not in particular. But for the child it would be better if I married someone who could have some feeling and love for her.'

'Yes, that is a very wise thought,' Begam Nihal agreed.

'From this point of view,' Asghar continued, 'I cannot think of anyone better than Zohra. She is Jehan Ara's aunt and the child is also attached to her. In fact, she has brought her up since her mother died. She is young, no doubt. . . .'

'No. A man remains young at sixty, and a woman grows old at twenty,' Begam Nihal repeated an old saying. 'I was only thirteen when I was married.'

'So you approve of it?' Asghar said, and his eyes brimmed over with happiness.

'What else could please me more than your happiness? May God keep you happy. . . .'

From behind came a soft miaow of a cat and a human voice muttering something. The voice came from the old Hunchbacked Aunt, as she was generally called. She was a distant relation and had come to live with them for the last few months. Her husband had left her long ago when, after the birth of her first child who was stillborn, she had become hunchbacked. Since then she had lived with different relations. She had ferocious grey-green eyes, and an ugly screeching voice. When straight she must have been tall, and even now when she walked, with the upper part of her body looking like a tortoise with the head sticking forward and the arms hanging back, her legs looked as long as those of a man. She was very fond of cats, and she had one which followed her about like a dog, and she treated her like a daughter and fawned on her. She lived all alone in the small dark room which had been allotted to her, and passed most of her time talking to Catto, the cat.

She had money of her own, and whenever she needed anything she produced a gold mohur from a bundle of rags, and asked some boy or Dilchain to change it for her. When they refused to do something for her she complained to Catto, as if the animal were human and understood everything she said. But the surprising thing was that the cat did seem to understand and miaowed at proper moments, gently, as if she seemed to agree with her mistress, or loudly, as though she disagreed.

Asghar had never thought that anyone else besides his mother would be listening to what he said. But Hunchbacked Aunt heard their conversation and muttered to her cat: 'The world is so selfish. Isn't it, pussy darling? One dies today, and tomorrow is another day....'

The next day Hunchbacked Aunt told Begam Jamal what she had heard, just by the way:

'Have you heard, sister,' she said, 'that Asghar is going to marry Zohra?'

'Hai, hai,' said Begam Jamal in a shocked voice. 'Are you speaking the truth?'

'Why should I tell a lie for nothing? God is my witness that I heard him talk to Elder Sister about it. And I told Catto. It wasn't so very long ago that Bilqeece (may God rest her soul) died. Even her bones would be still intact. What would she say in her grave? How selfish is the world!'

'May God keep you alive, sister,' said Begam Jamal. 'You have said the truth. It was only yesterday that he lost his wife, and he is already thinking of marrying again! ...'

She went to see Begam Shahbaz about this, more with a view to know her opinion than oppose it directly. Begam Shahbaz would never have agreed to the match, and she said:

'Heaven and earth might become one, but I will never give Zohra to him. I never knew that he could forget his wife so soon and then want to marry her own younger sister! ...'

* * *

Asghar had spoken to Mir Nihal and, apart from raising any objection, he had seemed pleased with his decision. 'Yes, my son, you should marry again,' he said. 'You are still young, and only a woman can look after the home. Your choice is also wise. The child's aunt would love her and treat her as her own child. May God keep you happy....'

And blind old Begam Nihal went to Begam Shahbaz and gave her the proposal for Zohra's hand. Begam Shahbaz put off the matter by saying that she must consult Ashfaq. When Asghar heard this reply he was filled with doubts and fears, for his relations with Ashfaq had become strained on account of Bilqeece, and he could not have any hope of sympathy from him. . . .

* * *

After her conversation with Begam Jamal and the talk with Begam Nihal, Begam Shahbaz told Zohra not to go before Asghar and to observe purdah with him. But the two houses were connected, and Zohra went to see Asghar secretly. She had listened to Begam Jamal's conversation with her mother, and reported it to Asghar. He got furious, for it had become a question of life and death to him. He came and told his father how Begam Jamal was opposing his marriage with Zohra. Mir Nihal got very angry, and shouted at Begam Jamal, saying that it had always been her habit to run others down.

It was evening when this happened. A mad faqir used to come to the house now and then. He was always naked and filthy, and the hair on his body was matted with dust and dirt. He carried a stick in his hand, and came in a doli, and usually stayed for a day or so. He was known as Blind Hafizji, and was mad. Yet everyone considered him a majzoob, a person who has reached a certain mystical stage when divine passion has come upon him and he becomes indifferent to his own self and the world. He always babbled to himself, and never talked connected sentences. He had become a majzoob at quite an early age and was said to be gifted with prescience.

When he came to Mir Nihal's he always asked for kabab or some other dish and it had to be provided for him. At night he would walk about shouting or muttering to himself, and Mir Nihal got disgusted with him, for he did not allow him any rest. When he was tired of walking about he lay on the floor besmeared with his own filth, stinking horribly. He would raise his hand and move his fingers quickly, muttering all the time tik, tik, tik, tik, tik, tik. As he lay there he looked worse than a Caliban, of the earth earthy.

On this evening Blind Hafizji had been raving more than usual. Perhaps it was because he had asked for pulao, but no pulao had been cooked and he could not get it. Dilchain came and told him:

'No pulao has been cooked today, Hafizji.'

He began to shout and beat the ground with his stick, muttering:

'Pulao, pulao. Kotha, kotha. . . .'

No one took any notice of him as that was his way. He walked into the by-lane and found his way inside the zenana, shouting:

'*Kothay wali, kothay wali.*'

When the ladies saw him they screamed with fright, and he was led out by Dilchain.

It was discovered that Begam Jamal had received some pulao from a relation that day. But she refused to give it to Blind Hafizji, saying: 'All sorts of madmen come to the house, and no one turns them out. I won't give anything to that shameless beast . . .'

'Sister, sister! What has happened to you?' Anjum Zamani shouted at her. 'You will never correct your ways. They are all God's creatures, and you never know when you might displease Him . . .'

And she sent the pulao to Hafizji. But he refused to eat it, and shouted so loudly that his voice could be heard inside the zenana. Begam Jamal was frightened a little, but she was very headstrong and never gave in.

When Hafizji's passion had subsided a little Asghar came and had a talk with his father.

'Aunt is opposing my marriage,' he told his father. 'I am not marrying for my comfort, but for the sake of that motherless child. What have I done to her that she should oppose my marriage?'

'What!' said Mir Nihal angrily. 'What right has she to oppose your marriage! She is very mean and always wants to come between people and their happiness. Was it for this that I had kept her in the house and treated her like my own sister! . . .'

He shouted and aired his anger against his sister-in-law.

The sweeper woman came to clean the latrine and sweep the floor which had been dirtied by Blind Hafizji. She heard Mir Nihal shouting at Begam Jamal. When she went inside Begam Jamal asked her what Blind Hafizji was doing, for she was feeling guilty of having annoyed him, and was afraid of the wrath of God.

'He was lying quiet in a corner,' the sweeper woman said. 'But, Begam, master seemed to be very angry.'

'With whom?'

'He seemed to be angry with you.'

'Why?' Begam Jamal said, flaring up.

The sweeper woman related what she had heard Mir Nihal say to Asghar.

Begam Jamal was hurt deeply and she began to boil with rage.

'I will have it out with him,' she shouted. 'What does he mean by calling me names, and before everyone! I have not run away with his daughter-in-law. Why should I oppose his son's marriage? . . .'

Anjum Zamani tried to calm her down; and when Begam Nihal

heard about it she reasoned with her. But the dam of her anger had burst, and she was bent upon having it out once and for all.

She could not go outside just then as Blind Hafizji was there. When he had left she went to Mir Nihal trembling with rage. Mir Nihal refused to see her or talk to her. But she was also obstinate, and was bent upon talking to him and finding out the source of his information.

'You've got to tell me who told you all this,' she demanded in an angry tone.

'I can't tell you,' Mir Nihal replied in an equally peremptory manner.

'Then I will leave your house and go away. When you consider me so petty and mean, when you have no regard for me, how can I stay on here?'

Mir Nihal began to cry. He had become so sentimental that the least thing touched him. Yet he felt he could not give his son away, and he said:

'Do whatever you like, but I can't tell you the name of the person.'

'Then I will leave after a week if you do not tell me within that period....'

She came away and wept and cried her eyes out. But the die was cast, and she had put an axe on her own legs. She was too vain to stay on after what she considered a great insult. Mir Nihal felt extremely grieved and had word sent to her that she should change her mind and stay on.

'Only on one condition,' she replied, 'that he promises to tell me the person's name.'

This, however, Mir Nihal could not do. So, after a week she shifted to a small house which belonged to her and had to be vacated as tenants were living in it.

The day on which she left with her sister-in-law was a day of mourning. She had lived here for forty years, ever since she had been married. The house looked deserted and lonely for days after she had gone. When a person has lived with you for some time the eyes become used to her gait, her features, her figure moving about from place to place. You know that she lives in that room, that this thing belongs to her. The ears become accustomed to her voice, the sound of her feet, the rustle of her clothes. But when she has gone the eyes look for the well-known face; the ears long to hear the familiar voice; but in vain. It seems that some dearly loved one has died, and her place is empty, and the heart is breaking with pain....

9

MIR NIHAL was stunned after this incident. He had been very fond of his dead brother, and had cherished his memory. In their boyhood and youth they had lived together, and together they had seen the death of the world in which they had been born. Their father had died of cholera soon after the massacres of 1857. He had left a good deal of money in the house when they were turned out of the city. But it had been discovered and looted by the Prize Agency. Most of their property was also lost, sold to the banias at ridiculously low prices by the English. The little of it that remained had kept their bodies and souls together. Mir Jamal was a year or so older than Mir Nihal, but there had existed great comradeship and love between them. And Mir Nihal was sincerely fond of his brother's widow. When she left Mir Nihal was greatly grieved and wept. But she was well-known for her temper and nothing could be done. . . .

He had already got disgusted with catching rats, and through the long days and nights he moped and lived on memories that were dead. His pillowcase and bed sheet became black with dirt, but he did not mind. His food was sometimes coarse and unwholesome, but he gulped it down. Often even Ghafoor grumbled at him and grudged doing things. His master had become old and witless, he said. Mir Nihal suffered the vagaries of life with the same grace with which he had lived through its splendours and joys.

Asghar had not yet received any definite reply about his marriage from Begam Shahbaz. He was in suspense and did not know what to do. Still, he hoped that it might all come right in the end. He met Zohra secretly, and she was willing to marry him. It was this fact which made him hopeful.

Habibuddin had not improved. In fact, as the days had passed his condition had become worse. So he took long leave and came home to be treated properly. He had become much reduced, and did not seem to be half his usual self.

He stayed in the men's part of the house to avoid too much company of women and for convenience. The hakims and doctors and friends could come and see him without the bother of purdah and getting the women away from the eyes of the strangers.

Hakim Ajmal Khan was called and he prescribed large doses of medicine which took hours to prepare. All night the herbs and dried roots were soaked in water. In the morning other ingredients were pounded and mixed with the herb-water. The mixture looked ugly and black, and its taste was bitter. But it had to be drunk.

The treatment continued for about a month, but it did not do any good to Habibuddin whose condition became worse.

Inside the zenana the women were anxious and prayed and talked.

'It is surely no physical disease, but the influence of some jinn,' said Begam Nihal.

Relevant verses from the Koran were read to dispel the influence of the jinn. But the women were not religious persons and had no knowledge of charms. So molvis were sent for.

Habibuddin had friends all over Delhi, and everyone brought a new cure or suggestion. One of his friends brought with him Bekhud, the poet, who was renowned for subduing jinns. He gave a charm to be kept under the pillow at night, and the dream which came to him in his sleep was to be reported. When Bekhud came in the morning he asked:

'What dream did you see?'

'I dreamt,' said Habibuddin, 'that I was walking alone in an expansive plain. I met a man with a red beard and a callosity on his forehead. In a golden voice he said: "Follow me." But as I looked, his beard vanished and red flames appeared all around, and the plain caught fire. It was hot and my throat was parched and I woke up.'

'Surely it is the influence of some ferocious jinn,' said Bekhud. 'But I will catch him. I have caught many jinns in my life. One gave me great trouble. He had fallen in love with a bania's daughter. She became pale and paler every day, and started remaining quiet and melancholy. The jinn often beat her and she howled and cried. I came to know about it and I said I would charm the jinn and get him into a bottle. . . .'

And he related how he had caught the jinn and freed the girl of his influence, and promised to do the same with the jinn who was troubling Habibuddin.

He started his charm whose course was of forty days. He ordered that seven fresh jasmine flowers should be kept under the patient's pillow at night and should be sent to him in the morning. Before going to his office Shams took them to Bekhud, or Masroor went. Bekhud himself came every third or fourth day and talked of jinns and poetry for hours. But his treatment did not do any good. Even when the forty days were over the jinn had not been charmed; and Habibuddin became weaker and thinner every day.

Mir Nihal lay on his bed and felt anxious for his son. A number of friends and relatives always gathered round Habibuddin. In the evenings and on holidays Asghar and Shams and Nazrul Hasan and others gathered and played cards. Habibuddin watched or helped one of them. Mir Nihal also enjoyed these things. He seemed less lonely and talked more and smiled and laughed. It was wonderful to have people you love around you.

*   *   *

When Hakim Ajmal Khan's bitter and huge doses of medicines did not do any good, Asghar suggested that Dr. Mitra should be consulted. So he arrived. He, of course, said that it was TB and that both the lungs were affected. 'Bot there is nauthing, Babu,' he said in his Bengali accent. 'He will gat vell soon.'

And he prescribed expensive medicines which were dispensed at his own dispensary; and he asked them to give Habibuddin more fruits and bottled chicken soup which, too, was to be bought at his shop to make sure that it was genuinely English. And every time he came he charged eight rupees and his tonga hire.

Dilchain had, in the meantime, discovered a small earthen doll buried under the oven when she was cleaning it one day. She went and showed it to Begam Kalim and Begam Habib.

'It is the effect of witchcraft,' she said, 'which is responsible for Mian's illness.'

The tender hearts of the women were filled with dread. They sent Dilchain to Aakhoonji Saheb, who wrote verses from the Koran on seven snow-white plates in saffron water. The plates were to be washed with a little water, and the water from one plate was to be taken for three days, a drop in the morning. Thus all the plates were to serve for twenty-one days, which was the course of this charm.

But strange things happened inside the zenana. A pot full of ill-omened things came flying in the air and struck against the bare trunk of the date palm whose leaves had all fallen. Another day some cooked cereal was found lying under the henna tree. From where it came no one knew. It had surely not been cooked in the house. A knife was seen whizzing past at night. All this was seen by Dilchain who was once a Hindu and had long ago been converted to Islam. Yet with the simple credulity peculiar to the people of India all these things were believed.

Poor women from the neighbourhood came, fluttering their burqas and dragging their slippers under them, and sympathized.

'He is such a fine man,' said one. 'He gave me a rupee once; and he is so ill now.'

'He helped my son and got him a job,' another said. 'I can never forget his kindness. May God cure him soon. . . .'

Thus they came and sympathized and suggested cures and medicines. One said to Begam Habib:

'You must go to the tomb of Hazrat Mahboob Elahi and pray. He is such a generous saint that your prayer will surely be heard. I pray for his recovery all the time.'

'You must give him water from the well at Hazrat Nizamuddin's tomb,' another suggested. 'It has magical qualities and has worked miracles. My husband had once fallen ill like yours and he got cured through the kind intercession of the Saint. . . .'

Begam Habib felt her heart sink within her as days went by and there was no sign of her husband's getting well. In fact, his condition was getting steadily worse and he could hardly sit up in bed, and bed sores appeared on his back.

* * *

Nazrul Hasan brought a Molvi Saheb one day. He wore a green velvet sherwani, a red paijama of silk, a golden conical cap on his head. He had a black oval beard, long curly hair reaching down to his waist, collyrium in his eyes. He was an expert at healing patients who had come under some spell or were affected by the evil eye. He read something and blew his breath at a butcher's knife and passed it over Habibuddin from head to toe seven times, then wrapped it up in a dark cloak.

'My charm can dispel the worst kind of witchcraft,' he declared. 'I don't claim anything for myself. The word of Allah is efficacious and great. . . .'

He did the trick for seven days. Then he asked for a snow-white cock, to be sacrificed, seven rupees for the prayers to the dead, two and a half seers of fine sweets. After this he never came. His charm had failed.

Mir Nihal saw all this, and fearing that the worst might happen he began to shed silent tears, and remembered Kambal Shah and his other Sufi and faqir friends who could surely heal his son. Begam Nihal also wept, and every day she sent for some flesh and had it passed up and down over her son's body seven times, and had it given to the kites who swooped down in great numbers and finished it in a moment. Begam Kalim had two goats sacrificed. Begam Habib prayed and did what everyone asked her to do, and was frantic with fear and grief.

But, alas, Habibuddin became more emaciated and weak. Hollows and black circles appeared under his eyes, and his face became wan and pale.

'This is a happy sign,' Sharfullah said. 'It always means that the patient is getting well, and is on the road to recovery.'

He brought a magician one day. Habibuddin protested. Perhaps he had realized the futility of everything. Yet Hope is a wonderful thing; and when everyone persuaded him he agreed to be treated by the magician as well.

The magician had had to eat human excrement to learn the art; and he had taken out a stillborn child of an oil-man from its grave, and had brought its spirit under his control. He made a doll of dough, pierced it with pins and needles, read out charms and incantations. Then he asked Habibuddin to cut it into two. The effect of magic was destroyed!

But no. Habibuddin became so weak that he had to be removed inside the zenana so that he could be nursed better and looked after properly. It was on a fine morning in early October that he was removed inside. When Mir Nihal realized how ill his son had become he wept, and sobs shook his bed. Then he lay there constantly, day in, day out, hoping and fearing, praying for the recovery of his son. Every day he was carried inside sitting on a child's small bed, and sat near his son for an hour or two. But he could not sit up for long and was brought outside in the same fashion as he had been taken in.

*   *   *

Relations had been coming and going constantly. Those who lived in the city came in dolis; others came from outside and stayed for days. Begam Waheed and Mehro also arrived when they learnt that their brother's condition had become very bad. When they saw the sickly pallor on his face, and the swelling on his cheeks and feet, they realized that he was a guest with them for only a short time.

In the daytime they were all near him, and at night they sat in the room by turns. They were not allowed to talk much in his room now. As they looked at his face a helplessness took possession of them and silent tears streamed down their faces.

One day Habibuddin caught his wife weeping. 'Why are you crying?' he said to her. 'I will get well all right. You need not be sad for nothing.' 'O yes, by God's grace you will be on your feet soon,' she said, hurriedly drying her tears. 'It was silly of me to cry. . . .'

10

THREE days before his death Habibuddin said to his mother:
'Please liberate me of all the duties which are incumbent on me for having sucked your milk. And forgive me for all that I may have said or done to displease you. . . .'

He asked everyone's forgiveness for all that he might have done to hurt or displease them. And his wife liberated him from the responsibility of paying her mehr.

After this he became calm and fell into a coma. He sometimes mumbled words and greetings to innumerable people who had died long ago. He often said how the fine old people came to see him and talked to him, many saints and persons clothed in white, all waiting to receive him. On the night of his death he said gently:
'It's beautiful, divine.'

Shams, who was sitting by his bed, said to him:
'Did you say something?'

'No,' he replied as if from far away in a different world. 'Grandfather Iqbal was giving me a very fine-smelling rose. . . . See, there is Uncle Jamal coming to greet me. . . .'

Then he became quiet and closed his eyes, and a blissful expression appeared on his face. Shams felt as if he smelt the fragrance of the rose. A cool gust of wind blew and he smelt myrrh and incense in the air. He began to read verses from the Koran and tears dropped from his eyes. He wiped them away and said to Habibuddin:
'Think of God and concentrate on Him.'

'Glory be to God,' Habibuddin whispered. 'I am in a wonderful place, and the finest people are near me. One of them is offering me . . .'

Then he became silent and a blissful yet distant look appeared in his eyes. . . .

*   *   *

About eleven in the night he quietly passed away, as gently as if he had
fallen asleep. His wife and Shams and Asghar were sitting near his bed.
But they did not see the change come over his face. They just heard a
slight gurgling sound, saw him move his body very gently; and his mouth
opened a little. When they realized what had happened a cry rent the
air. Soon the whole house was filled with the sounds of lamentation. . . .
    Begam Habib's glass bangles were broken and her ornaments and
dyed clothes were taken off. They all embraced and cried and beat their
breasts, and Mehro fell into a swoon. The women of the neighbourhood woke up, climbed upon the roofs, peeped, sympathized, shed
tears and went back to sleep. Mir Nihal beat his head against the
wooden side of his bed and sobs shook his heavy frame.
    Nasim, who had gone to sleep, awoke with a start. He did not know
what death really meant. When he saw everyone lamenting and weeping
he was stupefied. An unknown dread took possession of him. He thought
that his father was not really dead, but was in that long deep sleep about
which he had heard in stories. Still, he felt that he was coming to him
from a dark corner or a door, and his heart came into his mouth.
    No one could go to sleep, and everyone sat reading the Koran in the
room or outside. The first sudden outburst of grief was over. They
became quiet or wept every now and then as the memory came back to
them, or they thought of the things that Habibuddin had said or done
for them. . . .

                        *   *   *

In the morning they took his body outside to be washed. When Mir
Nihal saw it he was tortured as on the rack, and tossed about in pain.
The ghassal had come and began to give the corpse a bath. They had
forgotten to take off a gold ring from his finger and, finding an opportunity, the ghassal tore it from the finger and put it in his pocket.
    The relations had all been informed. Ahmad Wazir had gone round
to all the houses. One by one, in twos and threes, they began to arrive,
to meet, talk and weep, and see their loved one and friend to his final
resting-place. Hundreds of them gathered. Since there was no space in
the house they sat in the by-lane. The women came in dolis. The kahars
shouted, and amidst cries of lamentation no one paid them any heed.

                        *   *   *

When they had dressed him in his white clothes and had shown his face
to the women, they took him away on a bed covered with a winding-
sheet, amidst loud and heart-rending cries of grief. The day was warm

and dreary. Gusts of wind blew, lifting up bits of paper, dry leaves and feathers a little way up towards the sky to leave them to fall limply back to the earth.

Mir Nihal was carried to the graveyard in a doli behind the dead body, weeping his eyes sore. He sobbed; he muttered something about the futility of his life; he expressed grief for not being able to lend a shoulder in carrying his son's body to its final resting-place.

They said the prayers for the dead in a small mosque near the cemetery, so many hundreds of relations and friends. Then they reached the graveyard. But the grave was not ready. When at last it was, they lowered the body into the grave and Shams and Asghar laid it on the bedless floor, turned his face towards the Kaaba, put a piece of the sacred carpet which covers the House of God at Mecca on his chest.

On the fresh turned earth sat Mir Nihal inside the doli, but he could not see inside the grave as a crowd had come in front of him. Then the crowd parted. The kahars lifted the doli and put it near the edge of the grave. They were showing Habibuddin's face for the last time to the relations and friends. Mir Nihal's beard was unkempt and dirty. His white hair was dishevelled. His limp body was shaking with sobs.

The grave-diggers covered up the lower part of the grave with stone slabs, filled up the crevices with mud, and asked the people to put a handful of earth each into the grave before they finally filled it up. Mir Nihal's doli was brought near the edge of the grave again. He took a little earth in his trembling hand. His tears fell on the fresh earth in his hand, and limply he let it drop and covered his face. . . .

*   *   *

It was a sad crowd which came back home. No food had been cooked in the house, but it had been sent by Naseeruddin. Even the children had not been given anything to eat so long as the dead body had not been taken away. It was after three in the afternoon that they returned, and gulped the food down, for life must go on. And food was sent to the houses of those who had not stayed to take it at Mir Nihal's.

Asghar had just sat down to take his food when he saw Chanbeli standing in the by-lane, looking at him. He went hurriedly to her, fearing something else had happened.

'I had come in the morning too, but did not think it fit to deliver this letter which Zohra Begam has sent.'

With trembling hands Asghar opened the letter. On the top was written in pencil: 'Eleven o'clock of the night.' And the letter ran:

'I have just learnt that they are getting me married in the morning. . . .
I love only you. Tell me what should I do? . . . But God's will be done. .
. . Forgive me, and remember me now and then. . . .

Good-bye,

In distress, yours for ever,

ZOHRA.'

At the foot of the paper were written these lines, perhaps an after-
thought:

'Pain and sorrow and a cruel fate
Have brought me well nigh to a lifeless state.

'But go, my love, and may God be with you.
The parted will meet one day if fates allow.'

He looked at Chanbeli with deeply hurt and reproachful eyes accus-
ing her, as it were, for not having stopped the marriage or informed him
at least. She heaved a sigh and said:

'Who can meddle in the affairs of God? . . .'

Asghar forgot his food and, holding his head between his hands, he
sat there stunned and stupefied. . . .

*   *   *

Mir Nihal lay on his bed more dead than alive, too broken to think even
of the past. The sky was overcast with a cloud of dust, and one grey
pigeon, strayed from its flock, plied its lonely way across the unending
vastness of the sky. The oven which had been built in the morning to
boil the water for the dead was full of ashes and dust. On the bare top
of the date palm sat a kite and shrilly cried for a while and flew away,
leaving the trunk, ugly and dark, standing all alone against the sky.

His days were done and beauty had vanished from the earth. But life
remained over which men had no command and must go on. He was
weary and tired, limp like a shaken hand. His world had fallen to pieces
all around him, smothered by indifference and death. Yet he was still
alive to mope like an owl, and count his days, at the mercy of Time and
Fate.

He lay on the bed in a state of coma, too feelingless to sit up or think.
The sun went down and hid his face. The rooks cawed and flew away.
The sparrows found their nests. And night came striding fast, bringing
silence in its train, and covered up the empires of the world in its
blanket of darkness and gloom. . . .